WAITING

FOR

MOZART

A Novel about Church People Caught in Conflict

by

Charles Pilon

Caritas Communications
Thiensville Professional Park
216 North Green Bay Road, Suite 208
Thiensville, WI 53092
262.242.5049
dgawlik@wi.rr.com

Cover by Jane Anderson Design

Printed and bound in the United States of America
First Edition, March 2008

Pilon, Charles
Waiting for Mozart,
A Novel about Church People Caught in Conflict
www.charlespilon.com
ISBN 0-9799390-1-1

Early Praise for *Waiting for Mozart*

Waiting for Mozart delivers not only a story of human compulsion and conflict but also valuable insights into the Catholic Church in the years following the changes set in motion by Vatican II. As a Unitarian-Universalist, I knew little about the theology underlying those changes or the monumental import they had for institutions and individuals. *Waiting for Mozart* introduced me to both, as well as to a cast of memorable characters.
Nancy J. Ashmore, writer/editor, Ashmore Ink.

What greater joy could there be for the Catholic Church than the awakening of her faith-filled laity? The call from Vatican II in *Lumen Gentium* has indeed reached their hearts and minds and they are leaving behind the passive role assigned them by earlier generations. They're responding to their Baptismal call to be participants – players, at every level – in the salvific mission of the Church.

Waiting for Mozart is an engaging, passionate story about a parish working to embrace this vision and all the heartache and struggle that goes along with the reform of an ancient institution like the Church.
Margaret Benson, Director of Faith Formation,
St. Wenceslaus Parish, New Prague, MN.

Events of the 20th and 21st centuries have driven institutions with long traditions into new and difficult environments today. In the Catholic Church, these changes have had an impact in one way or another on priests, people (especially women) in religious orders, and hundreds of lay men and women on parish staffs as well as hundreds of thousands faithful lay people still in the pews for Mass on Sundays.

Sometimes a priest—especially a pastor—and other Church authorities, as well, have developed crippling and fearsomely defensive responses to change —new environments—in the Church. Taliban-like reaction to modern times by anyone with authority in the Church injures the *health* of a faith community and compromises the *effectiveness* of the Church in service of the Gospel.

Waiting for Mozart is a novel about real life in many Catholic parishes today – a story about conflict over the vision for Church in the 21st century. I've read the book. I recognize the characters. I know the story from my experience as a priest. It's a great read.

Fr. Kevin I. Clinton, Pastor, St. Wenceslaus Church, New Prague, MN.

ے۔ے۔ے۔ے۔ے۔ے۔ے۔ے۔ے۔ے۔ے۔ے۔ے۔ے

Call it a tug of war. Call it a meltdown. *Waiting for Mozart* got my attention on page one and as the story unfolded I discovered scenes and unexpected plot developments that amazed me. Inspired by real life situations in Catholic parishes, this story pits a pastor and his lay leaders in a power struggle that reflects different visions of the Church emerging from Vatican II.

In strong, crisp language the author depicts with profound insight the events of everyday life in far too many parishes. I liked his nuanced study of a spreading cast of characters who get drawn into the conflict. The pot really boils in this story and people involved in any aspect of parish ministry will recognize the contest as well as the characters in play on every page.

Terry Dosh, editor of Bread Rising.

ے۔ے۔ے۔ے۔ے۔ے۔ے۔ے۔ے۔ے۔ے۔ے۔ے۔ے

As you make your way into *Waiting for Mozart*, it won't be long before you begin to recognize experiences and characters from your own life in parish ministry. This fiction will make you reflect deeply on the ministry you do in the Church and why you do it. You may even say, "This isn't fiction; it's real life." The story spoke to me. It said: stay healthy; relationships count; discern carefully where you'll invest yourself.

Sister Ginny Heldorfer, OSF, Pastoral Associate,
St. Wenceslaus Parish, New Prague, MN.

ے۔ے۔ے۔ے۔ے۔ے۔ے۔ے۔ے۔ے۔ے۔ے۔ے۔ے

Waiting for Mozart is provocative, clearly written fiction and engaging commentary on the Herculean effort of a Catholic parish to implement changes and renewal mandated by the Second Vatican Council. Parishioners lock horns with a recalcitrant pastor who pays lip service to renewal, done best after Vatican II collaboratively with educated, enlightened laity. Readers will be drawn into the story from the outset as character after character deals with a priest who cannot get over it: father doesn't always know best.

Arthur E. Zannoni, biblical scholar and an award winning author of five books, his latest being **Tell Me Your Story: The Parables of Jesus.**

Meet with the author at your church, your library, school or local book store. E-mail at c.a.pilon@comcast.net or phone 651-484-5402.

ACKNOWLEDGEMENTS

I want to thank members of my family, colleagues in church work and other friends for helping me write *Waiting for Mozart*. I think of those who read the manuscript: Margaret Benson, Fr. Kevin Clinton, Sue Damyanovich, Terry Dosh, Barney Hanson, Sister Ginny Heldorfer, Bill Hunt, Michael Morwood, Jerry Roth, Wilmer Sigwarth, Jerry and Mary Skjolsvik and Art Zannoni. I am indebted beyond measure to these thirteen faithful readers, critics and commentators. Their praise for the story was encouraging and at the same time straightforward and honest.

It was a pleasure and such an education to work with an editor and writing coach like Nancy Ashmore of Northfield, Minnesota, and I consider myself fortunate indeed to have discovered David Gawlik of *Caritas Communications*, a supportive, insightful publisher. No one more than Terry Dosh facilitated the serendipitous coming together of events and people that brought *Waiting for Mozart* to publication. I am deeply indebted to him for that. And to Christopher Pilon, a simple thank you, son.

Finally, the words *debt of gratitude* could never describe what I owe to my wife of almost 37 years, who must feel she has read *Waiting for Mozart* at least 37 times. In fact, it took me only 15 of those years to complete the story, but year in and year out she read excerpt after excerpt, a chapter and then another one followed by others until finally she read and re-read the entire story, cover to cover, more times than I care to tell. It is to my wife Ana, a literary beacon trained as such and a proven, practiced critic of every kind of literature in two languages, that I dedicate this novel. Thank you, sweetheart.

As is true with most fiction, any similarity in this story to actual events or to real persons is purely and entirely coincidental. I created the *Waiting for Mozart* characters and story line in my mind and from my heart. If this story generates significant civil discourse about clericalism in the Catholic Church and would contribute somehow to a lessening of that crucial issue, this author would be more than gratified.

TABLE OF CONTENTS

TABLE OF CONTENTS

FOREWORD

They named it Vatican II, a reforming Catholic Church Council called for by Pope John XXIII in 1959. Between 1962 and 1965, some 2,600 Catholic bishops and other ecclesiastics and scholars from all over the world, including those from other faith traditions, assembled in Rome for four separate Council sessions intended by the pope to let some fresh air into an institution he believed had gotten musty.

Among other important things the Council accomplished, it set forth again the original understanding of the place that common people hold in the Church: While ordinary men and women are not consecrated—as priests are—by the hands of the bishop and the holy oil of ordination, they are marked with the water and the holy oils of Baptism and Confirmation. Consequently, God breathes and lives and moves in them as well as in the parish priest or the bishop.

This offered non-ordained people the basis for striking, historic changes in their lives. For centuries, Catholics had looked up to their priests as saintly leaders called and sent by God to be the source and the fountain of grace that would save their souls. Vatican II, however, proclaimed holiness—and social responsibility— for every person baptized, not just for priests. The point was crucial.

Many churches formed representative parish councils. The idea was a new one for Catholics, including their priests, and the transition to a post-Vatican II parish was often not easy. When left-and right-leaning factions disagreed over policy or procedure, the resulting anger and bitterness sometimes continued for days, even weeks and months. Ordinary people had been given *voice* in the Church, however, and they wanted to be honored and fairly heard. If it ever came to an argument, *that* was pivotal.

CHAPTER 1

Sunday, January 21,1990

11:30 a.m.

Father Joseph Burns, pastor for nearly 19 years at St. Mary's Catholic parish in Mapleton, Minnesota, a first ring suburb of St. Paul, returned to the sacristy after the third and final Mass of the weekend. The decisive homily he prepared so carefully had gone well enough, he thought—better, at least, than on Saturday evening and at the Mass earlier that morning.

Megan Roberts, a member of the parish council, drew the pastor's attention as she entered the sacristy. He signaled her to remain right there and wait, indicating it would be just a minute or two. Megan waited nervously, determined to confront the pastor. *Crossed the line, he has—and not just mine. His ugly use of power and brutal control over people—abuse, really—has gone on long enough. Since he got here, in fact. And now, today, he claims that trusting him and the Church measures a person's trust in God. Imagine this man—this brute—preaching nonsense like that! Garbage! We've had enough. Make it snappy, priest. I'm done waiting.*

After the pastor finished talking with a young couple who had come to the sacristy to register in the parish, he began to remove the Mass vestments. He looked around for Ted Kroenig, another member of the parish council who had served as Lector at the Mass. He handed the chasuble to Ted, who hung it in the tall vestment closet. "Thank you, boys," he said to the altar servers, who were about to leave the sacristy. "You sure you have it all put away?" They assured him that everything was in order.

He looked over at Megan, who was facing him squarely, arms folded tightly. *Can't put it off any longer,* he groused to himself. *Get it over with.* "Yes, Megan?" He motioned her over from where she was standing. *Easy to tell—she's furious. And a witch. What's she want this time?*

"Yes, Megan. What is it? What can I do for you? That was a young couple who would like to join our parish," he explained. "They've heard a lot of good things about St. Mary's and want to register as members."

Megan scoffed inadvertently, wondering why anyone would do such a thing, but made no further response. Instead she planted her eyes squarely on the pastor, fighting furiously for composure.

"I am here to insist, Joe, that you never say again, as you did in your sermon this morning, *twice,* that trust in the Church is the same as trust in God. It is *not.* I don't and I will never believe that."

"My, oh my, Megan! You're one unhappy woman this morning. It's written all over you." He felt a fire inside him and looked away for relief. *It's always something with this bitter, bitter woman; a bucking bronco to deal with and one I never should have let onto the council—a ton of trouble, right from the start.*

"*Never* tell me that again, Joe. And, yes, you bet I'm unhappy. I have learned a lot in my first year and a half on the parish council about you and your ways and now today you boldly dared to make an announcement to our members about parish council issues that are extremely complex and difficult. It was out of order." *To say the least! Add that he doesn't keep his word; changes rules to serve his own purposes; gets abusive on a moment's notice; says one thing, does another. Lies. Plays God.*

His face twisted. Just the sight of Megan as she entered the sacristy had put the pastor on edge. "Listen to me, lady," he snapped. "My record in this parish speaks for itself. My work here has always been judged good—*very* good, as a matter fact. And I have the archbishop's full support to continue here as pastor, in spite of some problems. It's malcontents like you who are the problem. People like you need to get on board."

"Your *record*, Joe! Would that include stomping out of meetings, endless staff turnover, changing prepared agendas without notice and—just a year ago—that awful chapel fiasco? Listen to me, Joe." She paused, trying to steady her voice, finally quitting the effort. "There are two factions in this church," she continued sharply. "A situation you have created by your behavior. You hear only the people you favor. There is no way for a parish to survive this."

The pastor's lips tightened over his teeth. "Don't tell me about factions, Megan. There aren't any in this parish. The people in this church don't want all this trouble. They just want to save their souls—as *you* should be doing!" He watched her face freeze and backpedaled a bit.

"I assure you, we'll get the parish council back on track, Megan. There's no reason you can't be a part of it, if you want to be." He motioned for Ted to not leave the sacristy just yet. "Perhaps you think I'm trying to fool you—*lying* even, about this, maybe?" His eyebrows rose, inquiringly. "We *will* have a parish council at St. Mary's, Megan. Trust me on this."

"*Lying*? Yes, I'd say so," she snapped. "In fact, I believe you are *routinely* dishonest in the way you work with people. It explains years of contentious staff meetings, abrupt resignations from the parish council and a lot of other things. You've gotten away with your clerical ways for nearly two decades in this parish, but I'm telling you, here and now, that those days must come to an end." She raised her voice caustically. "What help can a parish council be if you continue to work with it deceptively—promising things and not delivering, teaching and promoting one thing, then doing another, and..."

Joe Burns ignited, stung by the challenge made in public, within earshot of people still in the church and in front of the altar boy who had returned, looking for one of his gloves.

"Megan, my dear, what can you do about it?" the priest sneered. "Leave this in the hands of God and of the Church. I am the pastor at St. Mary's, named so by the archbishop. If you can't see that and get on board with it, then I cannot help you," he taunted, pointing a finger directly into her face. Trying to compose himself, he slowly lifted the stole from his shoulders, folded it and held it out for Ted to take from him.

"I'm not *asking* for your help," Megan snarled, stabbing back, nearly poking him in the chest. "Nor do I need it. It should come as no surprise to you that many of us believe this parish would do better without you as pastor."

"So you think you're going to get *rid* of me?" the priest scoffed. "Get serious, Megan." He grabbed her, pressing his thumb into her forearm, and pulled her aside so that Ted could place the stole in the top drawer of the vesting counter.

Noticing, Ted looked intently at Megan as he closed the vesting counter drawer. "Easy now," he said to her, stepping back to wait for the pastor to remove the alb. She jerked her arm free, disregarding Ted's look and the suggestion.

"That's correct," she blustered. "There are hundreds of members in this parish who have had enough of you as pastor. You can no longer *boss* this parish community. Do you know how deeply many people here *despise* you as pastor, but say nothing about it?"

"Megan, please, for heaven's sake," Ted pleaded.

"Go ahead and believe whatever you want to, my dear," the pastor replied snidely, dismissing her with a swipe of his hand, fighting to appear unruffled. "Go ahead—listen to the lies you've heard, dear. You're mistaken. Or worse, misled."

Scowling, Megan squeezed her right hand into a fist at her side until the knuckles showed white. "Listen up," she shouted. "Do not call me *dear*. *Never*. Is that clear? I am *not* your dear. I am not your *child*. And I object to you talking to me as though I were."

"Shut up, woman!" the pastor yelled. "Just...shut up! I'm sick and tired of you and of everyone else *like* you!" He pulled the alb up over his head and shook it firmly to straighten it. He handed it to Ted, who nervously hung it in the vestment closet and closed the door, concerned that the matter was tipping out of control.

"I'm not discussing this any further," the pastor shot back, stabbing fiercely at Megan's face. "I've been right every time I've made changes to improve this accursed council and I was right in what I said this morning. Get over it, woman," he blared.

Bob Talbot, a member of the parish council and the pastor's closest confidant from the day Joe Burns arrived as pastor in 1971, rushed into the sacristy to find out what the uproar was about. He'd heard the hollering halfway back in the church where he'd been speaking with other parishioners. Ted mumbled an explanation, but Bob couldn't hear over the continuing hubbub. "Do you need help?" Someone was calling from somewhere near the front pew in the church. "Should we call the police?"

"No, no need for that," Bob yelled into the church as he poked his head back out from the sacristy. Leaving momentarily to assure parish members who were clustering noisily at the front, he announced loudly to be heard throughout the church, "Ted is in there and together we'll be able to handle it."

Hearing his name and the growing commotion in the church, Ted caught the pastor's eye, seeking assurance he could safely leave for a moment to help Bob calm the parishioners. Joe Burns nodded and Ted hurried out of the sacristy, glancing back over his shoulder as Megan began shouting again.

"You taught us well, Joe, so that now we're smarter than you think and maybe than you intended." Megan's two daughters who were waiting for her at the back of the church heard their mother's yelling and flinched, alarmed at its shrillness.

"And a lot of thanks I get for it," Joe Burns thundered.

"The Church is baptized people, not just priests and your pope," she screamed back. "You taught that to this parish many years ago and now you don't like what it means, though you claim to. That's what this is about."

"Say some more, Megan. Come on," the pastor taunted, motioning for her to step forward, as if she might want to duke it out with him.

"We're on to you, Joe, and to your type of priest," she shrieked into his face. His eyes turned hard, glazed with rage. She proceeded. "There are lots of people—all *over*—who know your type now, Joe—*hundreds* from this parish. You, however, don't seem to get it. You're out of touch, Joe. You're a lousy priest. I, for one, am going to fight this to the end."

Joe Burns turned away abruptly, intending to leave her with her thoughts and her own vile words ringing in her ears, but then suddenly something gushing and boiling in him burst. He whirled on her, put his hands on her shoulders and drove her into the closed door of the vestment closet. Her head snapped forward from the impact and her eyes clicked shut. The pastor jammed his left elbow and forearm up under her neck, chopped at her flailing arms with the fist of his right hand and then dug at her neck with both hands.

Megan tried to reach for the priest's neck, but her smaller body and shorter arms were no match for his fury and the six-foot, four-inch frame that he was pressing against her. Mouth open, teeth bared, Joe Burns grunted against her upper body, struggling for leverage. He reached back with his right leg to push with his foot against the base of the vesting counter behind him. Unable to reach it, he shortened his stance again. Insane with rage, he loosened the choking grip and used his right hand to begin pressing wildly on his left arm to crush her neck straight on from the front.

The woman's eyes popped open, bulging. Her mind raced in terror. Fearing for her life, she struggled for air. There was none. Two inches from her own, the pastor's eyes were wild and hard. She clawed at the arm as it pressed, a fence post across her neck. She tried to turn. There was no room.

The priest pressed harder, his eyes protruding, saliva leaking from the corners of his mouth. She clawed again at his arms and hands, tore her nails into the scalp on his balding, sweating head, and raised a knee for his groin. She struggled to spit into his face. There was no saliva.

The pastor licked his own saliva back into his mouth, twisted his tongue, and bit on it fiercely. He struggled to press the last breath of life out of her, a woman he had hated from the first time he heard her speak, from the moment she first opened her stinking, blaspheming mouth against the priesthood of God. He leaned against her harder, pressing furiously in spurts, standing now on one leg, then the other, searching for the leverage he needed to finally silence this witch and every other bitching scourge she stood for, man or woman.

Outside the sacristy with the concerned parishioners, Bob and Ted had heard the crack of Megan's head against the vestment closet door and the thumps, grunts and desperate shuffling that followed. They'd turned for the sacristy immediately, but Ted tripped on the first of the four marble steps to the sanctuary and slammed his forehead on the edge of one of them, opening a gash above his left eye. After nearly falling himself, Bob yanked a handkerchief from his back pocket. He helped Ted get it pressed against the cut and then dashed with him up the remaining steps, stumbling into the sacristy, winded and frantic about what they'd find.

"Joe!! Father Joe," they shouted. Ted tossed the bloodied handkerchief aside and ran a step ahead of Bob to begin trying to free Megan from the pastor's punishing, suffocating crush. Bob drove his shoulder into the pastor's hips and thighs with all the weight and force he could muster, jarring him loose for the split second Ted needed to grab the pastor around the neck. Together they pulled the crazed, drained man off Megan and wrestled him to the floor.

CHAPTER 2

Two and One Half Months Earlier

Tuesday, November 7, 1989

Joe Burns entered the parish council room at 7:28 p.m. and, without a word or sideways glance, took a seat at the antique table that was the room's centerpiece. He fidgeted in the formal, high-backed chair, shifting it left, then right and finally pushing back slightly from the table, he coughed and began drumming his fingers on its mahogany surface.

At the opposite end of the room, six of the seven council members who had already arrived continued pouring coffee and chatting among themselves and with several other parishioners who had come for the parish council meeting. By turning just a bit and appearing casual, they were able to observe the pastor's demeanor and restlessness—signs, perhaps, of another explosive meeting. Some believed that one day a simple matter in this room could blow up and morph out of control, even into a matter of some historic significance.

A hand stuck casually into his brown woolen pants, Bob Talbot studied the pastor tapping persistently across the room. It was a weary man he was watching, he knew.

Twenty years now this man's confidant and there's still a whole landscape inside him I don't know. A fine priest though—and many agree. Ordained before Vatican II but known for aggressive application of its directives. Appointed our pastor, he threw himself into shaping us into a contemporary kind of Catholic community. Some considered him—and Joe thought it true—to be one of the enlightened, new breed of Catholic priests in a Church busy reforming itself. Who could argue it?

Bob sipped from his coffee, recalling with a certain pride those early days after Joe Burns became the pastor—*liturgy better than in most Catholic parishes—more carefully planned and spirited—truer to Vatican II; volunteer song leaders and lectors better prepared than those in any nearby parish; ministry to teenagers strong enough to attract kids from other churches—who then became leaders in the program here.*

He needed help, of course—and got plenty. Hired the best staff he could, introduced solid management principles and got parishioners to help write a personnel policy for laymen and women working for the Church—the first in the diocese. Called for strategic planning early on and, of course, formed this council to help him set policy and manage our affairs—a Catholic parish quite unlike those of only ten years earlier.

An accurate assessment, Bob thought. *And fair.* Sipping his coffee again, he peered over the top of his cup at the pastor. *Yes, but there've been problems and mistakes, too, over the years—like his sharp, critical bearing, for example; disappointment and bitter dissension at meetings and often for much of the time in between; decisions made abruptly—autocratically—that have cost us talented staffers and volunteers, poisoning talk around the parish.*

Bob crossed the room to say hello to the pastor. He patted him lightly on the back and then rested his hand on the priest's shoulder. Joe glanced up and pressed it.

"Where's Jensen?" he asked gruffly. "It's time to start."

"It's snowing, Father Joe. He must be delayed."

"Seven-thirty is starting time. Everyone else is present, right?"

"He'll be here, Joe," Bob assured, tapping him again on the shoulder before returning to the group gathered at the coffeemaker. He opened the refrigerator. "Muffins anyone?" he asked, reaching in for two plates of baked goods left from those served with coffee on Sunday after the Masses. "Can't resist 'em, can you?" he joshed, making his way around the circle that formed. "Neither can I," he smiled, patting the slight bulge he carried just above the bottom buttons on his tan sweater.

After a bit more banter, conversation slowed and then stopped. The room went quiet, except for the sound of the pastor's renewed drumming. That stopped with a quick double rap at 7:40—when council chairman Jim Jensen hurried into the room.

"Let's get going, everyone," he urged, shaking snow from the maroon jacket he wore. Hanging it on the rack in the corner, he took the chair at the head of the table.

The members of the council drifted toward their seats, some nodding to the pastor. They received no sign, not a word in return. Bob Talbot and Ted Kroenig, both in their 60s and both serving their fourth three-year term on the council, refilled their cups before sitting in the remaining chairs—the ones beside and directly across from the pastor.

Visitors sat in folding chairs behind the council. They were present as observers by virtue of the pastor's long-standing policy that a council meeting was a parish-wide agenda and the door should be open to anyone who wanted to be present and listen.

The custom at St. Mary's since shortly after Joe Burns' arrival as pastor was for a member of the council to offer the opening prayer for each meeting, a practice intended to indicate that laypeople, not just priests, were capable and empowered to lead church prayer. Jim nodded to Sheila Martinson, 40, a wife, a mother of three and the vice president of marketing for a large real estate firm, to begin the prayer. She prayed for the parish and the meeting at hand and then for the U.N. General Assembly, where delegates were preparing for conferences on the rights of the world's children.

"It's great when people pray like that, original and from the heart," the pastor observed without looking up.

Megan Roberts, 38, a dentist and divorced mother of two girls, shifted in her chair and began twisting the sapphire ring on her right hand. Jim squared his folder on the table and then adjusted it a tad before thanking Sheila for the prayer. He started to welcome the observers.

"Get on with it," Joe Burns blurted out. "We've got a lot to do, and I've still got half a night of work left when we get done here. Let's cut the talk and get going. The chatter never ends."

Jim shifted his solid six-foot frame in his seat and stared at the pastor. "Joe, I'd like to finish my sentence."

The pastor tapped his sharpened pencil twice, kicked his legs back and locked them under the chair, his cheeks flushing.

"Yes, I know, I understand." He rolled the pencil between his palms. "We've got to get going here, folks. I've had a longer day already than most of you and ..." He studied the pencil, then pointed it at Jim, conceding. "Alright, fine. Go ahead. Get on with it."

Jim tried a smile. None came. *A rotten way to start,* he thought. *There's better places to be on a pretty and snowy evening in Minnesota.* He glanced out the window where snow was falling into the light of a streetlamp. *That'd be nice!* Deliberately, he completed what he'd intended to say. His mouth clicked dry at the end.

"I want to get going here," Joe Burns declared a second time as soon as Jim finished. "This council needs to know right away, tonight, that I cannot even consider the proposal you've prepared for this meeting."

The chairman stiffened. Bob set his glasses on the table and massaged his forehead. They weren't the only ones unsettled by the pastor's announcement. Megan was twisting her ring again. Tom Andrews, 34, stole a glance at the pastor and froze. Priests had been his heroes from the day he became an altar boy in fourth grade. Others closed their folders or studied their hands. Sheila was examining faces.

This won't work, Joe, Bob thought as he drained his coffee cup. *Used to be that a suggestion by a pastor, even a hint, could change an agenda, start a program or torpedo something that'd been months in the making. People figured, why waste time on stuff the pastor says isn't necessary? He would know, right? That was then, Joe. It won't work tonight. Ted, Tom, and Megan worked too many hours on this report, over too long a time. And Jim's not going to back off. Not after what happened with the chapel.*

Bob shuddered, remembering the time when Joe decided to convert an alcove honoring the Virgin Mary, the church's patron, into a self-contained chapel for weekday Masses and small weddings and funerals. After months of discussion, the council was ready to support his proposal.

In the meantime, however, the plan came to the attention of four charter families of the parish for whom a prayer in the Marian alcove had been the first stop in the church every Sunday for better than 50 years. "Whaterya doin'?" they challenged the pastor. "She's God's mother. She's always been there for us in that alcove. You do this, we're goin' to the bishop."

They argued their case at meetings of the Altar and Rosary Society, the Funeral Guild, the adult leaders of the parish Boy Scout troop, and the parents of the Altar Boys—who took their concerns to the parish council, filling meeting after meeting with heated rhetoric. The debates delayed action on the chapel for the better part of two years. Still, some considered the process a model for ways members of the parish could weigh in on an important matter. Just a year ago, everyone who wanted to speak seemed to have done so.

The council scheduled a decision for its November meeting. Without warning, Joe pulled the matter from the agenda and dismissed the feasibility committee that he had appointed, reserving the right to make the decision about the chapel by himself—later, at an unspecified time.

The move angered everyone. Those who had participated in the endless discussions felt the pastor had wasted their time. Others feared that he'd wait for the ruckus to die down, then reintroduce the proposal, thereby starting the fight all over again—or worse, that one day he'd just build it—without consulting *anyone*. Members of the parish council were the most incensed of all. The process had dishonored—gutted— the very idea of collaborative work and ministry formulated at Vatican II. The council chairman resigned immediately and quit the parish the next day. Despite his own fury, Jim, the vice-chair, agreed to stay on and serve as the council chairman.

ダ ダ ダ ダ ダ ダ ダ ダ ダ ダ ダ ダ ダ ダ ダ

Breaking the ponderous silence that had followed the pastor's newest ruling, Ted got up for more coffee. Coming back with the pot, he topped off his own cup and then, jittering, reached for Sheila's, which he filled to overflowing. Three people jumped up for napkins. "I'll get it," Ted snapped, flustered. He returned, paper towels streaming from his hand.

"I don't see any reason to consider this proposal you've prepared," the pastor repeated, ignoring Ted, who was reaching in front of him to dry the table.

"It's not a proposal," Jim contended, swiping at his fluffy, slightly receding red hair. "At this point it's just a report, a study, done by three members of this council. A study you approved, by the way. Just six months ago. In fact, you requested it."

"Don't interrupt me, Jim," the pastor snapped, brushing sharply at a sleeve of the grayish tweed jacket he wore over his black shirt and Roman collar. "There's no longer any point to it. Sunday offerings are down, so we can't even *consider* staff salary adjustments for some time to come. This discussion you've got planned, this proposal or study or whatever you want to call it, will serve no purpose. I'm tabling it."

A dragon stirred around the table, whispering and sniffing.

Finally, Sheila spoke. "Help me understand." She tugged lightly the buttoned white cuff showing from one of the sleeves of her navy business suit, then folded her hands in front of her. "Father Joe, when you and I prepared the agenda two weeks ago you agreed to consider this report. You've told us in the past that you don't want to control matters in ways that hurt the work of the council. I'm asking you to remember that now. Let us proceed with the agenda, including a report on the salary study you requested."

Joe Burns knew that when the affable and self-possessed Sheila Martinson spoke, people listened. Invariably she drew wandering eyes and minds back to the council table and the issue at hand. And she had always been unremittingly gracious with him personally. He fingered his collar as he studied the classy redhead with the stunning eyes, a woman he appreciated—even esteemed. His past public admiration of her cordiality, however, trapped him now. He paused, deliberating.

What's a priest to do when a guy like Jim Jensen issues a challenge as vile as this one? If it were anyone but Sheila pressing me on this, or someone like Bob, I'd just run the chairman over and not look back. There's something different here tonight, though—this meeting. What's up here?

Jim twirled the chairman's gavel slowly between his hands, tapped it once on the table, lightly, and then, cautiously, laid it down.

"You've done this before, Joe," he accused. "Have you already forgotten the chapel incident last year? We've allowed that kind of thing too many times. We can't do our job this way. I don't see..."

"I know you don't see, Mr. Jensen," the pastor heckled. "It's hard for you to see *anything*, period. I know..."

"Just a minute," Jim countered, raising his voice. "Please don't talk to me that way. We are here to serve this parish, as you are, Joe. It doesn't help when you make light of the role we play."

Brushing a hand over his silvering hair and stroking at the few strands above, Bob studied the two men, the pastor and the chairman, the priest and the former priest, contrasting their backgrounds. Little more than a decade separated them, but even a few years could make a significant difference in how a priest came out of the seminary. Ordained in 1967, Jim had studied for the priesthood during Vatican II. Unsettled by what he sometimes specifically and literally called the Church's fearsome, oppressive ways of doing things, he had prized ministering freely and creatively as a priest and, truth be told, Bob mused, probably admired his own daring—a thing almost unimagined for men ordained just a few years earlier—men like Joe Burns. Joe had gotten the theological education and the seminary discipline and training given to young men since the late 1500's.

Faced now with Jim's blatant opposition, the pastor slouched back in his chair, arms hanging at his sides, almost to the floor. The pose accentuated his large frame, a physique that, combined with his authoritative style and the aura of the priesthood, had made him an overwhelming, frightening presence at St. Mary's over the years. He straightened up and took a deep breath. Leaning forward, eyes closed, he pressed his palms together in front of his face.

"Jim," he said, eyes still shut. He waited, breathed deeply again and exhaled. "There's no money," he asserted, his bulging brown eyes open now, glaring at the council chairman. "Look at me."

The pastor waited, breathing audibly. "Jim, I told you to look at me," he demanded. "There. Is. No. Money," he repeated, rapping the table with each word. "The Finance Committee does not support additional expense for salaries. Bob will verify that. And the Finance Committee is

15

the *only* parish committee that Church law requires a pastor to have. I'll remind you all, as I have time and again: Canon Law does not *require* a parish council."

Jim and Megan exchanged glances at the warning—the threat, in fact—that Joe Burns often uttered when he was feeling pressured.

"So, sir, what do you want to do?" the pastor continued, singling out the chairman. "Waste everybody's time?" He looked around, hands at his hips, then extended them, signaling the assurance he felt. "It isn't worth it, people. I know what we are able to do in this parish. And I know for certain that we can in no way do *this*. There's no *money*, I tell you. You can submit your lousy report if you want to and I'll read it. But we can't pay any more in salaries." He pulled at the lapels of his jacket and brushed at a shoulder before sitting back. "That's the end of it."

The room went silent again. A door slammed someplace down the corridor.

CHAPTER 3

Tuesday, November 7

8:10 p.m.

"This can't be the end of it, folks," Jim said finally, yanking at the knot in his tie. He ran two fingers around inside his collar to loosen it and get some air. "Time is up, Joe. This has to stop. This council will not permit you to override it again with a snap of your fingers. You can't make changes to an agreed-upon agenda and, worse, reject out of hand a report that you yourself specifically requested."

The pastor sniggered, running his eyes over the parish council room. *A pastor's little Vatican,* he thought, *where important church work could happen—ministry shared by a modern, up-to-date priest and the members of his parish. Sure, it's just a renovated classroom, but redecorated with an eye to* significance, *not just function—the table on an island of plush red carpet, intended to evoke fiery tongues and the outpouring of God's Holy Spirit on the work done here; formal, heavy drapes to complement the carpet; portraits of recent popes; shelves with books and magazines on scripture and theology and ways that parish councils could operate effectively—yes, my own Vatican, where I've given the only life I had for my people. Work, nothing but work—selfless, all of it. God's work, surely.* The pastor's eyes focused again as he slowly surveyed the council.

"I'm tired, people," he moaned. "So very tired." He laid a hand on the table. *If they'd just leave me alone—let me do the work, the work I've been ordained for.* He massaged his forehead, studied the perspiration on his fingers and rubbed it into his hands. *It's always something. And it used to be so simple—men of a parish would pull together around a pastor and get done what needed doing. Now? Every day is a struggle. No honor. No respect.* He lowered his head, massaging his temples again.

"Cooperation, that's all I need," he lamented. "I just want to get my priestly work done. A man can't even set the agenda for his own work any more." He leaned forward, an elbow on the table.

Ted pressed softly on his thin mustache now, waiting to be sure the pastor was done speaking and then moved to the edge of his chair. Along with Bob Talbot, Ted served as one of the two parish trustees, who together with the archbishop, his vicar and the pastor, made up the legal corporation of St. Mary's Catholic Church. Ted had always taken it as his responsibility— a calling—to speak at council meetings for those who had no direct voice in parish affairs. "Father Joe, I understand what you're saying and I sympathize. I have to admit, though, that I think this may not be the best way to go. We worked hard on this," he added. "What could it hurt to listen?" He slid back in his chair and stroked his graying beard. "Once you've heard our report, Father, it'd still be yours to decide. We'd back off."

Jim pulled at his collar again and stood up, fighting to hold himself together. "The pastor can reject a report just because he wants to?" he muttered, half to himself. *Sure! Refuse the work you asked for! Go ahead! Do the obscenity!* He glared out the window, then back at the table. *No, not this time. Not tonight.* "That's not good enough, Ted," Jim contended loudly. "A boundary's been crossed here and as the chairman I, for one, will not permit it. A pastor may not refuse to review a report and thereby change the agenda for a meeting just because he wants to. I know most of you here agree with me and there are hundreds in the parish who would, as well." He looked straight at Ted before he sat down. "We cannot permit this." He pulled off his glasses and slid them onto the table with a jerk.

"Permit? Cannot permit?" the pastor stammered. "What's this about *cannot permit?* Tell me, Jim," he taunted. "What's to *permit?* You don't run this place, Jim Jensen. It's not your show, sir."

"I'm telling you, Joe, this won't work anymore. It's too late now. You've run out of time."

"Too late? What's too late?" the pastor mocked. "A *priest* is responsible in every parish, Mr. Jensen. And it's to the bishop that he's responsible, I might add. Not to the Jim Jensens of the world. Stand down, Jim. You have nothing to say about boundaries. The Church sets the boundaries, and they are very clear here. This council is advisory. I don't care what you say. The pastor is in charge."

Megan twisted in her chair, stewing and squinting acridly. *I'd hoped to make a difference here, but so far this priest's been the same every meeting. Predictable. Arrogant. Making unilateral decisions and repeating trite speeches. Try as he may, the man never comes up with what's needed. Jim is right—time's up.* Joe Burns continued, pontificating now. "Your priest was here yesterday, he's here today and he'll be here tomorrow. Can't say that about laypeople, now, can you? So let's stop wasting time," he demanded, his face lined with anger. "As I said, I've got more work left today than most of you have done since you got up this morning. I'm sorry. There's no money to increase staff salaries and that's all there is to it. I'd like to. You know that. We can't, however, and you know that, too. Move on."

"Okay, Father Joe, you're the pastor," Ted volunteered. Sitting tall, he ran large weathered hands up and down over the leather vest he wore with a checkered shirt and a new pair of Levis. "As I said, I would wait some if I were you, but if that's what you want, it's good enough for me."

Megan pushed the sleeves of her brown corduroy jacket up tight on her forearms. Lips drawn tightly over her teeth, she fired back. "It's *not* good enough for *me*. No, sir! That just won't do around here any longer. We've talked about this habit of yours, *so* evident this evening, ever since I came on to this council. You agreed to stop it." She fought to control the tone in her voice, but the tightness there trumpeted the rage in her belly. "There are a couple of important things here," she declared, pointing at the pastor. "First of all, you owe it to us to..."

"Owe?" the pastor echoed, his face twisted. "Owe?" he chided. "Tell me about owing, Miss Roberts. Don't you ever, *ever*, say that I owe you or

•

anyone else in this parish *anything*." He exploded. "I have given all there is to give. Find me a priest who has given more. This really steams me."

"Steam all night if you want to," Megan snarled. "Priests like you no longer scare me. I am going to finish what I was saying. You owe it to us to..."

"Megan, I'm warning you."

"You owe it to us to give this report every consideration."

The pastor got to his feet.

She waved him off. "We went into this with your specific approval—at your request, in fact. Secondly, I know firsthand that some people on staff are excited about this review of parish compensation and are expecting the study to be completed and reported on. Soon."

"Staff, you say? Who, for cripessake?" the pastor demanded. "Who's been talking to you about this? Staff members have no right to be talking with parish council people about this or any other matter—not without prior clearance from me. Until the Church decides to do things differently, that's the rule," he scolded.

"What rule?" Megan demanded.

"The rule *here*. In this parish. In *any* parish."

Jim fingered the gavel. "That *used* to be the rule."

"The person in charge is the pastor of the parish," Joe snapped, spitting p's on Ted to his left as he sat down.

"The person in charge has to be a *leader*," Jim rebutted.

"That's crap, Jim, and that'll be enough of this, thank you. Staff can't go around the pastor to talk with any fool council. That's the rule, here."

Ted nodded, approving the points the pastor was making.

Sheila studied the pastor in the silence that followed, then leaned into the table, reaching toward him with both hands. Her jacket lifted on her shoulders. "In business, Father Joe, we have to do things better than we sometimes do them here at St. Mary's."

"What things?" the pastor scowled.

"Things like listening. And teamwork and planning and follow-through. I know you don't like business ideas and standards applied to the Church, but it fits here."

Joe Burns rocked from side to side, then pulled his chair closer to the table. *Can't let her do this. There are moments of absolute principle, after all. This is one of them and not even Sheila can cross that line with me.*

He tried not to stab when he pointed at her, but the moment carried him away. "That's right, Sheila. I don't like parish affairs referred to as business." He cracked his knuckles. "This is the Church. You can have all the marketing theory and business crap you want in your real estate empire, but in the Church it doesn't count for anything. Nothing at all. That's the trouble with people today. That stuff may work..."

Sheila cut in, meeting the burn in the pastor's eyes. "Father, you've said that you want a Church for modern times. You want a council to help you insure good management and up-to-date business practices and..."

"Sheila, that's enough. Let's move on." Red-faced, Joe pushed his fingernails along his scalp several times, blotted the sweat onto his pants and stroked his scalp again.

After a pause, Bob, who had recently retired from his position as an executive with the YMCA, smiled as he claimed the pastor's attention. "Father Joe, you know as well as I do that we cannot be successful this way. We agree on the vision, Joe. This is about how we get the job done."

Arms folded, leaning back, the pastor studied a man he trusted. *It'd be easy if every voice was like Bob's, true in tone, authentic. But people lose their way. The Lord said it—they need a shepherd. A priest does the best he can for his flock, but a guy gets tired sometimes, dammit.*

At the same time, Bob was considering his pastor, reviewing the evening's performance thus far. *Pathetic,* he concluded. *Definitely not what you'd hope for after so much effort with him over the years. Is it a crisis? Perhaps.* Flashing his easy, gracious smile once more, he tried again.

"Joe, the days are gone when you could just do what you want as the leader of an organization. Your finer instincts tell you that. We've talked about it frequently—right here at council and you and I, privately. You don't like Church work referred to as business? Okay, that's fine with me. I try to never use that word in your presence. But, Joe, whatever you choose to call it, *this* isn't going to work. A leader cannot share leadership and power with people and then arbitrarily take it back."

The pastor could barely breathe. "Bob, you know I like you," he confessed, face drawn, leaning forward, trying to engage his friend. "But let me tell you something—and we've talked about *this* before, too. People lose sight of the big picture—God's plan for the Church. They get confused and start thinking the Church is a business and can be run that way. This council will come around. I know you will."

Bob knew it for a lie, knew the pastor didn't really believe what he had just said, even as he softened his words to continue.

"Look, friends. I don't care. You're good people. I appreciate you, but listen, folks. You don't have the full picture. There's no way you can see it from where you sit. I'm just trying to do what's right here. We've come a long way in this parish, as you've often said, Bob. And, Ted, you remember it, too. Way back—when we started together."

"You're right, Father. Those were great days," Ted affirmed, humping his shoulders and tugging lightly at his vest. "What in the world happened to change it all like this?" He didn't wait for an answer. "We have to work together better, that's what. As I said before, Father, I think it might be a mistake for you to dump this report. But folks!" he pleaded, massaging the fleshy base of one thumb. "Come on now, folks. This is Father Joe. How would you like his job, trying to manage all this?" He relaxed and passed a hand back over his thinning hair.

Joe Burns read the room again. Most of the heads were down. *Look at them! Not a nod, no agreement, nothing.* It was clear now. Ted's words were having no impact. They weren't getting it.

"Look, folks," he appealed. "All that priests ask for is a little help. You can do that. Just don't get in the way at every step. This is the Kingdom of God, remember, and that's what I was ordained for. You can help, I assure you. Just don't get in the way."

"What in God's name are you talking about?" Jim scoffed. "The Church is the *people*, Joe. It's the *people*, not just priests and bishops."

The pastor's eyes narrowed to slits. "Shut up, Jim. You could have had a part in this. You were a priest of God, for cripessake, and like a fool you decided to give it up. Now stay in your place."

Jim bristled, his mind racing. "*That's* a lot of crap, Joe," he blustered. "We're fighting for what it means to be the Church today. We're not kids here, trading marbles."

"You don't like the way I do things around here? Then get out," the pastor shouted, standing up and pointing to the door. "You became chairman by the rules of the council. I never liked it, but I live by the rules, and now we've got the proof about you. We'll get a new chairman, that's all. I'm the priest here. I've got the call from God, Jim, not you.

Now stand down or get out."

"I am not going to get out, Joe. This is my Church as much as it is yours. I repeat, you do not *own* this Church. You do not own *us*. And, by God, you do not own *me*."

The pastor dropped heavily back into his chair. "People, my people," he moaned, cradling his head in his hands, hiding his eyes. He waited several moments before looking up. When he did, the corners of his eyes were moist. He paused and then proceeded in tones barely audible. "Honestly, people, you owe me more. What do you say about this?" He studied the people at the table, awaiting a response.

"Tom?" he said finally.

Many meetings ran their course without Tom Andrews either offering an opinion or being asked for one. He had no idea where the words were coming from when he finally replied. He just felt the leap.

"Father Joe, I have to be honest with you." His face rigid, he peeked at the pastor, then locked his eyes on the center of the table. "You know how I respect you and how I appreciate the chance you gave me to serve on this council, but I have to say, Father, I think you should hear the committee on this. I'll support you, of course, but I think you should hear us out. At least in this case, Father Joe."

The pastor's fists tightened under the table. He looked to Rosa Perez, his personal choice to represent the growing number of Latinos in the parish.

Profound cultural reverence made it difficult for Rosa to offer an opinion opposed to or even different from that of a priest, but under his gaze now, she quickly smoothed back her silky black hair and asked for the pastor's permission to speak. It didn't come. She swallowed hard as the pastor's hand moved slightly. She took it for yes.

"Please listen to me, Father Joe," she pleaded. "You are a good priest. I will always stick by my priest. He is God for me. *Que te bendiga La Virgen de Guadalupe*. But, Father Joe, this, in my humble opinion, is not right. Listen to Sheila. Pay attention to Bob. I know Jim makes you angry, but you've got a lot of help here. We want this to be the new kind of Catholic parish that you have been telling us about for so many years. What you are asking people to be tonight is the old kind of Church."

"Stop right there, Rose," Joe demanded.

"Rosa," she replied softly, looking directly at the priest.

Joe Burns shook his finger at her and then expanded the gesture to include everyone else at the table. Two observers got up to leave.

"Go," the pastor shrieked. "Go on. Get out." As the door closed behind them, he sighted down his long arm and stabbed his finger again at Rosa. "You," he growled through gritted teeth. "You should talk about a new kind of Church. You haven't helped me one iota with your people. Don't talk to me about the new kind of Catholic Church. Get your own conservative, timid people in order before you come to your pastor, trying to teach him a lesson or two."

He stood abruptly, snapping, "That's what's wrong with these councils. People don't *know* enough. I don't say they're stupid. They just don't have the big picture. They don't see what our bishops see and as pastor I work for the bishop. Remember that."

He began to pace around the room. "I can't do this any more," he muttered. "It's out of control. You may not think so, but I know I am a good priest. God knows what we've been through for twenty-five years."

Clamping his eyes shut, he slapped a fist into the palm of the other hand, then bit down on the fist hard enough to score the skin there. He resurfaced a minute later.

"I've had enough," he mumbled. He looked around the table. There was no help. Megan was bent forward, shielding her eyes. Dave Hanratty, the director of parish volunteers and the only member of the staff to attend council meetings, had been quiet the entire evening as expected, and was tapping the table with his empty Styrofoam cup. Sheila's hands were folded in front of her.

When his eyes reached Jim Jensen, the priest's entire body trembled.

"You! You're the damn problem here," he raged. "You're the one stirring the pot. Every priest I know talks about types like you. That's the problem. Your kind," he stammered, glaring and shaking.

He pointed his finger at Jim like a gun, then pulled the trigger. "No more!" he bellowed. "That's the end of this." With that, he stormed out of the council room and down the hallway.

The council members regarded each other in silence. It had finally happened. Joe Burns had crossed the line one time too many. The consequences would be historic—worthy, they'd say when it was over, of the Council Fathers in Rome during the 1960s.

CHAPTER 4

Tuesday, November 7

9:25 p.m.

To anyone who was willing to listen, Ted Kroenig could—and would—tell the war stories about Joe Burns' years as the pastor at St. Mary's. He'd begin with the one about the hash the pastor was served by his predecessor, Father Charles Williams, who had tried to close the parish school in 1970. While most Catholics had always considered as sacred any idea that a priest might offer, proposing to close a parish school was not one of them. When Father Williams did so, there was a deadly, dreadful fight. Ultimately, the archbishop transferred Father Williams to another parish and named Joe as the pastor. The school remained open.

During the summer of 1972, as Joe began his second year at St. Mary's, he learned that three of the nine nuns who taught in the parish school had made petition to leave their religious order. He was forced to replace them with lay teachers, a financial burden for which the parish was totally unprepared. Early in the spring of 1973, he gave up hope of replacing them with other women religious and, bowing to the inevitable, recommended closing the school to resolve the budgeting impasse. In a split vote in June, the parish council supported his proposal.

It seemed to many parishioners that the new pastor did not care about the school. Some even accused him of coming to St. Mary's with his mind made up about it. Ted maintained emphatically that Joe had worked hard to clarify his position, but he had to confess that the pastor's tone hadn't helped with what he had to say.

"I don't see what the problem is here," Joe had announced at a parish meeting that filled the school gymnasium. "It's clear as the nose on your face that we don't have the money to support a school. There are no nuns. Get it?"

He insisted that he had not arrived at St. Mary's with a preconceived plan to close the school. "My ideas develop," he said. "I'm always thinking. Always reading. Always studying." In the end, he explained, the development of his thought on the school had been organic.

Somebody asked what it had to do with music.

Ted would admit that Joe might simply have smiled at the misunderstanding and continued, because many parishioners were amused. Joe Burns wasn't, however.

"Organic, for godssake, people! *Organic!*" he repeated in frustration. "From its center! Naturally. *Not* like the organ in church, for cripessake!" He spelled out the word and continued. "My ideas grow organically. One idea leads to another. They all come from my heart, from my center. Why do you accuse me of lying about the school? It was an organic development in my thinking." By now he was shouting. "It was all there for you to see. It was honest. You saw me shaped and changed before your very eyes by events over which I had no control. If you knew how hard I tried to get nuns here, you'd get off my back. I didn't become a priest to run a school."

For some, the school issue and the priest's open contempt were early signals that even though this priest preached about its merits, he had neither the intention nor the ability to work collaboratively. While Ted judged it unfair, many predicted that the pastor's professed commitment to shared decision-making and to valuing the insights and convictions of Catholics in the pews would come to nothing. The school was closed.

Two years later, at another public meeting in the gym—this time to resolve a controversy over whether the pastor could remove the Communion rail that stood between the priest at the altar and the people in the pews—parishioners asked how the matter would finally get decided. Someone referred to the way the decision had been made to close the school.

Pulled back into the old argument, Joe again ended up speaking dismissively. It was too much for some people to take, priest or no. "More of the same," they said. "*This* is what he means by sharing decisions?" some asked. Others walked out mumbling, "Democracy in the Church? Ain't a priest born who could do it." To some, however, it made little difference. "He's the pastor. Let's go home."

It was the first time Ted heard people call the pastor a brute.

☙☙☙☙☙☙☙☙☙☙☙☙☙☙

Nearly half an hour had passed since Joe Burns stomped out of the council room. As he had on similar occasions, after the pastor left the meeting, Dave Hanratty had excused himself to work in his office nearby. Jim was now contending—for the third time, by Ted's count—that a triangle was no longer an appropriate image for the Catholic Church, with priests and their bishops and the pope at the top of the organization—in power. In that model, non-ordained, ordinary people were at the bottom—powerless, without voice.

"It's a circle," Jim repeated, shaping it with his hands. "The Church, first of all, is the *people*."

"Okay, a circle, a circle. We get it," Ted barked. "It's a circle, but damn it, you can't build *anything* unless you've got your priest with you." He got up to make more coffee. "What do you think? Should I do both?" He held up two decanters. There was no reply.

"Put them both on, Ted," Sheila said finally."

We're about done here," said Jim. "We don't need that much."

Ted shrugged. "I'll do one."

"I'm with you on this, Jim." Megan Roberts tapped the papers in front of her, straightening them for her folder. She leaned her slender body forward, arms folded on the table, her thin face intent. "Friends, we don't have to put up with this every meeting. I consented to serve on this council because I believe some changes are needed, like sharing responsibility and broadening how decisions are made in the parish, but this priest consistently and arbitrarily decides what will come to the table and what will not."

"We're lucky to have the man," Ted asserted again, retaking his chair. "True, he doesn't always say things the way you'd like, but we've got to stop beating up on him." A project manager for forty years at Kroenig Construction, the family firm that built the parish church in 1916, Ted had a one-step-at-a-time approach to life—something he attributed to his work in construction. He liked things step-by-step in church, too. The pastor was a good man, he maintained, and the parish should build on that.

"I don't get it, Ted," Megan shot back. "You couldn't put your buildings up this way, could you? If you ran your projects the way Joe runs this church, you'd be out of business."

"This is different."

"No, Ted, it's not," Jim snapped, mussing his hair. "We make too many excuses for this guy. There are better ways to do things in the Church today."

"I know that," said Ted. "But why in the name of God do you have to start talking like that, Jim? So bitter and *sharp*? It always starts the war."

Megan searched the table and then looked at Ted. "Can you imagine someone asking for a report on something that's important for our parish and for our staff and then refusing to even look at it? That's nuts—insane!" She twisted the silver and turquoise bracelet on her wrist.

"That's enough, Megan," Ted scolded, a razor's edge on his voice. "I don't want anyone suggesting the pastor is mentally ill."

"What would you call it, Ted?" Megan asked rhetorically and continued. "I'm no psychiatrist, but this man seems unhinged to me. All that twitching, tapping, pacing... He's barely able to manage himself, much less successfully pastor a church. We should take steps now to get a change."

"You could never get rid of a priest," Ted contended. "It can't happen. It won't." He yanked at his vest.

"Yes, it can," Jim argued.

Ted bucked the chairman. "The archbishop's his own man. He won't be pushed around. I tell you, it won't happen." He reminded the group that five years after Joe had become pastor, he was certain he had a commitment from Walter Meuncher, the newly appointed archbishop, for an associate pastor to help with the ever-increasing workload at a growing, busy suburban parish like St. Mary's. Instead, plans changed and the archbishop sent the intended associate to Rome for advanced studies.

Joe had prepared two members of the council to speak for the parish in a discussion with the archbishop about the need for an associate pastor at St. Mary's. Ted was one and the chairman of the council was the other. It was an opportunity, he pointed out, for laypeople to acquire the experience of collaborative Church ministry at the diocesan level. Things didn't go as planned. Joe ended up seeing the archbishop alone.

"The chairman and I were at the rectory by 3:30, as arranged," Ted explained. "But that morning the archbishop had asked the pastor to be at the chancery at 3:00, saying he didn't think it was necessary for members of the parish council to be present. Joe was disappointed, of course, but in the end, he said, he had to go along with the archbishop's decision.

"We asked about all the work and preparation that went into this. Joe told us to be reasonable and to remember that theory is fine, but things don't always work according to theory. It was a matter of accepting God's will, manifest in the decision of the archbishop."

Ted looked for confirmation to Bob Talbot, who'd been a member of the council at the time. Bob nodded. It was a true story.

"That was the end of it," Ted went on. "So you won't get anywhere talking to this archbishop about replacing Father Joe. He's not about to sit down with any parish council today any more than he was ten or fifteen years ago."

Jim looked at the clock on the wall above the refrigerator. "The bottom line is this, Ted: There'll be no peace at St. Mary's while Joe Burns is the pastor."

"That's bunk," Ted replied.

"It's hard to learn how to do old things in new ways," Bob noted thoughtfully. "Joe's been slow to develop the skills a person needs today to lead other people. He likes the idea of change but has a hard time getting it done in ways that work."

"Ted?" With delicate fingers, Sheila Martinson felt her pearl necklace, waiting for the man to look at her. "No matter how difficult it may be, Ted, a leader today has to move beyond simply *understanding* new ways of doing things. You've got to be able to get the package off the shelf into somebody's hands. Unfortunately, in the ten years I've been a member of this parish, Joe has never been good at doing the stuff that makes the ideas work."

"I don't care what any of you say. We're lucky to have this man, given the shortage of priests," Ted protested. "Yeah, Joe's got some problems managing things, but everyone's got problems. Most parishioners are willing to excuse the things he does as a matter of style or simply a short-coming, and this council should, too. Maybe he shouldn't act the way he does sometimes, but nobody's perfect. Let's get off his back and give him some support."

Pressing a finger to her lips, Megan tried to slow the anger coursing through her body. She began deliberately.

"The worst part of all this is that it's bigger than just this parish alone and this one priest." She raised her voice slightly. "I've heard it even from patients at my clinic: Priests act like feudal lords—lords of the manor, one fellow called them. People can't stand the arrogance of these men—and Joe Burns is the worst, at least in my experience." She fingered the pin on her lapel. "That's it. That's where I stand. It's time to do something."

"Then find another parish," Ted demanded.

"I won't do that."

"There are thousands of Catholics who agree with me," Ted contested. "Sure, the Church needs some change. But it's happening. For twenty years Joe has been talking with us about Vatican II. We've learned a lot and done well. This is a fine, new kind of Catholic parish."

Megan placed her hands flat on the table and waited, fingers spread. "Here's my point. I will not leave the Catholic Church again, the way I had to when I divorced. It's *our* church, Ted. They've taught us that. This kind of priest either has to make some personal changes or make way for somebody else. I don't believe priests like this will survive. They can't. We can't let them."

Ted took a deep breath, bringing himself under control, and looked straight at Megan, noting her simple beauty, as he had often done before—blonde hair, wispy all around and tied up loosely in back, eyes blue—*pretty* actually.

"Megan, let me be clear about this. I won't be part of any move or meeting that is out to get rid of the pastor. That's wrong. We both want the same thing for St. Mary's and that's what counts."

Megan met his gaze. "I don't know about that, Ted. I believe that what you want and what I want are totally different. And how we get there is a problem, too. I'm not turning back this time.

"I agree with you on one thing for sure, Ted," said Sheila. "The likelihood of removing a pastor by protest is pretty remote. The archbishop can't give in to that kind of pressure."

"Whatever we do, it has to be good for the whole parish," Tom peeped safely, folding his arms over his sweatshirt.

Rosa rubbed the stubby, soft fingers of one hand with those of the other. "It's been hard for priests," she offered.

"It's been hard for *everyone*," Jim reminded her. "We've tried everything—petitions, resignations, letters of protest. We've done them all and nothing changes. They're pointless."

He looked at the clock again and grimaced. "It's almost ten o'clock, folks. We're not going to resolve this tonight, in any case. Looks to me like it's time for another special meeting. We can have it at my house again."

"We don't need that and if you schedule it I'm not sure I'm coming," Ted retorted. "As I said, I think Joe should read the report, but he's not going to and for most people that's fine. The pastor's the pastor."

Jim adjourned the meeting. Ted shook his head. He'd had the last word, but he hadn't carried the day and he knew it. He joined in as everyone helped to straighten chairs, clear the table, rinse out coffee pots and wipe the counter. Gathering up their coats, the council members headed for the church to pray together, as was their custom. Bob poked his head into Dave's office to pick him up en route.

Dave opened the side door to the church with his key. They entered, signing themselves with the blessed water, and then took places to kneel in the front two pews. They peered into the dimly lit sanctuary, blinking and leaning forward, looking harder, squinting. Heads bobbed, jerked left, then right to see better, to be sure. One by one, certain now, numbing now, they looked away, stunned.

Eyes closed like the lens on a camera, Joe Burns lay atop the altar, twitching, his knees pulled tightly to his chest.

CHAPTER 5

Tuesday, November 7

10:15 p.m.

It seemed an eternity, kneeling there. Megan felt her skin crawl and she wanted to run, but stayed a moment to look again at the scene. "This is nuts. Let's get out of here," she muttered finally to Rosa Perez. Behind them, someone bumped a kneeler. It struck the floor sharply, the crack resounding throughout the darkened church. Joe stirred on the altar. Others of the council began to sidle out, following Rosa and Megan, who peeked back over her shoulder, shuddered, and then hurried out the door.

"I'd better get him," Ted murmured to Bob. He left the pew, genuflected to the tabernacle, and ascended the four steps into the sanctuary. He stood in front of the altar, arms extended, ready to catch his priest in the event he began to roll off. He stepped forward and an easy squeeze on the pastor's right shoulder woke him.

Opening his eyes, Joe sucked for air and collided with the situation. He lurched to get off the altar. "You're okay, Father. Go easy," Ted said, restraining him.

"Ted! Ted Kroenig. My God! Thank you. What's going on here?" He maneuvered to get down. "Where am I?" Again he lurched, pushing against Ted. "What am I doing here?" he fretted. *Who else is here? Head jerking, he scanned the area. Did anyone... the rest of the council... see me? Damn!*

Bob hurried up the steps to help Ted ease Joe down from the altar. Together they inched their way to the bench in front of the first pew. The priest sat with them there for several minutes before he moved to get up.

"Sure you're okay, Father?" Bob asked. They got up as a threesome. Bob and Ted removed their hands slowly as they assessed whether the pastor could stand alone. After swaying slightly, he steadied and, one on each side, they helped him make his way out the church door and through the snow and ice to the rectory.

"Everyone saw me, I suppose?" Joe muttered at the door of the enclosed back porch.

"Well, yes, Father, they did. We go to pray after meetings, remember?" Ted said gently.

"I was on the altar? They saw me there?" he fussed, looking to Bob, knowing.

Bob nodded.

"Cripes!" He pulled the porch door open.

"Forget it, Joe. It's fine." Bob checked his watch by the light over the porch stairs. "It's almost 10:30. Are you sure you're okay now?" Joe nodded. "You need to get a good night's rest, Father."

The pastor could only nod again, his head heavy. He turned around halfway, motioning to say thank you and good night, and entered the darkened rectory. He felt his way down the central hallway, went into the study and shuffled to the leather recliner. He dropped into it and sat motionless in the dark, stunned, reviewing what he thought might well be his worst night in nearly thirty-four years of priesthood—not embarrassed by the events of the evening, but *stung* by what seemed entirely unfair to a pastor who had sacrificed so much, a low blow to a man who had given his whole life to the priesthood.

Headlights from the schoolyard parking lot raced around two walls of the study. *Has to be Bob and Ted—they stayed to talk? In the snow? What time is it anyway?* He searched out the glow of the small digital clock facing him from a bookshelf. It said 10:38. His eyes closed quickly and within a minute he began to snore loudly until he woke with a jerk half an hour later.

Rising slowly, he went to the bathroom across the hall, ran cold water and cupped handfuls of it onto his face. Then he ran his wet hands several times over his scalp and held them there, pressing his head from the side, at the cheeks, as he looked into the mirror. He stared, losing track of time, studying the eyes in the mirror. Was there ever a day he hadn't wanted to be a priest? he wondered. *But at what price now? What's it worth, like this? Thirty-four years—a few more to forty. So forty years I'll be a priest and for what?* He dabbed his face with the hand towel and looked into the mirror again. Suddenly, it hit him. *Ken. I've gotta see Ken.*

Joe Burns and Father Kenneth Halpin were members in one of many priests' support groups that formed after Vatican II. Priests sensed the need for a time and place where they could pray together, confess their weariness, be openly angry at the new pressures under which they were doing their work and in general find assistance in managing their lives in a Church that was changing dramatically.

Joe and Ken's group of eight priests brought together a wide range of experience as well as theological and pastoral perspective. Joe had been a member of the group for ten years, Ken for just six—since his appointment as pastor at St. Rita's, a neighboring church half the size of St. Mary's. Quirks of suburban expansion in the area had limited the geographic boundaries of St. Rita's. Joe often kidded Ken that life had to be twice as easy for a priest with half the number of people taking pot shots at him, jesting that his success at St. Rita's could be due to that alone.

In fact, after ordination Ken Halpin had been sent to Europe for advanced studies. He did not complete the dissertation that would have made him a doctor of theology, however, and he requested that the archbishop change the plan to place him as a seminary professor and assign him instead to a parish in the diocese. His original and only passion anyway had been to be a parish priest and to face the challenges of being a pastor guided and formed by the documents and the principles of Vatican II. The archbishop did so, and they agreed that he would also call on Ken to use his training and schooling abroad for special assignments in the diocese.

There was something—a peaceful heart, perhaps—in the way Ken Halpin did his work that Joe admired. He often tapped Ken outside the support group for his insight and advice on implementing change in the Church. And frequently they went ice fishing together once the area lakes froze over for the winter.

လ၁လ၁လ၁လ၁လ၁လ၁လ၁လ၁လ၁

Joe flicked off the light in the bathroom, strode to the study to call Ken, thought better of it because of the hour, delayed and then made the call anyway. Ken picked up the phone.

"I'm in a mess," Joe confessed candidly. "A big one. Got some time? I know it's late."

"Of course, Joe. I'm still awake, just reading. C'mon over."

Joe was out of the rectory in five minutes and arrived at St. Rita's ten minutes later. Ken was at the door before Joe could ring the bell. "Come on in for heaven's sake. What's going on?"

Inside, Joe reached for his friend and fell onto his shoulder. "It's too much, Ken."

Ken held him awkwardly for a moment and then led him to his study where Joe sat down in an overstuffed chair and leaned forward, elbows on his knees. Alternately, he rubbed softly, then pressed firmly on his skull behind the ears. He slid back into the chair. "I can't do this anymore."

The younger priest had seen his colleague upset before, but never in a meltdown like this. "Tell me, Joe. What is it?"

"It's out of control."

"What is? What happened?"

"I'm supposed to be their leader, for cripessake."

"And I'm guessing it's your parish council. Sounds that way."

Joe nodded and stumbled through his version of the meeting. "In the end, I just walked. Got out of there. No one can lead these people. How could *anyone* do it? Take a man like Jim Jensen, for instance!"

"We've talked about Jim before."

"And that Roberts woman!"

"Megan."

"How can a pastor lead people like these? Tonight was the limit. No one—not a *one*—stood with me at the end, so I walked."

"Joe, I want you to listen to me. We talk together often, you and I, about our work and a lot of other things, but this time I want you to just listen. It's not as though I haven't said these things to you before, but tonight I want to be very direct—maybe more so than on other occasions.

"Joe, leadership is earned. Followers allow it. They grant it. I truly believe the Lord wants the Roman Catholic Church to reform itself at this time and—just as important—lay members must take part in shaping the reform. There's more than one way to do things and we make progress whenever the people have an impact on their own future. Sure, there will be mistakes, but we make them together. The Church has been so top heavy, Joe—*clergy* heavy! That's understandable, in the light of history, but it's no longer excusable in the light of Vatican II. It's a new day, Joe."

Joe tried to interrupt.

"Just hold on, Joe. Let me finish. For many reasons and for long periods of time the Church defined and legislated matters with rigid, absolute certainty and righteous, unbending ideas about God and Church practices that Jesus probably wouldn't agree with. Supposedly the official, institutional Church had everything figured out. There were no more questions to ask and little room for public discussion before Pope John opened the windows at Vatican II. People began breathing fresh air and the reform of the 1960's was underway."

Ken lifted his hand to keep Joe from speaking.

"It seems to have happened overnight, but really, you know as well as I that the groundwork had been laid fifty, maybe a hundred years earlier with all kinds of study and scholarly research done quietly behind the scenes, resulting in the rebirth of some of our original, ancient theology. I'll tell you, Joe, studying to be a priest in the light of Vatican II was the most wonderful, liberating experience of my life. This one Church Council, however, does not mark the end of things. There'll be a Vatican III someday. It's a mistake to think that we've got all the truth or that all the right ideas have been expressed and explored already. Or that we have to get everything done in a single generation. Okay, Joe, go ahead."

"Sure, there'll be a Vatican III, but for right now we've got number two. And all the changes ordered in the '60s now rest on the shoulders of the bishops and their priests. If *we* don't do it, Ken, it'll never happen."

"I'm not so sure about that, Joe. There's a divine presence that's driving this, not the bishops and priests. It's not *ours.*" He paused, waiting for the other priest's eyes. "I really try to *listen* to the people of my parish, Joe. I don't have to control everything nor be responsible for all the results. People are good, Joe, and in astonishing ways I find God is present in things lay people do as part of this crucial reform of the Church."

"Of course, Ken. God is good and faithful and present and all that, but you know the story as well as I. The Lord said don't stand around all the day idle. Go to the vineyard and work. There's not supposed to be much standing around, much waiting."

"Listen to me. The waiting around that you distrust and dislike so much is the waiting we do for *Mozart*, Joe. We have to *wait* for Mozart."

"Mozart?"

"Yes, you bet. Let me tell you how I know that and what I mean. One Sunday afternoon a few years ago I sat in my study here, stretched out, resting, listening to the man's Third Violin Concerto in G Major. I found the second part, the adagio, totally, unbelievably *stunning—superbly* beautiful—just plain *perfect*, you could say. Of course, there *isn't* anything that's absolutely, totally perfect in life, and that afternoon I finally understood and conceded that point, once and for all. We have to *wait* for perfection—wait for *Mozart*—who became for me a metaphor for the perfect world—a reformed Church, improved liturgy, better preaching, world peace or whatever else it is that I dream of and value.

"We work, we wait, and then we reverse the order, but the Lord seems not to be in that much of a hurry. Basically there's some waiting to do. Not just standing around idle, mind you, but *waiting*, being *patient*—creatively, with imagination—and never taking our ears off the music. If we're too quick to decide what's perfect and how everything *should* be—reformed perfectly to the vision of Vatican II, let's say—then we've gone too far and said too much and we end up playing God. Only God is perfect—and that guy Mozart, I'd say, especially in the adagio of his third concerto." Ken waited until Joe looked over at him. He smiled at the older priest. "Adagio means *slowly*, Joe—not to be hurried, at *ease*. So that's why we wait. Mozart isn't here yet. It's on the way. We have to do some waiting and be creative about it."

Joe squirmed forward to get out of the oversized chair, then settled back slightly. "Those are good thoughts, Ken, and your Mozart idea is all fine and dandy, but I'd have to think some more about it. For now, you know that I can't be a priest that way. I respect you and your way of doing things, but I can't buy it because I don't think it's right. I make the Mozart. I'm ordained for that. A priest has to make the music."

"Well, Joe, my friend, I can't agree with you. And I can't force you to be something you're not. I believe there are many ways to be a priest today and a lot of different styles and perspectives that will work. I take time to consider them all, but I must tell you—in my opinion, what you've just said won't work. Call on me any time and we can talk about it some more if you'd like to."

It was past midnight when the pastors parted company, still friends.

From the doorway Ken watched Joe back out of the driveway and turn for home. As he thought about Joe's response to Mozart, it saddened him—about Joe, not for himself. It somehow brought to mind the last time he'd been to the Highway 61 Bait Shop, almost a year ago now, to pick up the minnows for their first afternoon of ice-fishing the previous winter. Still standing in the doorway and staring out into the street as he recalled the occasion, his heart ached and he felt chilled by more than the early winter night.

"Terrific day for it, Father," Gus Lindstrom, the owner of the bait shop and a long-time parishioner at St. Rita's, had said as Ken entered.

"Yup, it's great to get out for an afternoon." His sunglasses fogged as he stepped further into the shop. "It must be getting pretty busy in here now."

"Yes, and we like that," Gus grinned and motioned Ken to follow him back to the minnow tanks. "What'll it be, Father? The same? Three dozen or so?"

The priest nodded. "That should be enough."

Gus pushed a net eighteen inches square into one of the tanks, snaring the minnows. He shook the net carefully to slide them off into the pail, then dipped back into the tank and pulled another couple dozen out. "That's for good luck on the first day out, Father."

"Thanks, Gus. I appreciate that. What do I owe?" Ken asked, pulling out his wallet.

"*That's on me, Father. It's nothing.*"

"*Well, thank you,*" Ken said, bowing slightly toward Gus. "*I don't expect that.*"

"*It's my pleasure. You have a good time this afternoon.*"

Resuming his place behind the counter, Gus tidied the containers of inexpensive bobbers and sinkers there, then looked up at the priest. "*You're out with your regular partner?*" At Ken's nod, he continued. "*So, how is Father Burns these days? Excuse me, Father Ken, but he's a strange one. Don't know if I should say so, but I hear about him in here year round, Father. Always seems angry about something, people say. A priest ought to be better'n that, they say. I've always wondered but, well... It's okay if I talk to you like this, isn't it, Father?*"

"*Of course it is, Gus. What you say is safe with me. Yes, there are people concerned about Father Burns. He puts a lot of pressure on himself. He wants to make the Church the best it can be and that's a lot of work.*" He slipped the wallet back into his pants pocket. "*It takes time for things to happen in the Church, Gus. We've got to give everybody a chance to change at their own pace. Priests, too. Not everyone accepts change the same way. I say a prayer for Fr. Burns every day.*"

"*Well, that's your affair, Father. You're a kind man. I appreciate that. Your friend is a case, though. That's the word out there, anyway.*"

Ken offered again to pay for the minnows. "*No, that's for you, Father. It's nothin'. You guys have a good time.*"

Ken closed his front door and turned off the outside light, wondering what more he could have done. How much better could he have said it? Joe just didn't get it. A good man destroying himself? Perhaps.

CHAPTER 6

Tuesday, November 7

10:20 p.m.

J im Jensen drove slowly through the streets of Mapleton, through the parish, rather than take the interstate highway home. He called Peggy, his wife of fourteen years, from an all-night gas station to tell her the meeting was over, but he'd be stopping briefly at Edenberry Park, as he often did after parish council sessions.

He drove to a favorite spot that overlooked park paths and walkways lit by tall, arched streetlamps. With the windshield wipers set at high to brush aside the snow that had resumed falling, he let the scene take him in. He adjusted the car seat, leaned back and closed his eyes to review the evening. It struck him that Joe Burns personified a nineteenth century phenomenon of the American West. His punishing, destructive behavior illustrated, in color, the evil assumptions and policies of Manifest Destiny, which conferred upon one people the unparalleled right to crush another. *Sure! Take the land, shoot the buffalo, build the railroad, and steal gold from sacred hills. Do whatever you want, when you want to do it!*

And who will challenge similar tyranny in the Church? It's from God, after all, this destiny—unknown by the unwashed, by those with no franchise, but supposedly manifest even so. The power—the destiny—presumes what it wants to. The earth is flat. The sun goes round the earth. Who can argue?

So go ahead, oppress us, most believers say. Have at it. Others, they say, smarter than we, have questioned it or boldly raised objections. But we're average people—too much to lose by objecting. You want it this way? Let it be, then. What you say is true? Fine. It's destiny. It's God's will. So be it.

Jim shifted his weight in the car seat and stared past the moving wipers out into the falling snow.

I will not buy into this destiny, will not be intimidated. There's only managing it, coping, living to change it where you can. Manifest Destiny in the Catholic Church is bad air that people breathe—both the oppressors and the oppressed. The wheels are off that wagon. It's bunk, has no coin as a worldview. No more taking the land or shooting the buffalo, nor may you rape the people. Clerics may no longer act as if they alone are a Church intended and established by Christ.

There's better air available—really fresh air—and if you don't create more of it in the Catholic Church, if you don't open the window for others, then you've lived in vain after 1965.

Jim blinked. *Frightening—all of it!* He shut off the wipers and allowed the night to snow him in for a while before turning the ignition key and clearing the windshield. He headed for home.

Turning into the driveway of his green-shuttered two-story colonial home, he pressed the garage door opener on the visor above him. He checked the window of the master bedroom upstairs; the lamp lit there confirmed that Peggy was waiting for him.

He grabbed his folder thick with council reports and papers, and slowly walked to the front door. He leaned his forehead against the doorjamb, seeking the cold that sometimes fizzed the coals that burned in his brain and his soul after council meetings. Inside, stepping into the kitchen, he poured a glass of milk, wrapped half a dozen chocolate chip cookies in a paper towel and brushed through the day's mail on the table before he began to make his way upstairs.

"Daddy, I'm hungry." It was Joan Marie, Jim's five-year-old, standing at the top of the stairs in pink, footed pajamas. "Can I have a cookie?"

"Sweetheart, it's late. You should be in bed," the father declared. The tone belied his words, however, and his face said it's so good to see you as he looked up from the second step. "But, sure, here. You can have one of mine."

He set the milk on the top stair, between the spindle and riser. "There. Nobody can kick it over now." He seated himself beside her and, opening his hand, let her pick a cookie from the stack, marveling all the while at his good fortune.

Joan Marie was the last of Jim's four children. She came unexpectedly when Peggy was nearly forty-two, after Joshua James, almost thirteen, and the twins, Jeremy John and Judith Ann, now ten—all of them named, at Jim's suggestion and because Peg was gracious, after biblical saints and prophets.

❧❧❧❧❧❧❧❧❧❧❧❧❧❧❧

There had been a previous marriage, just a year after Jim left the priesthood in 1972. Angela was a woman his age whom he had known in college, before major seminary. After six months, the impulsive marriage performed by a Justice of the Peace ended in divorce. Jim, who had begun courses at St. Cloud State University toward the business degree he wanted, transferred to the University of Minnesota and continued taking a course or two at a time while supporting himself by working full time as a janitor.

It was during this time that he met Peg; they fell in love, and in 1975 they married. The Church could bless the marriage and did so, and his life with Peggy and the children had afforded him personal peace and well-being he hadn't imagined possible previously.

With a loan from Peggy's father and mother, Jim eventually earned a degree in business administration, emphasizing organizational development and marketing. An interest in volunteer organizations and small, independent family businesses led to his involvement in a capital building campaign for the YMCA near Jim and Peggy's apartment—which a year later led to a position at Summit Development Corporation, the firm retained by the Y to manage and insure the success of the campaign.

After five years with Summit, Jim had started his own consulting firm. His flair for strategic planning and organizational development, paired with his considerable skills in communication, was helping small business-es and not-for-profits market their services and products with great suc-cess. He was doing business all over the state of Minnesota as well as Wisconsin, Iowa, and South Dakota. Jim flew his own twin-engine plane to the more distant sites, a skill he learned from Peggy's father, who had been a commercial pilot for Northwest Airlines.

಄಄಄಄಄಄಄಄಄಄಄಄಄಄಄

Joan Marie was taking tiny, conserving bites until she motioned for milk, then dunked the last quarter of her cookie and finished it off. Jim pressed her firmly to himself. She turned her face up to kiss him.

"That's enough now, sweetheart. It's time for bed."

"Okay, Daddy, I'm tired now. Will you tuck me in?"

In the bedroom, Jim leaned over the girl and lingered, looking deeply at her in the vague shadows thrown by the night light on the wall behind him. She seemed asleep. He kissed her again softly, remained a moment, and left the room.

At the stairway, he bent down to pick up the milk and the last cookie before making his way to the master bedroom door. He knocked and poked his head in just far enough for Peggy to see his forehead.

"So. Talking with your little girlfriend," she teased, laying aside the book she was reading. "Nice. I didn't want to interrupt you two." The plain nightgown she wore could not diminish her dazzling beauty—curled blonde hair to her shoulders, mussed a bit from the pillow, warm blue eyes that smiled assurance, a shade of lipstick left from the day, a touch off color.

"It's the cookies. I'm irresistible." Jim closed the door and crossed the plush carpet to the rocking chair. He plopped into the rocker and waved the last cookie toward Peg, feigning an offer, before he set the cookie and the glass on the table. He checked the digital clock on Peggy's side of the bed. It was 11:20. He leaned back and rubbed his face, then his eyes, and peeked at Peg. "Mind if I shut the window?"

"No, it was getting a bit warm in here so I opened it a crack—go ahead, shut it and tell me. Was it a *big* truck? You look run over."

"How's about a different topic?"

Peg knew. "It *was* a big truck."

Jim smiled. As was usual after council meetings, his wife had no trouble seeing through him. "You're wondering about the meeting," he stated as he leaned forward, reaching to loosen the laces on his brown Florsheims. "What a night." He pulled off the first shoe.

"Tell me about it."

He explained how the pastor summarily dismissed the report he had specifically requested six months earlier and ended up stomping out of the meeting.

"Sounds familiar. Everybody said the usual things?"

"Yes, of course."

"Again."

Wiggling the shoe off with the other foot, Jim rocked in the chair, head back, eyes closed. Peggy waited.

"And then, listen to this, Peg." He leaned forward again, almost sliding out of the rocker. "After the meeting, the creep goes to the church and, get this, we find him lying on top of the altar."

Peggy stared at her husband.

"He was just *there*, I don't know, to *pray* or some damn thing?" He shrugged. "I have no idea. Anyway, when we went to the church, as we always do for a prayer after meetings, we found him there, lying on the altar, facing us, curled up, fetal."

"What?" Peggy hung her legs over the edge of the bed, staring at Jim. "What?"

"That's what *I'm* saying. *What?*"

She fell back onto the pillow and buried her eyes in the bend at her elbow. "What was he *doing* there? *Sleeping?* Was he looking *out* at you or what?"

"I couldn't tell, Peg. No one could. Who knows? He looked unconscious."

"So then what? How did he get down?"

"Ted."

"I suppose."

"Ted and Bob got him. The rest of us just hightailed it out of there, Megan and Rosa ahead of everyone else. As soon as we got to the parking lot, we got into our cars and split. We didn't stop to talk it over, didn't even want to acknowledge we'd seen this sorry man like that."

"He's unstable—and it's not the first time. What'll he do next?"

Jim went to the closet for his pajamas and then to the three-quarter bath off the bedroom. He brushed his teeth, put on the pajamas and slid into bed. He lay on his back, one arm bent back under the pillow.

After a long silence, Peggy spoke. "Jim, I want to ask you something." She waited, weighing the words. "Do you think, maybe, Jim, it's time for you to let go of all this—to just let it go?"

Jim grew still.

Peg waited.

Jim's breathing was shallow. "Let it go, sweetheart?"

Peg turned onto her side, facing Jim, and draped her arm over him, coaxing him closer to her trim, shapely body. "Yes. Would it be possible for you to put your energy elsewhere for a while? You've done your share for this parish. It's going to kill you, honey. You can't win this." She looked up, checking, seeking his eyes.

They were closed. "I can't, Peg. I can't let this go."

"You've done more than your share, Jim. There are others. Let them carry it for a while."

"Somebody's got to stop this man."

"*You* don't have to do it—not all the time."

"You can't expect the average parishioner to stand up to a person like this, Peg. The power difference and the fear of doing so is overwhelming. I wish people *would* speak up or talk back to a priest, but I know that's expecting too much, even when there's a principle at stake."

Principle, Peggy Jensen thought, *damnable principle.* Her husband came by his craze for principle honestly, she knew. As Jim saw it, both his grandfather and his dad lived by principle and paid the price for it.

※※※※※※※※※※※※※※※※

A union organizer for warehousemen in St. Cloud where he and his wife Mary were raising a family of five boys, Grandpa Jensen believed in fairness for everyone, even employers. An employer had to eat and feed his kids and wife, too, he said. Good things should be spread to everyone at the table. He wouldn't—couldn't—stomach the dark, crooked tactics that sometimes marked labor union activities.

Other union leaders, peers and those above him, couldn't stomach Harold Jensen and his talk. In August of 1949 Harold took a baseball bat over the head and then, as he lay unconscious on the ground, additional strikes to his knees. He regained a blurred consciousness, but not his mind or his ability to walk. He sat in a wheelchair, drool escaping from his disfigured mouth, until the day he died, two years later. Jim was eleven.

Just a year later Jim learned the lesson a second time. A teacher at a Catholic high school north of St. Cloud, Clarence Jensen, Jim's father, was considered an outstanding teacher by his peers, able to help his students make connections between their school subjects and their lives. Not one to shy away from controversy if it would help a classroom discussion, he went so far as to make obscure resources available to students, occasionally even an opinion or a chapter found in a book within the Index of Forbidden Books, designed to safeguard Catholics from unapproved ideas.

Agitated and vocal parents objected. The school fired him—on orders of the bishop in St. Cloud. There was no warning, no explanation, no severance, no opportunity for Clarence to offer an explanation of how his teaching might fit with Catholic standards for orthodoxy. He eventually found work in the public schools of St. Cloud. During the transition, however, the family used up a small savings account intended eventually to help provide higher education for the five children. Still just a boy, Jim had learned the price often paid for principle.

❧❧❧❧❧❧❧❧❧❧❧❧❧❧❧

Jim lifted himself up onto his right elbow to face Peggy.

She knew. "You're thinking you'd like a bat."

"Yeah," he exhaled with an empty chuckle.

"It's not necessary, Jim. And you know from grandpa and your dad that nothing good can come from intolerance or violence and the evils they imply." She reached toward him and gently caressed his cheek with the backside of her graceful fingers. "This is only about the Church, remember. Do you think God really cares all that much about this Roman Catholic Church you worry about so much? Honey, you don't have to bring this man down. He's not your meat to put on a hook and haul into the cooler." She passed her hand delicately over his cheek again.

Jim laid back, fingers locked over his stomach.

"You're taking on too much, Jim. I'm afraid for you. You're so angry. You think it's all up to you." Taking a breath, then folding her arms over her breasts, Peggy continued. "I'm talking about your single-minded-ness, your inability to do things more slowly, more in moderation. Follow the advice you give your clients, sweetheart—ease up a bit. It will make you more effective in the long run. You're much better at business than you are in church, Jim."

She's good at pushing back, Jim granted. *A guy makes his points better if he has a sense of humor—gets more done, more easily. And right, Peg, I do it better in business than at the parish. Still...*

"There's so much more at stake here, Peg."

"You don't have to fix the Church."

"Then who's going to?"

"You've done your share, Jim."

"My share of talking, maybe. We've got to *do* more. Hold back in the basket on Sundays maybe—hit them in the pocketbook. That'll fix 'em—bring 'em to their knees."

"It might. There are consequences to that, however, and they're seri-ous. We agreed, I thought, that the harm of that might easily outweigh the gains in the long run."

"Whatever." Jim snorted. "It isn't going to happen anyway. All they want is a Mass on Sunday. 'Just say Mass, Father. Don't let them bother you.' Can you imagine, Peg? This man believes that crap. He takes it as approval from the people."

"It's not?"

"They don't know what they're saying."

"They don't? You think they want anything else from him? Just give them a Mass, make the decisions and take care of things in the parish. Pay the bills, keep the property looking good and equipment in working order. Be there when you need him, like for funerals and weddings and when there's a new baby for Baptism. That's really all they want, Jim. You're kidding yourself. They *know* what they want."

"But that's not enough."

"Who says, Jim? You're no Joe Burns, to be sure, but excuse me,

Honey, sometimes you can be very sure of yourself in deciding things for others."

"Let's give this a rest, Peg. God takes care of some things."

"*Some* things?"

"Let's call it a day, sweetheart. Thank you."

Knowing they had reached the point where they'd usually start repeating themselves, to no good purpose, Peggy relented. She clicked off the bedside light and pulled up the covers. She and Jim turned in the bed, got their arms around each other lightly and eased into sleep. It was well past midnight.

CHAPTER 7

Tuesday, November 7

10:20 p.m.

Megan Roberts drove the four miles from the church to her mother's house where she had left her two girls, Janet, 12, and Jacqueline, 9, for the evening.

"How'd the meeting go?" her mother asked.

"The usual. I'd rather not talk about it, mom. The girls got their homework done?"

"Yes, and in a hurry, so I turned on the TV for them upstairs."

"Okay, ladies. Time to go," Megan called up to her daughters.

In short order the girls had packed their school bags, grabbed a cookie from the cookie jar and kissed and thanked their grandmother before piling into the car. Ten minutes later they were home, getting ready for bed.

Megan ran through the mail quickly and changed into jeans and a sweatshirt before she plopped into her favorite chair in the living room and put her feet up on the hassock. The girls came to give her a good night kiss. "Hope you feel better in the morning, Mom. A long meeting, huh?" the older child said.

"Yes, and it was hard, girls. Here, give your mom her kisses. Good night, my sweethearts." They left for their bedroom and Megan was alone.

She sat quietly for ten minutes, surfed the network channels briefly and then got up to put on a pot of water for tea. On the way back, she slipped an old audio of Christian hymns into the tape player. "Rock of Ages" came on. She sank into the chair again and put her feet up. The night had been insane. She set her mind to forget the meeting and, for once, it worked. Somehow, the music took her. She thought back to her childhood and her religious upbringing.

Not exactly the usual! They must have thought me a brat—those priests and nuns who taught me as a youngster. And with good reason. They were never able to sell me on what they were trying to teach those Saturday mornings or on Wednesday afternoons. To start with, I thought it was no life they had—unmarried, living in the convent or the rectory. The Brides of Christ. Yeah sure! I never bought it after eighth grade. That's when I knew, somehow, in some way, that many of these people weren't healthy.

Could they see that on my face? Maybe I unconsciously stepped away from them a bit or frowned or turned up my nose or something. Somehow I think they sensed I wasn't comfortable near them. That might be what prompted them to single me out whenever they could—for missed home-work, dirt under a fingernail, scuffs on my Sunday shoes.

For reasons that she never understood or accepted, Megan didn't make her First Communion until the fifth grade, two years after her classmates. The first time it was because she missed words on the test for the Act of Contrition. The next it was because she arrived late for the practice for First Communion—the procession into church, how to walk and where to sit, how to fold your hands and bow your head.

In any event, she and her teachers at the church grated on each other early on. It began to show near the end of eighth grade when she received the sacrament of Confirmation—which was also when she finally began to not care any more. And so, the brat.

The teapot began to whistle, bringing her back. She went to the kitchen, chose a teabag, poured boiling water and picked up some vanil-la wafers while she waited for it to brew. She made her way back to the living room and her chair, chomped on a cookie, then another, and sipped tea. It took only a moment to lose herself again in her thoughts.

It didn't get any better in high school. To my surprise—and keen disappointment—my parents sent me to a Catholic high school, of all places! I laid low in religion classes where I thought I might easily be exposed, but got good grades there because I was able to parrot back in exams what they taught. I graduated a Catholic with honors, my earlier experiences with the Church unattended to.

It wasn't until she studied dentistry at the University of Minnesota and got active at the Newman Center that her formation in Catholic Christianity really jelled. She read widely and engaged in discussions about many challenging subjects and world issues, including matters of faith, the Catholic Church and world religions. She found herself affirmed in her thinking and in her faith by staff and students alike.

Soothed by the music and feeling sleepy, Megan sipped her tea and reached to the table at her side to shut off the lamp and relight it at the lowest setting. She pulled up an oversized comforter folded on the floor at the side of the chair and arranged it over her body, tucking her shoulders in at the top.

Her mind continued to churn the past. She recalled what a crippling shock her divorce had been. She and Jeremy stayed together for seven years, but their love lasted for only a couple of them. Not only were they busy raising two daughters, but Megan had gone into practice with her father and was involved in developing a rapidly expanding dental clientele.

Then her dad died suddenly, five years to the day after she got her DDS. She had to determine from various options how the clinic could best serve the growing business. She decided to construct a new, larger clinic. It was a strategic move financially, but too soon she found herself overwhelmed with the complexities of building a new facility. She had been enchanted with dentistry. The business end of it crushed her. When she wasn't working on financing, she was reviewing construction plans. When she was home, she wasn't really present.

All of it left her husband alone and she knew that. When he complained to her about it, she agreed with him completely—not to say it really addressed the issue. They grew apart, more so than she was aware. More than she could admit.

Then one day she discovered, almost by chance, that her husband had had a love affair. Supposedly that was over, and with counseling they managed to get past it. But within six months he was seeing another woman occasionally and then there was a third.

Megan sat quietly for some time before she found herself weeping, overcome by the evening, the thought of the girls, her busy life and the failed marriage.

We might have stayed together in some kind of separated, broken relationship, but for Jeremy, too, the marriage was for better or worse, and he could, he should have known—he was told—that this pressure from the ill-timed death of my father was temporary. When he said he couldn't wait, I divorced him.

She took another cookie and drained the cup. In the kitchen she checked the water in the glass pot, found it needed reheating and waited for it, legs stretched out beneath the table, reflecting on the worst part of the divorce, the part that still enraged her.

It was six months later, at Christmas time, that she experienced some form of repentance and returned to the Church. She decided to go to Confession and that's where she met her first dragon priest. She told him she was divorced, but why she did so, she has never been able to figure out. It led to questions about marital fidelity and sexual relationships that she might be having and the declaration that if she were doing something like that and did not seriously intend to stop it, he could not forgive her sins and she could not presume to take Communion at Mass.

As if that wasn't bad enough, the creep reminded me that masturbation was still a mortal sin and—according to the Catholic teaching we grew up with—enough to send me to hell forever if I would die in that sin. The fool offered that to me, he said, as information he thought I would find important and valuable. I was furious. I hadn't asked. I knew the rules and I likely would have broken this one and continued to receive Communion anyway whenever I attended Mass.

The teapot whistled and she brewed a second cup, noting that the clock on the wall above the counter said 11:30. As she returned to the living room, she reversed the tape in the tape player. It began with "Just a Closer Walk with Thee." She took another vanilla wafer, wiggled into the chair slowly to not spill the tea, sipped it carefully and rested her eyes, head back.

And that's when I changed parishes, hoping to never, ever see that man again, she reflected. *I joined St. Mary's and continued going to Mass on Sundays with some frequency and to receive Communion at Mass—whatever the rules—but I no longer considered myself a member of the Catholic Church. I had left it. I didn't want—didn't need, wouldn't tolerate—a Church that would hold beliefs and opinions like those proposed by the cleric I met that time in Confession.*

She took the last two cookies and finished her tea, then pulled the blanket up tight to her neck and snuggled into it, recalling how she got involved at St. Mary's, volunteering for the parish committee for religious education and later permitting her name to be placed in nomination for the parish council. She'd had encouragement from Clarice Morgan, the director of the religious education program, and because of Clarice, she received the support—the votes—of many members of the parish who had children in classes at the church.

She developed a visceral reaction to Joe Burns and the clericalism and sexism he brought to his exercise of Catholic priesthood. Neither she nor Jim Jensen could walk away from that kind of a challenge. For both of them, she knew, it was personal.

Foolish me! I thought I could bring to my relationship with a priest like this the same precision and effectiveness I take to a difficult tooth extraction or a root canal. But that hasn't worked. The pressure he can bring to bear on any conversation or matter under consideration at a council meeting makes me edgy. And then angry. It's almost impossible to be civil at those meetings. The five feet three inches in my bony frame belie the rage that courses through my body at times. I feel it every time I'm in that man's presence.

"Time for bed," she mumbled to herself. *One church meeting and this much thinking about it is enough for one day.* She went to the girls' room, pulled their covers up tight and gave them each a kiss. She signed them with the cross and left the room.

CHAPTER 8

Wednesday, November 8

12:30 a.m.

Back at the rectory, Joe stepped into the dark hallway for the second time that night and thought it a metaphor for his current predicament. Worse was Ken's Mozart idea. "I don't think so," he muttered to himself. We know what the Lord set up for his Church. And what priests have to do. Ken has to think about that some more.

He flopped into the recliner in his study to relax and reclaim himself, but he dozed off quickly, only to be awakened after ten minutes when Mindy, his cat, jumped onto his lap. He eased her back to the floor, stood to shake off his drowsiness and then walked the hallway half a dozen times, steadying himself at each turn with two fingers on the wainscoting. He returned to the study and paced slowly for several minutes in the dark, then went to the kitchen and prepared himself a bowl of breakfast cereal. Into a second bowl on the floor he dispensed cold water from the refrigerator for the cat, who darted from the hallway into the kitchen.

Seating himself in a wooden chair at the table, stretching his legs beneath it, he ate slowly, fiddling in the bowl with every other bite before bringing the spoon to his mouth. Looking out into the night from the window next to the table, he thought about sleep. *That's the worst part of these fights—not sleeping. People get over the fighting and come around— never saw a time they haven't. But a priest never gets his sleep back.*

When the bowl was empty, he took it to the sink, hit the light switch as he left the kitchen, returned to the study and pulled the door nearly closed, leaving it open a crack for Mindy. He turned the desk lamp on to its lowest setting. It illumined the telephone, a wooden crucifix, and a 4 x 6 framed photograph of his father and mother on their wedding day. He straightened the crucifix a touch and then surveyed the room.

It was the largest one in the house, fully twenty-five feet long by fourteen feet across. One wall, floor to ceiling, held bookcases crammed with books and theological reference volumes. Another ten feet of shelving along the adjoining wall was filled with neatly filed periodicals and journals. On the wall at one end hung portraits of John XXIII and Pius XII, duplicates of the ones in the parish council room. Behind the desk, sheer curtains and heavy, patterned drapes framed a grand triple window.

He took off his shirt and collar and, clad in an undershirt, stepped over to the recliner. He plopped into it again and settled back, feeling light, almost buoyant. He rested his arms easily on the soft leather padding and kicked off his shoes. He extended the leg rest to view his toes, rubbing his stockinged feet together. Lowering his head, he closed his eyes and exhaled through his nose, hissing loudly. Mindy, standing at the door, turned back into the hall. Joe lay still, considering his life, the life of a priest.

What was it, anyway, that made a boy want to be one — a priest? What about all that training —minor seminary so early in life, boys just fourteen, most of them, and right out of eighth grade? And I? Just thirteen, having skipped third grade. And what of that fearsome God who called *you? It was a* vocation, *wanted or not. You are selected for a system you don't choose. It finds you. Which is to say, God does. He calls you. And you'd better take the call or there could be trouble in your life.*

Mindy jumped onto his lap again. The priest opened his eyes for a moment, blinked, squinted, stroked the cat, and fell asleep.

ぺ→ぺ→ぺ→ぺ→ぺ→ぺ→ぺ→ぺ→ぺ→ぺ→ぺ→ぺ→ぺ→ぺ→ぺ→ぺ→

A finger quivered, pushing his eyes open. The clock on the book-shelf moved to 1:20 a.m. Drained, the priest sat staring, his mind shuffling through his life as a boy as if it were yesterday.

All those sins! No touching, especially. Any place. No thinking about touching, either. No sex, ever, at all. Don't even start. You can't look here. Or there. Don't think this or that, either. None of it. And it made such sense—back then, anyway—because, after all, who had the answers? The Church, of course: the priest, the nuns. They must *be right, you figured as a kid. They would know about the sins and about the hell you'd get for committing them—hell forever.*

That's it then! I'll be a priest. I'm bad, probably, and this way I can be good and right. And safe, too. Besides, then I can tell others what's right and good. They'll save their souls, and they'll thank me for it. Yes, I'll be a priest and help people serve God. I'll be right and safe and go to heaven for sure and *I'll help others at the same time.*

What is *it that happens, then, when a man puts on that black suit with the white collar? Priestness, maybe? Rightness? Yes, he joins rightness. When does he find that it's nice to be there? That it's more than safe. It's nice, and officially right besides. Prestigious, too—in the Church anyway. People look up to you. They need you. They bless you. They give you value.*

Waking with a start half an hour later, he felt perspiration dotting his forehead. He swiped it away, wiping his hand dry on his shoulder. Reaching for a small pillow on the floor at the side of the chair, he tucked it behind his head, breathed heavily, and coasted further into the recesses of his mind and the life of a priest, replaying familiar scenes, responding to a million critics. He knew their faces and where they sat for Mass on Sundays.

So tell me, people. What if one day your priest finds himself over-whelmed, crushed even, by the very Church he's trying to serve? He poked the pillow, seeking a comfort that was stubbornly eluding him. *What if, deep in his heart, a priest begins to wonder whether his Church, maybe, isn't everything it claims for itself?*

Could priests turn into false *prophets, maybe, in their black suits and white Roman collars? Certainly a priest knows the primal fear of God in the*

*hearts of his people. He knows his own fear as well. They, he—all of them—
eat and drink their fears, then sleep on them. A priest could one day come to
see, couldn't he, how the Church controls its children—of all ages.*

Giving up on getting the pillow to support his head as he wanted
and sweating profusely now, he got up out of the recliner and slowly
shuffled to the chair by his desk. He ran his fingers over the crucifix
lying on its surface, one that had adorned his grandfather's casket. He
rolled the chair back a bit and stretched out completely. He drifted off
again into scenes made familiar by repeated viewing over the years, rang-
ing through his own life and the lives of a thousand priests he knew.

*And then, you who know everything! Imagine! An enormous wind
blows from the mind and the heart of God! A Catholic Church Council is
born, and it comes at a point in the billions of years of God's universe and
in time to catch, to* include *your priest, your pastor. Imagine, people! It
comes in time! He's still alive! He's been a priest for some time now, but still
a young man not yet forty. Sure, he's got baggage from childhood, a lot of it,
like everyone, but certainly within the bounds of good health. Your priest
gets re-educated by that Vatican Council of the '60's by that Spirit of God,
and he sees new possibilities, new freedoms—for himself, as well as for his
people. He sees a new world, a new Church.*

"Anything was possible," he muttered. "A fresh start." He snorted. *So,
you critics! You want to run the Church? Tell me, then. What's a priest to
do if he feels himself renewed like this and then later discovers himself hope-
lessly blocked, shredded, by his own Church—the patriarchy, the mistakes
of history, the power, the money, the unbending tradition? Then what?
What does he do, you who know so much?*

"What. Does. He. Do?" he demanded, mumbling in his sleep.

*Changes come in bits and pieces. Minor improvements need worldwide
consideration and evaluation before anything can happen. Gotta have trial
periods and endless waiting before even the most insignificant, lousy, stinking thing can be changed. And yet...*

He sighed.

*And yet the world has changed and in the Church it's like a rolling river,
up and over its banks, relentless, ever widening, powerful and taking out
unexpected landmarks and what we thought were unmovable barriers and
obstacles to change. There seems to be no limit to where the Spirit is taking*

this Church, the Church a priest grew up in, the Church where he gave his life to save people.

He pressed back into the desk chair, shaking his head from side to side, working out a kink in his neck even as he mumbled and whispered, lamenting the predicament.

Imagine! He makes a run at creating a new kind of Catholic parish— puts every ounce of energy into reformed worship; into fresh strategies for passing the faith on to children; creating for adults a vision for collaboration and collegiality. There would be Church governance and organizational structures to make it happen, even new church buildings with architecture to support a vision of community rather than of hierarchy. Everything *becomes a statement about a new kind of Church, a new people of God.*

He got out of the chair, buoyed by the memory of those happy times. "What a vision your priest had—and right from the start!" he muttered as he bent over to stroke Mindy's head, relishing the way the cat arched into his touch. "Right, Mindy? All the right things, at the right time. I read all the documents, bought all the books, went to all the seminars and summer schools and got myself re-educated. Right?"

Joe returned to the recliner, stuffing the pillow behind his head as he continued. *And so, he ends up a reformed priest with a new spirit, a new life. The Church would have councils and boards to help make decisions.* He stretched and then burrowed deeper into the chair, letting his fatigue reclaim him. *Yes, people would have a voice. They, too, have their gifts from God, after all, talent as valuable as that of the priest or the bishop—better in some ways.* "What a great time that was!" His eyelids dipped. "A great time to be a priest," he whispered, his voice trailing off.

The phone rang some time later. He woke, shaking, confused, and let it ring until the recorder took the message.

"Father Joe, this is Bob. I know, it's the middle of the night, but I'm just wondering how you are. Upstairs asleep, I hope, and not hearing this. I know it's been a tough night. Call if you want to."

He got up for the bathroom. "Too much coffee," he mumbled at Mindy, a blur on the floor, near the nightlight. Returning to his chair, he reclined it and sniffed once. Pressing his eyelids tightly shut, he dove again, deeply, digging into the distant corners of his life.

There's other things, too, like appreciation. Like never really getting any. Are people too busy to be grateful? I'll tell you about being busy. You wonder why some priests don't connect with people? I can tell you about that, too. People say some priests don't have the right style for today's world. So? Everybody has a style. Thing is, a priest usually gets things right. But then, what if he can't ever sell the package? What if he puts people off, including his bishop sometimes? And so, for all the vision and leadership, for all the success, he's never okay. Never affirmed. Always alone. No woman. No bishop. Few friends. Maybe none. Always working. Keeping the faith. Sharing the vision. Shaping it. Sharpening the focus. Upping the ante, but never, ever, anything for himself. And so, people, there's your priest! No appreciation. No life. A lot of grief. How do you like him?

People complain about what I say and what I don't say. They maintain that things I say always come out wrong. I never say good, kind words. Never offer praise, compliments, support. It's never right, you know.

Restless, he shifted in the chair, growing more agitated.

Doesn't seem that way to me! People have to be tougher, you know. It's thin skin, that's all. What I say has to be said, that's the trouble.

He twitched and muttered himself back to consciousness. "Listen to me, dammit! Baptized people shouldn't have to be thanked. *Or appreciated. The work is for God, after all. Why do things always have to be said a certain way, people? Why can't you just take my words at dictionary value and leave me out of it?*"

I know, sometimes anyway, my face and, okay, maybe my eyes, sometimes, are hard. "But you have to get past that, for cripessake. Just take my words and my meaning." *Not my face, not my intensity, not my gestures, nor criticism and putdowns, nor my devaluing your so-called unique, stinking personhood.*

Joe Burns stirred in the recliner and cracked his eyes open. It was 3:15 a.m. Mindy leaped back onto his lap. The priest closed his eyes and slept what remained of the night.

CHAPTER 9

Wednesday, November 8

6:20 a.m.

Waking with a start, Joe shivered at the thought of the night just passed. He reached to the floor at one side of the chair for the comforter he kept there, stood up to wrap it around himself and then slid his feet toward the desk for the phone.

"Good morning, Bob. Joe here. It's not too early to be calling, is it?"

"No, Joe, this is fine. I'm awake and accounted for. What's up?" He knew, of course.

"I'd like to see you this morning for breakfast, if I can. I really need to talk with someone, you, if possible."

"Last night, the meeting."

"Right."

"That'll be fine, Joe. I'm free until ten this morning. Perkins?"

"Yes, Perkins."

The pastor remembered it was Wednesday. Bob heard him mutter something about the 8:00 Mass.

"Is there something you need? Something I can do?"

"Naw, never mind. I was just thinking about the scheduled Mass this morning, but I'll call Lorraine and have her distribute Communion. I hate to do it this way, but seeing you comes first."

"That's fine. What time?"

"Give me an hour."

"Seven-thirty, then, or whenever you get there."

డ్రాడ్రాడ్రాడ్రాడ్రాడ్రాడ్రాడ్రాడ్రాడ్రాడ్రాడ్రాడ్రా

Lorraine Larsen, the parish liturgist, was the fourth person to hold that position in the past seven years. She worked with the pastor, a part-time director of music and other staff to prepare the worship and other prayer services at St. Mary's. Joe considered her the most creative and energetic person he had hired for that position in all the years he'd been the pastor. And best of all, she was a team player that a priest could count on when he needed one.

Joe studied the phone on his desk for a moment, then pressed the numbers from memory. *Good morning, Lorraine,* he thought. *Here's your wake up call.* He let it ring twice and hung up.

He pressed the numbers again. Jack Larsen picked up on the second ring.

"Hello, Jack. Father Joe. I know it's early, but may I speak with Lorraine? I've stumbled onto a problem this morning and I need her help. Would you be able to put her on the line, please?"

"Good morning, Father. Yes, sure. Just a minute." Joe heard Lorraine's husband waking her.

She took the phone half-asleep, spluttering at her husband.

"Joe Burns," the pastor declared with some play in his voice. "You know—your embattled pastor. I'm sorry to call so early, Lorraine, but I've got a problem here this morning." He waited. "Hello? You awake?"

"Yes, Father Joe. I'm okay. A problem? What problem?"

"I can't offer the 8:00 Mass. The reason why isn't important right now. I'll explain later. I need you to be at the church to distribute Communion."

"Gosh, Joe, I'm sorry," the liturgist replied, trying to focus. "I've got to take my son to school first thing to meet with his teacher. This really won't work today."

"Oh boy, that's bad, Lorraine. Any chance of moving that to later? Or what about tomorrow? Could you take Jimmy in tomorrow? I really need this."

"I'm a bit out of it yet, Joe. Can you hold for just a minute?" Lorraine covered the phone mouthpiece, resting it on her stomach. She stretched to a quiver, relaxed and yawned. Her husband, propped up on one elbow regarding her darkening expression, ran his fingers through her jet-black hair.

Lorraine retrieved the phone. "This is *not* a good morning for me to come early, Joe. As a matter of fact..."

"Lorraine, let me stop you. I hate to call like this but I really need the favor. I know—we've got to get other members in the parish trained to hold Communion services. We keep talking about it. What do you think?"

"What do I think about what, Joe?"

"What do you think about covering me at 8:00 so I can take care of this problem?"

"What do I *think?* I *can't,* Joe. I told you. I have an appointment. Our son is doing terribly in math this fall."

"Lorraine, we had a bad council meeting again last night. This Jensen fellow will be the death of me yet. I just got off the phone with Bob Talbot. We're on for breakfast at 7:30. I need someone for 8:00."

Lorraine had been in this bind before with the pastor. She tapped her forehead with the back of the receiver, pondering what she should do.

A Communion service isn't the same as Mass, but don't forget—people are gathered in the name of Jesus to hear the Scriptures and to receive the Eucharist; so, true to his word, Jesus must be there, present. It foreshadows the day when a woman will actually be the priest.

"Hold on a minute, Joe." She covered the mouthpiece again and turned to her husband.

"I'll take Jimmy, if it's important," he said. "Go ahead."

"Joe, look, okay," Lorraine conceded. "I've told you before that I like to be given notice about these things, but okay *again* this time. My husband will take our son and I'll be there before 8:00. Have a good breakfast. I hope you get this fixed. What happened anyway?"

"I've got to go, Lorraine. I'll fill you in later. Pray for your pastor, will you?"

Joe hung up the phone and debated about a change of clothes and a shower. *A quick snooze'd be better.* He slipped off his pants and wrapped himself tightly into the comforter again before he slid into the recliner and popped it back. He was feeling good in spite of it all—clean in his heart, exhausted from work considered essential and eager to get on with this latest battle, knowing it had to be fought.

ᕦᕤᕦᕤᕦᕤᕦᕤᕦᕤᕦᕤᕦᕤ

Just past 7:00 Joe's head jerked to the left, waking him. The kitchen timer he used for naps, kept on the floor at the side of the recliner, sounded a moment later. He shaved quickly, threw on a fresh pair of khaki pants, a long-sleeved tan shirt and his U of M sweatshirt. Grabbing his overcoat, he left the house briskly and caught a wet wind and a mix of snow and rain in the face on his way to the garage. He shivered as he waited for the garage door opener to do its task. *Getting colder. And a foot of snow by tonight, they say. Too soon for winter.*

As he drove the mile and a half to the restaurant, the rhythmic left right, left right of the windshield wipers provided curious comfort. He snapped off the radio to hear it better. Left right, left right, one two, three four. *Regular. Dependable. A guy needs that.*

ᕦᕤᕦᕤᕦᕤᕦᕤᕦᕤᕦᕤᕦᕤ

Comfortably ensconced in his Oldsmobile Ciera, Bob Talbot used the forty-minute drive from his home north of St. Paul to ponder what lay ahead.

A recently retired executive of the Greater Minneapolis YMCA, Bob had spent many hours with Joe over the years, sharing his experience and the significant challenges he had faced while learning collaborative, less directive and top-down ways of working with others. Knowing that churches weren't unlike voluntary systems like the Y, Bob had tried to pass on to Joe what he had learned. He found the pastor a willing student, with good and laudable intentions, albeit a plodding learner.

An exit sign reminded Bob of the lake, off to the left a mile or so, where years ago he had spent an entire summer afternoon catching crappies and sunfish with the pastor, listening to Joe's story about the path that brought him to the priesthood. It rang clear as a bell in his mind as he mulled it over.

In the last half of the nineteenth century, a colonization bureau was selling thousands of acres of farmland in west central Minnesota to Irish immigrants—invited to Minnesota by the celebrated and fiery archbishop of St. Paul at the time, John Ireland, who headed the bureau.

Joe's great-grandfather bought one of the farms in 1882 and it had passed to Joe's own father by the time Joe was born in 1931. The Burnses never forgot to whom thanks was due for the comparative prosperity they enjoyed. They prayed for John Ireland at table every day and at their bedsides every night, asking that God bless the archbishop for all he had done for them. For thirty years the archbishop's framed photograph hung on the wall in the farmhouse living room.

Joe was eleven when his father up and left the farm, taking his wife and four children with him to St. Paul, because a year earlier Joe had told his father he was feeling a call in his heart to be a priest. The dad figured no better place for Joe, therefore, than in St. Paul, the archdiocesan Church where John Ireland had been so successful a servant of God and the Irish people. Eventually, the family purchased a home in St. Paul's North End district, within sight of the dome of the Cathedral built by Ireland. Joe went from Catholic parochial school to the minor seminary and entered the major seminary in 1950. He was ordained a priest in 1956 at the age of 25, the youngest in his class.

There was a time that Joe had had reason to believe he would be tapped to take his years of theology in Rome and then complete other studies that could lead to a career within the diocesan chancery office, perhaps one day even to being named a bishop. It didn't happen and Joe settled for what he held had been his call from God anyway—being a parish priest.

Still, the idea that he might have been honored that other way suggested he could be something special as a priest, a bright light, a developer of new ideas and challenging possibilities, a new frontier fighter like the great prelate who had blessed his family with opportunity and had become his idol. It wouldn't be about farms and jobs and immigration now but rather about a booming American Church, expanding into the suburbs of larger cities like St. Paul and Minneapolis and prospering in every lovely smaller town throughout the archdiocese.

And who could say for sure, Joe figured. If done well, his work as a parish priest and pastor could arguably provide good reason for him to still get the call to the episcopacy someplace—in Duluth, maybe, or Winona, if not St. Paul. He was out of touch in that regard. I never told him.

Bob checked his wristwatch. *Halfway,* he thought. *Plenty of time.* He adjusted his hold on the steering wheel and rolled his shoulders several times to stretch and relax. His mind was stuck on the pastor and the parish. *Trouble like this is nothing new at St. Mary's,* he reflected, knowing the history of bitter conflict in the parish long before Joe Burns came on the scene.

Archbishop Ireland brought in French-speaking priests from Montreal and Quebec to work among settlers north of St. Paul, many of them farmers, most of them French Canadians, until he officially established the parish of St. Mary's there in 1916. He named Father Guy Leclercq the first pastor and told him to build a church.

Father LeClercq died just two years later and when the archbishop made clear his intention to appoint an Irish pastor to replace him, it caused a rumble north of town. Community newspapers published in French across the state raised a stink, letters were written and visits made to the chancery in St. Paul by parish leaders who demonstrated no stomach for a break from the tradition—French-speaking pastors for French Canadian parishes.

It was a battle they would have lost. Not one to change his mind or back down in matters like this, Ireland was in the last year of his life and apparently decided not to force the issue in this case because a French-speaking priest followed Fr. LeClercq as pastor.

It had been a fight and the people at St. Mary's took the outcome as a victory, free and clear. The story of how a French-speaking parish once wrestled down a cleric—and won—is still told around here, now some seventy years later. That they actually believed they had battled John Ireland, and beaten him, must have made Joe's blood boil, though I never heard him say it.

He signaled to exit the interstate.

I've never doubted that angry people can be true and loyal to the Church. It's possible, I think, to stake out a place for yourself and remain faithful as you believe God sees things, but perhaps outside an understanding that your bishop might approve.

Jim and Megan! Such intense passion about St. Mary's and the Church as a whole! They'd be more effective, I think, if at times anyway they could give things a rest. And yet—was it John Foster Dulles? Someone, anyway, cautioned against treadmill policies that hold people tight in an organization and give them no movement whatsoever, in any direction, until they drop, exhausted. That's what gets Jim and Megan going—they fight the treadmill like a wildfire. Gotta give 'em credit. Seems to me anger can be an ally; apathy cannot.

He turned to cross back over the freeway and came to a stoplight just two blocks from Perkins.

A complex man, this Joe Burns—a fearsome and twisted priest, some say, but there's that gracious side to him, too, and his talent for organization and hard work—accomplished most of what many lesser men, surely lesser priests, would only have imagined. The dark, brooding side, of course, does him no service.

He pushed his head back against the headrest and closed his eyes. The image that appeared of the pastor lying on the altar not ten hours earlier horrified him. His eyes popped open; his fingers twitched on the steering wheel.

Will Joe survive this? Possibly not.

He noted the second, maybe third, time that thought had crossed his mind in five minutes.

ৡৡৡৡৡৡৡৡৡৡৡৡৡৡৡৡৡ

They arrived at the restaurant from opposite directions but at the same time and found parking spots side by side.

"Short night?" Bob asked carefully after he got out, meeting the pastor's eyes over the roof of his car. Joe tried to smile but it came out sour as they stepped towards the entrance to the restaurant. They hung their coats and kicked off their overshoes and without a wait were seated at a window booth.

As Joe looked around the restaurant, he sensed an ease there—twos and threes conversing over breakfast or just coffee, almost in slow motion. It seemed... peaceful. He found himself relaxing. It was good to be here, good to be with Bob.

The waitress brought coffee. "Great—we need that," Joe declared. He filled two cups.

"So. A short night," Bob said directly. "Get any sleep at all?"

"Not a lot, but I dozed some. Got a few winks on the altar, of course." He examined Bob's face. It was steady. He relaxed further.

As always, it's safe with Bob—he knows about change and how hard it is in the Church, complex and tangled—burdened—with a history that's also a part of its glory. Nice to be with a man who understands, who'll hold securely anything a priest might say.

The waitress stepped up to take their orders—a waffle for Bob and oatmeal and toast for Joe. She asked to be reminded when they needed more coffee.

Joe sipped from his cup and put his hands around it to warm them. He looked at Bob, who was waiting.

"Terrible meeting last night, Bob. You wouldn't believe what this has done to me."

"Try me."

Bitterly, deliberately, Joe spent twenty minutes relating the story of the unsettling night as it came back to him—up the whole time, past three anyway, dozing off, waking again, then sleeping some, restless, sweating, going over his life. No appreciation. Disappointment, endless change, frustration—every day, at every turn and never, ever, any rest. Resistance, even from bishops, who ordered change in the first place. Totally shattering, that last point.

"Say more about all that."

"It's about more than the meeting."

"Go ahead."

Joe looked around, assuring himself he wouldn't be overheard. He put his hands around the cup again. "They tell me I put people off, Bob." He looked out the window, studying the parking lot. He turned back, searching Bob's face. "That I don't have the skills you need today." He added a touch of cream to the cup, stirred and rapped the rim with the spoon. "Relationships," he snapped, trying to keep his voice down. "They say I don't *relate*—that I come on too strong."

The waitress brought their orders. Bob poured syrup on his waffle and began eating while Joe continued, touching neither oatmeal nor toast.

"What's wrong with my intensity, Bob?" He rapped the rim of his cup again, spilling coffee this time. "I can't always be worrying about how people *feel*. Religion is not about feeling, for cripessake! What's right is right. I can't help it."

"I've always been a rebel, Bob. I'm *different* and they've never appreciated that. I've done my best. Everybody's got baggage and, sure, I've got plenty, I know. But why can't people just take me for what I am? Let's get on with the work. It's what I've given my whole life to. And for what? A rebellion like this? No thanks. What's all this fuss about the way I do things?"

Why the fuss? A peculiar question. Has he forgotten the chapel project? And twenty years of other equally maddening stunts? Pulling that chapel matter from the table that night just a year ago lit the match for last night's explosion.

They sat quietly, Joe mopping at the spilled coffee with his paper napkin.

"How's your breakfast, gentlemen?" the waitress asked as she passed by. "More coffee?"

"Yes, I think so, thanks," Bob answered, also noting that Joe needed another napkin.

She returned quickly with several, one of which Joe placed flat between his hands. He slid them lightly, nervously, over it and then leaned forward again.

"I have a lot of good relationships," he said finally, sounding hoarse now. "I don't understand why they make relationships the key to everything—even to getting the work done. It doesn't figure. We're all working for the kingdom of God, aren't we?" He cocked his head and jerked his hands open. It seemed so obvious.

Bob looked around for the waitress and the coffee decanter.

"All this relationship stuff is killing me, Bob. I have to be careful how I *say* everything," he scoffed. "If I don't say good morning, they think I'm mad. I hate that crap. Why can't we just do the work?"

The waitress returned with coffee and poured for them. Joe bit into his dry toast, washed it down with some coffee and continued ranting, trying to keep his voice down at Bob's hand signal that he do so.

"They claim I'm abusive. That that's supposed to be at the heart of all the so-called problems at St. Mary's. *Abusive* for godssake! I've done a good job in this parish," he insisted, emphasizing the point bitterly, a finger pointed straight onto the tabletop. "Faithful." He tapped the finger. "Thirty-four years a priest and a good one. I'll stand before God assured." He tapped again. "I stayed *in*. No leaving the priesthood for me. Oh no! Not me! Bills paid, property in good shape, great reputation for our parish everywhere, even outside the diocese. I get compliments on my sermons. People tell me that things I've said at funerals have helped them for years. So, what *is* all this, Bob?"

"That's a load to carry, Joe, and sometimes a person can't handle these things alone." Bob watched as the priest fingered one ear, then the other, massaging them softly before he looked up.

"It's a rough business, being a priest today," Joe sighed. "You get to feeling beat up."

"What about some additional help, Joe? Some outside counsel, maybe. Would you consider that?"

"The guys in my support group, Bob. I get tremendous help from them. They know best what I'm dealing with."

"Joe, when I was struggling in my work, it was important for me to get face to face with someone who could give me perspective—a counselor, someone away from the job who could help me with *myself*. Because that was the issue. I had to make changes in my thinking, my tone of voice, my attitude toward some people. Only then could I work effectively. With counseling and other outside help, I began to get better results for what I believed in."

There's a reason, thought Joe, staring at his oatmeal, *why this man is my best, most trusted confidant in the parish—smart, upbeat, experienced— and no one, but no one, tunes in and listens the way he does—watching your eyes, nose pointed at you as he listens. You move, his nose follows. He's present, he's got you in his sight; you know you count; you're worth something.*

"Think about what Sheila brings to the table, Joe. She thinks results—outcomes, always outcomes. You want something specific to happen in a given situation? That's where you start. First you determine the results you want; next you develop a plan on how to get it done."

Joe poked his spoon at the oatmeal again and pushed it away. Bob waited for the pastor to look at him. "As a matter of fact, Joe, I *have* heard parishioners say that you abuse people. It seems a harsh word to me. I have to tell you, however, I can feel it sometimes. Not for myself, of course. We understand each other. Others do feel it, though. I think you should pay attention to that."

"I don't think I should get all twisted up over it, Bob. I'll tell you, though, what they say about a man can hurt him."

"Yes, it can." Bob touched Joe's hand with one finger.

"I'll have to think about it, Bob."

"This issue with the council could be bigger than you think."

"Could be," Joe allowed, "but I doubt it."

"I'm not a doctor or a psychiatrist, Joe, and I know the dangers of pretending to be one. I also know what counseling did for me. It works. You should look into it..."

The waitress arrived to clear the table. "Anything more this morning, gentlemen?" She noticed Joe had hardly touched his breakfast. He motioned her to take it away, and she put the check on the table.

They moved to get up from the booth and Joe grabbed the check to pay at the counter. At the door he handed Bob his coat from the rack, took his own and they slipped into their footgear. Snow mixed with rain was turning the parking lot into a sheet of ice. Gingerly, they made their way to their cars.

"I appreciate your seeing me on short notice, Bob. Thank your dear wife Jeannie for me, too."

"You're welcome, Joe. Call me any time. Think about it, though—this getting some help—will you? "

"Thanks, Bob, but I think I'm going to be okay now. It's nothing I can't handle with the help of good friends like you."

Bob shuffled to his car and slid behind the wheel. He fumbled with the keys before turning the ignition, then looked to his right. Joe had already left. He wondered if he could have done something more, something better. Joe had seemed more than a bit unhinged.

ళళళళళళళళళళళళళళళ

The pastor returned to the parish and immediately went to the front office in the old school building. After he routinely slid a hand in and out of the mail slot assigned to him, he told Betty Halvorsen, his secretary and the faithful and trusted office manager for eighteen years, to schedule a staff meeting for 3:30 that afternoon.

"Staff is pretty well scattered today, Father Joe. I'm not sure I can get them together for you."

"They're not volunteers, are they, Betty? They have work hours, after all." *A man should be able to have a staff meeting when he needs one, for cripessake.* "Start calling around, please. Set it for 3:30 and tell them we'll be starting precisely on time."

"I'll do my best, Father." She handed him a message. Sheila Martinson had just called. "Says she has to see you for sure this morning sometime and can arrange her schedule to do so."

The pastor folded the note. "It's important to have them all at the meeting, Betty. Be sure you get everyone. Three-thirty sharp."

"How'd it go?" she inquired.

"How'd what go?"

"The meeting. The council meeting last night."

"Oh, yes. The meeting. Badly," he mumbled. "Badly," he muttered to himself, absentmindedly checking again for messages in his mailbox.

"It's short notice for a staff meeting, Father."

"We don't have meetings on notice, Betty. We have meetings when I need them. I need one today. Please get everybody together."

"I'll do my best."

Joe tucked the note to call Sheila into his shirt pocket, grabbed a tablet from the counter in front of the mailboxes, and left the parish office for his study in the rectory.

CHAPTER 10

Wednesday, November 8

7:30 a.m.

D ave Hanratty was organizing papers on his desk when the phone rang. It was Clarice Morgan, the parish's director of faith formation.

"Got some time?"

He checked his watch and rolled back the desk chair that comfortably accommodated his hefty frame. "Sure, Clarice. What's on your mind?"

"This won't surprise you. Megan Roberts just called. Can we talk?"

"Your place or mine?"

"Up here. I don't want the pastor to see us huddled this morning. I know he looks to meet with you after a council meeting to get your take on it."

"I'll be right up." Short on sleep after the long and disappointing meeting, Dave pushed out of the chair, rolled his broad shoulders several times and reached forward, locking his fingers out in front of his face.

Joe Burns had hired David Hanratty as the director of volunteers at St. Mary's ten years earlier. It was a new position at the time. The pastor explained to the parish council it was necessary due to the decline in the number of nuns and ordained priests available for ministry assignments since the 1960s.

Dave understood the need differently. He had left the seminary a year before ordination, thoroughly schooled in theology, and knew well the place of ordained priesthood in the Catholic Church. He was committed first of all, however, to the Church of baptized, ordinary Christians. Institutional change of this magnitude didn't come easy or quickly, he knew, but he had been resourceful in developing personal strategies— he called them rules—to keep his vision largely unclouded by the problems a priest like Joe could bring to parish ministry.

Clarice had been hired to address the problems faced by any parish that no longer had a school where nuns worked ten hours and more a day on elementary education and the religious formation of children. The pastor had made it her principal responsibility to involve parents in the religious education of their children, and she'd been so successful at it that Joe regularly could—and did—point to Clarice's work as proof that his parish modeled new ways of doing parish work and was on the cutting edge of reform within the Catholic Church.

A stout woman of medium height, with a splendid smile and exquisite taste in clothing, Clarice brought personal charisma to her relationships with parents and teachers in her program as well as with the children themselves. That charm belied the severity she could—and often did—bring to her relationship with Joe.

భావాలు భావాలు భావాలు భావాలు భావాలు భావాలు భావాలు

Physically fit at 45 from regular and strenuous exercise, Dave took the stairs two at a time to the second floor. He noticed that tables and folding chairs were scattered around the space and made a mental note to remind the maintenance staff to clean and straighten up the area.

Clarice began without ceremony, motioning Dave to take a seat in one of the two padded straightback chairs in front of her desk. "So— what was it this time?"

"You say Megan called."

"Yes, she said the meeting last night was another circus."

"That's a good summary. He slammed the door on us. Said he hadn't even looked at the report they prepared and had no intention of doing so—there was no need for it and in any case there was no money. Then he stomped out. Again."

"What's this about the altar?"

"She mentioned that?"

"Of course."

"After the meeting, when we went for prayer in the church, we found him there, on the altar."

"*On* the altar!" Clarice's face twisted. "He was *on* the altar?"

Dave nodded.

"That's just plain creepy. He may finally be losing it."

"Tell me about it!"

"I can't even picture it. Was he kneeling or what?"

Dave shook his head. "Lying there, in a fetal position, eyes pressed shut. Shaking pathetically."

"Well, who got him down? What happened? Did anyone talk to him afterwards?"

"Ted went up the steps to the altar. Bob stayed, too. The rest of us left without saying much, not even in the parking lot. It was just too weird."

"Megan's right. A circus." She shook her head. "Jim wants to do something about this man, she says."

"The archbishop won't tolerate a power move on a pastor. It won't happen."

"There's no hope for this parish short of a change in pastors, Dave. Joe Burns is a bust in today's Church."

"It's a lot bigger than this one priest, Clarice. Joe is a tiny part of the picture and it's a mistake to get bent out of shape on his way of being a priest. Soon, none of this will matter. The entire landscape is changing."

Clarice waved his point off with her hand. "I understand that. This pastor doesn't, however, and that's the problem. Here's what bothers me. Neither you nor I could change jobs and be sure it was going to be any better in a different parish. It's the same all over. Priests have the power and they use it to take control of what pleases them. You know how this place revolves around Joe and whatever he's up to on any given day."

Dave regarded his colleague kindly. *Easy on the eyes, this woman—enjoys life, a keen sense of humor. Yet, brings rigor and fury to these matters—makes her less attractive. She ought to go easy—more slowly.*

"This is about the future, Clarice. What's the priesthood going to look like down the road a ways? Who will qualify? What new skills will be required? Priests like Joe will not make the cut, in my opinion."

"The man is a dinosaur," she declared. "You may be willing to wait, Dave, but I know a lot of people who will not. Teachers in my program, for one. You don't think the Jim Jensen types are going to wait, do you? And Megan Roberts! You think Megan's going to stay around? Guess again, Dave. People are *angry*."

"Megan certainly is."

"What about you, Dave? He stays out of my department, thank God, but you have to work with him closely. You've got your personal strategies—rules, you call them—for working with him, but it must drive you nuts. So often it seems like you're outside the action, unable to get justifiably angry about it." She locked eyes with him.

"I *am* angry, dammit," Dave asserted, his gaze meeting hers without wavering. "You know that very well and you also know the strategies I've created to manage my anger, to keep my sanity and remain healthy."

Yes, my rules! Dave acknowledged to himself, passing a hand over his mouth, exhaling loudly through his nose. *Number One. The pastor is the boss. A good rule and so obvious! It's important to be completely clear about it, however, and be willing to live by it every day. His appointment by the bishop gives the pastor that standing and many people expect him to be that first of all, the boss. Over the years many have forgotten that and have gotten themselves into trouble, staff in particular. They lost their jobs. You'd expect that in most organizations.*

Number Two. Without question, categorically, Joe Burns is the enemy. No kidding, the bloody enemy. There are so many things that this priest does that are fundamentally opposed to what I stand for that I have to think of him that way. He's the enemy. Crazy, you say? Yes, it often feels that way, working here.

"You do take a lot of chances with this man," Clarice conceded, adding with a smile, "and I admire you for that. You speak your mind at staff meetings and Lord knows what you say to him in private. But is it enough? I've told you a hundred times, there's no way your mental gymnastics would work for me, no way I could be so philosophical about it all. My gut always gets involved."

"I call it vision, not gymnastics," Dave replied evenly. "It's the way I look at things."

"Vision. Right. Okay."

They laughed about it. The sticking point was a familiar one. This conversation wasn't going to get much further, but they chatted amicably about other matters for a few more minutes before Dave left, hoping the pastor wasn't waiting in his office for a council meeting wrap-up.

Clarice pushed back from her desk and ed her chair several times, finally making a complete circle. Had the pastor been awake on the altar, she wondered—playing the scene, a pathetic, twisted man? Or was he actually ill? And how would they deal with the situation, in either case? *Who* would deal with it?

ᏁᏁᏁᏁᏁᏁᏁᏁᏁᏁᏁᏁᏁᏁᏁᏁ

Midmorning Joe sat in the swivel chair in his study, feet propped up on the desk. He fingered the yellow legal pad resting on his thighs and pulled a pen from his shirt pocket. With it came the note reminding him to call Sheila.

That can wait, he decided, sliding the message into the binding at the top of the tablet.

He leaned back farther in the chair, stretched and locked his fingers together above his head. Shuddering, as if shaking off a chill, he relaxed his arms and let them drop.

Too much to do, he brooded, *too many people to call.* He scratched names on the pad: Sheila. Harry Droesch. Sister Janine. In a second column, he wrote: Staff meeting. Thanksgiving—two weeks. Christmas.

Lowering his feet to the floor, he picked up the phone and punched the numbers that would connect him with Harry Droesch, a priest eight years his senior and the pastor at Divine Mercy on St. Paul's West Side. He'd known him for years, ever since Harry was assigned as a young priest to the parish where Joe's family was registered. He had inspired Joe when Joe was a seminarian—and today they were part of the same priests' support group that included Ken Halpin.

Harry Droesch had a particularly hard time adapting to the changes set in motion by Vatican II. Twenty-five years after the fact, he still rued the loss of regular, private Confession and the traditional, felt obligation to attend Mass on Sundays under pain of serious sin. Not to mention the elimination of the rule about meatless Fridays, which had resulted, in Harry's opinion, in hundreds of thousands of Catholics letting go of the ancient discipline of abstaining from pleasure temporarily for a greater, postponed good.

He considered these serious matters and spoke of them often—and at length—with anyone who would listen. With fellow priests, he focused on the need to salvage what they had expected in the priesthood and find ways to do what they had cherished most when they studied for it.

He'll understand, Joe was thinking as the phone rang once, twice. *If anybody's going to listen, it'll be Harry.*

"Father Droesch here."

"Parish council meeting last night, Harry."

"Augh," Harry replied with disgust. "Those. I hate 'em."

Joe wasn't embarrassed to be talking with Harry about his battles. One priest was always safe with another. Quickly he told Harry about the conflict and how he'd stormed out of the meeting.

"I've done it myself. So?"

Crusty buzzard, that Harry, Joe mused. *I love him. Feet up, too, probably. Twins hat on, tummy pushing out, stretching his t-shirt.*

"They don't get it, Harry. People who support you don't control the mouthy ones, the ones stirring the pot."

"Your chairman. Jensen."

"Right."

"He's crazy. Or on some kind of crusade. At least a bit nuts, I'd say." Harry chuckled.

"I'm afraid so." Noticing that his feet had knocked the letter opener and the paperweight on his desk out of position, Joe nudged them back where they belonged.

"It's the same all over, Joe. They have only a piece or two of the picture."

"I keep telling them that. They lock into their own agendas and forget the big picture."

"The big picture, Joe. Don't ever lose sight of it. Things are always bigger than just your own parish."

Joe related for Harry his restless night, sitting in his study, going over his life as a priest, and then about his breakfast with Bob Talbot. "It's a mean trip some days, Harry. It helped to talk with Bob about it. He's a good man."

"You've told me."

"He's been through a lot of this stuff, too—you know, managing people. He had to make a lot of changes—style changes, you know?"

"Tell me about change, Joe. Nobody's had to deal with it the way priests have. Nobody. I've said it a thousand times."

"The thing is, Harry, a guy can't do it all by himself today. There's too much to be mindful of, too many things you've got to be *good* at. You need people to help you."

"Maybe, maybe not. I use them sparingly. All I need is two or three. Two is fine. I know they're saying you need more today, but it takes too long—it's too much work."

Joe contemplated his friend's response and what came next— what he wanted to reveal. After an awkward pause, he began.

"There's something else...After I stormed out of the meeting, I went to the church to pray. Somehow, I ended up doing it on the altar. *On* the altar, Harry. I dozed a bit, and the next thing I know these council people are coming into the church for the usual prayer after the meeting and they find me lying on the altar, exhausted, *stoned*, I'd say..." His voice trailed off. "You hate to have them see you that way, overwhelmed like that."

It took Harry a moment. "On top of the altar?"

"Yes, for godssake. I fell asleep up there." He gave an embarrassed snort.

"They wouldn't understand, Joe," Harry said after another pause. "They couldn't. *I* can, though. I've never done that myself, not that way, up on the altar, but I sure do get close sometimes when I'm alone. You've got to. You need it. You need some place, some thing, to hold on to."

"Exactly," Joe replied, relieved at Harry's non-judgmental response. "Still, I don't think I did myself any good with some of those folks."

"Nonsense. You did it. It's past. It's fine, Joe. Move on."

"Bob suggested this morning that I get some counseling," said Joe, testing the waters, wondering what Harry's take on the idea would be. "'Look into it,' Bob says. He reminded me that he got professional guidance and help when he needed to be more successful at his job."

"You're better off close to the altar. Pray to the Lord, Joe, and depend on your fellow priests for your counsel."

Joe released a breath he didn't know he'd been holding. "I think I've been a good pastor here."

"Of course you have! Remember, you report to the archbishop, not to some council in your parish. If he thinks you need help, some counseling or something, you should go get it. If not, don't worry. After all, a priest doesn't have the grace of God to do *everything*. The grace of the priesthood lets a man help other people. Hundreds of them. Thousands. That's what it's about. All this council stuff, the consultation and collaboration, it can be a lot of hooey. Be a priest, Joe. That's what you were ordained for. As a priest, that's your grace of state."

"The grace of state—exactly." Joe relaxed. "You're solid, Harry. A rock."

"Don't kid yourself, Joe. I'm tired, too. I do the new stuff because I have to, but I do it my way. We've got a council here to help the pastor— I figure that means it's *mine*. So I set the rules. You've got to do it that way, Joe. It'll kill you otherwise. The Church is not a democracy. We don't operate that way."

"Thanks, Harry. I mean it—there's no lift like the one I get from the guys in our group."

"That's what it's for, Joe. I'm glad you called. You take care now."

Rolling back from his desk, Joe reflected for a moment, pulled the reminder to call Sheila from the tablet, and walked down the hall to the kitchen. While coffee brewed, he sat at the window in the kitchen, eyes on two birdfeeders. Not fifteen feet away black-capped chickadees were pecking at birdseed and scattering the exposed, wet seed and the snow that had covered it. The long night caught up with him, weighing down his eyelids, his head. Elbow on the table, he softly and slowly fingered and patted his scalp.

When the coffee maker beeped, he poured a cup and sat again at the table, tracing the medallion embossed on his mug. SolutionS, it said. It was a souvenir from a management seminar in St. Paul ten years earlier.

That reminded him; he was supposed to call Sheila. Pressing the numbers for her direct line at work, he discovered she was away from her desk. At the tone he left a recorded message.

"This is Joe, Sheila. I can see you at 11:30 today, in my office in the old school building, if that works for you. Otherwise, give me a call at the rectory; we'll find another time or place."

Returning to his study, he sat back in his recliner. Within ten minutes his head was bobbing. Moments later, giving way to exhaustion, he slept.

෨෨෨෨෨෨෨෨෨෨෨෨෨෨෨

"Sheila's here, Father." It was Betty, calling from the parish office, Joe realized finally. He stared at the phone that had somehow made its way into his hand. "You scheduled her?"

"Yes, yes, I did," he mumbled, his mouth thick with sleep. "Tell her I'll be right over." He stopped in the bathroom to rinse his mouth and relieve himself. Snagging a parka at the back door, he hurried to his office.

"Sheila, for heaven's sake, I'm sorry," he explained, hustling into the waiting area. "It was a long night. I closed my eyes an hour ago to rest and fell asleep in my chair. Come in, please."

Gathering her coat from the chair where she had laid it, Sheila delayed a moment, studying the framed painting of Archbishop Meuncher on the wall. *Looks happy, even if just a bit heavy. And a charmer, I've heard. Does he know what's going on here?*

Joe offered her a seat in front of his desk, taking her coat and hanging it on the back of his office door as he closed it. "You comfortable there, Sheila? Can I get you anything?" He glanced at her warily, then seated himself in the black, high-back padded chair behind the desk. "We could meet in my study in the rectory, if you'd like something more private."

"No, this is fine. Thanks for making time for me."

Sheila looked around the room, familiar from the many times she had been there. As vice-chair of the parish council, she helped the pastor prepare the agenda for the bi-monthly parish council meeting. She had been trying at the same time to educate him about what she did for a living as a vice-president for marketing and how that might be useful in pastoring a parish church. Done casually, without pressure, it had suited the pastor just fine. A lighter touch—even banter—often helped. In fact, there were occasions when she believed it was only the bit of fun in her voice that kept him in conversation.

"I suppose you're here about the meeting last night." Joe folded his hands and rested them on his stomach as he described his disappointment at the council's action the night before. He told her about the breakfast he had with Bob Talbot earlier that morning and, almost parenthetically, explained that he had been praying when he fell asleep on the altar.

She decided not to respond directly to that. Nor to question it. Instead she fed back to him the message he had been preaching for years: the Church is not just priests and bishops; first of all it's the people. "You've said it many, many times, Joe. You alone as the pastor in the parish are not charged with the work of Christ any more than I am or any other member of the parish. Our roles are different. That's all. No one is privileged in the circle or higher than the other."

They sat in silence for a moment, the issue squarely on the table.

"It was a bad idea to not receive that report last night, Joe. How you respond in the long run to recommendations from a parish council is one thing. But short term, on this occasion, you should not have refused to consider a report that you had requested in the first place. The task force worked hard on it and..."

The pastor stiffened. "You really think the people of this parish give a rip about this stuff, Sheila? Frankly, I doubt *anybody* cares."

"I'm sure that bishops and priests don't want to hear this, Joe, so I'm going to say it carefully." She smiled at him. He reciprocated, if dryly. "It's true, isn't it, that Baptism is more fundamental in the Church than is ordination to the priesthood." It wasn't a question. "That's what you and others have told us, as I said just a moment ago. Well, we *bought* that, Father Joe, and so we *care* about it. A *lot*."

Thank God, this lady's not one of the crazies, the ones who make me nervous. She has sense. And you can josh with her.

"So, then, let me check this out," he said, plainly trying to banter. "Tell me, pastoress! What would you do in my position? Think, now, before you answer. What would you *do*? In this day and age? When each person, educated or not, good Catholic or not, is so rock-hard positive that he or she is correct about any given subject?" He wasn't bantering as he finished.

"That's easy, Joe, and you already know what I'd do. I'd have someone develop a committee of volunteers who understand that marketing the Church is about benefits and solutions. That's number one."

The pastor smiled, sure that Sheila was joshing him. "And number two?"

"Number one is enough. At least to start with. After that, things would never be the same, so I don't know what number two would be. Probably something a member of the committee would think of. That's what this is about, you know. It all begins someplace *outside* that rectory of yours. It starts in your *market*—outside, in the *parish*. Some people— you, for one—get itchy about using business terms and concepts in a church setting, but there is nothing to get uptight about."

"On your say-so," Joe replied directly without reprimanding. "Jesus didn't come to give us benefits, Sheila. He came to tell us about the truth and what is right. We've got to hold on to that and defend it."

"That's one of your standard responses, Joe. It may be true, but it's not enough and it's becoming less and less persuasive in today's world as you stated it." She got up to end the meeting.

"You need to do some things differently, Father Joe. This is a good parish, but it's been a battleground for too long. I've heard the stories from the day I got here. I'm willing to work at it, but I don't invest in hopeless causes. Unless things improve, my husband and I will probably look for a different parish."

"Don't do that, Sheila." He rose from his chair, wincing at the thought of losing her counsel. He studied her quiet face. It wasn't an immediate threat, he decided, extending his hand. "We need to stay in touch on this, Sheila. Don't worry. We'll work it out," he assured her. "We always do." As he helped her on with her coat and saw her to the door, he requested that she pray for her pastor.

"I can do that, Joe," Sheila said, but taking her leave added, "I'll tell you again, however—I won't invest myself where it's hopeless."

CHAPTER 11

Wednesday, November 8

3:30 p.m.

"I said I wanted everybody here and on time for the staff meeting." Joe glared at Betty Halvorsen.

"Sister Janine says she'll catch up on the meeting later, Father Joe."

"That's not good enough."

"Everyone's here except for Janine, Father. It was very short notice, and today's her day to visit nursing homes."

"We ought to be able to have a meeting when I need one," he grumbled. "What we do here this afternoon is crucial for everyone. She should be present."

He surveyed the staff room, slowly sliding his hands back and forth on the table, a work of art crafted by a founding father of the parish. Movable partitions within the room, a renovated classroom, provided a place for informal pursuits like reading or discussion or informal prayer, as well as places to display photography and artwork done by members of the staff or parishioners. He spotted a new piece, a watercolor by a Native American parishioner, Peter Featherstone, of cattle grazing in South Dakota. It softened his tone.

"Forget it," he told Betty. "I'll see Sister Janine about it myself."

He viewed the room again quickly, eyeing each staff member individually, as well. "Let's get going, people. We've got work to do. Jim Jensen was disruptive again last night at the parish council meeting—a *terrible* meeting! We've got to figure out how to handle him."

"So, is that the agenda for today's meeting?" Clarice Morgan asked.

Agenda! Riding her hobbyhorse again! The pastor fought to control muscles he felt quivering in his face and neck. "I need you to understand the situation," he pleaded with them, "and appreciate the position I have to take with Jensen on this so-called personnel study done by members of the parish council."

"'So-called study,' Joe?" inquired Clarice. "Why do you say it that way? It belittles the work done in good faith by parishioners, doesn't it?"

It's always something with Clarice. One day, the agenda. Next day, somebody's feelings. Then, something's not convenient, not relevant or some other thing—for fifteen damn years now. Why not just fire *the witch!*

But one thing at a time. She does good work, better than anyone else I could find nowadays. Parents love her, and that keeps them out of my hair. No malcontents complaining to me, killing time, yapping about schedules, teachers, curriculum. She writes good letters home to parents; anticipates problems. It's just here, at staff meetings, that she drives a person batty. So give it a rest for now.

"If you want, Joe, I can fill people in on the situation," Dave Hanratty volunteered.

"Thanks, Dave. I've got it covered," the priest snapped. "Clarice, they have no idea of what something like this could cost. They'll bankrupt us." He decided to be sure—again—that that they all had the full story—especially newcomer Gary Pirot, hired at the end of the summer to serve as the director of youth ministry. So he started at the beginning, recounting how the parochial school had been draining the parish financially for years before he arrived, how Father Charles Williams, his predecessor, had helped because he introduced the idea of closing the school before he, Joe Burns, arrived as pastor. The parish had been working fiercely ever since to become financially healthy.

"Every year, expense still outruns Sunday collections," he concluded ten minutes later. *Any idiot could see—there's no money.*

The pastor rolled a fist on the table, cracking his knuckles before he continued. "In spite of that, I think we've done pretty darn well for staff. You are all paid fairly." He stared at Clarice, knowing she'd dare to contradict him. "Good salaries and wages for the fine work all of you do. Still, expense increases as we expand our staff and our programs. We also pay more every year for your insurance—health and dental coverage. We have to be careful," he continued ruefully.

Dave Hanratty tried to get the meeting back on track. "Could you explain, Joe, why you didn't want to give consideration to the report prepared by the salary administration committee last night?"

"It's not a *salary administration* committee, Dave. How many times do I have to say that? Maybe if they were personnel people, you know, people who know something about personnel matters and the costs of personnel, maybe then I could trust them to do the job right. These are just council members."

Sure, just council members! With staffs and businesses to run, thought Luis Alvarez, the maintenance manager on staff. He let it go, reaching to straighten the hood on his sweatshirt. He would never interrupt and besides, Dave was already making that point with the pastor.

"Most of them are in business, Joe. They know how expensive personnel is these days."

"Yes, but they don't really know what it's like to run a parish. They don't understand ministry and what it means and what the priorities have to be. There are reasons we don't get paid what other people do."

Clarice watched the interplay, wondering. *Is Dave distracted in the least by the image of the pastor lying on the altar the night before?* She had seen it herself a dozen times. *Disgusting. Every time. Is Dave sickened by it at all? Or has he summoned up a new rule to manage it or make it go away?*

How does he do it? she thought. *So many* rules! *All this personal strategy, just to manage his work with this man.*

She turned her gaze to the pastor. She shivered involuntarily, trying not to show it, imagining him lying on the staff meeting table, another altar on which he might offer himself. *Could he, would he? Could he have been conscious on the altar the night before, gambling, hoping for support, even for pity, in the latest argument?* She couldn't rule it out.

"Give me a chance here," she heard Dave say. "I've been at the council meetings, Joe. I think I can help. Okay?"

The pastor leaned forward, pressing his forehead with the palm of one hand, rubbing left to right, back and forth. Dave took it for yes.

"Joe is right. I misspoke in calling it a salary administration committee. It was simply three members of the council, appointed to review the parish salary administration program. They're not saying that staff should be paid more or that we're underpaid or anything else."

"Yes, but that would be up for discussion," Clarice pointed out.

"You see?" the pastor jumped in. "There you are. That's what we can't have. We never had this kind of thing before."

"Joe, let me finish," Dave pleaded.

"No, sir," Joe snapped. "I don't need help on this. I've been managing parishes for more than thirty years now."

"This is about retaining good people by compensating them decently," Clarice fired back.

"What you want, Clarice, and what the rest of the staff may want, is one thing. What we can afford is quite another."

"Excuse me, Father."

A furrow on the brow of his handsome young face, Gary Pirot raised his hand hesitantly. It was his first staff meeting, but the youth director had learned early on to tread carefully with the pastor. "Could I get a little background and clarification on Jim Jensen? I'm new here, but I've gotten the impression that a lot of people admire him and..."

"Not at all." This was an easy one and gave the priest a chance to breathe, free of Clarice, if only for a moment. "Jim Jensen is a long-standing problem. For five years now, ever since he was elected to the council, he's wanted to be in control of the parish. Frankly, you'll find him a bully."

"By the way, Gary, welcome to your first staff meeting," the pastor continued, summoning his best pastoral cheer, given the rotten situation. "Don't worry. You'll catch on in a hurry to what's going on around here."

"Why are we here today, Joe?" Clarice asked. "I still don't understand. Our time is valuable and the parish is paying for it. This is another example of why we need a prepared agenda."

"Aw, for cripessake," the pastor snapped, struggling not to yell.

"Again, the stinking *agenda*! People expect me to do everything, including prepare an agenda for a lousy, simple meeting. I'm a *priest*, Clarice, not a manager. I don't care about agendas. I know what has to be done in this parish. We don't need an agenda while I'm talking. So get off my back!" Despite his best efforts, he was nearly shouting.

Dave and Clarice glanced at each other and slid back from the table. Luis moved to the windows, ostensibly to check the progress his assistants were making with snow and ice removal on sidewalks visible from where he stood. Lorraine, Betty and Gary watched the pastor pulling for air and holding it, then puffing through his nose. He rubbed his sweaty scalp.

"Look. Let me start over."

"Joe, I think we know," Lorraine said, straightening the blue blouse she was wearing.

"You don't. This is crucial. We can't afford this."

"Afford what?" Dave asked. "Joe, there's no request or even the suggestion that salaries and wages be increased. The council simply wants to see where we stand on a pay scale. Not how we compare with 3-M or General Mills, but how we compare with other *churches*—with our market."

The pastor's hand twitched and his face turned red. "We don't have a market, Dave." His emphasis made the word a profanity. "This isn't a business."

He pulled himself together. "Be that as it may, we've got to move along. So, go ahead. Bring everyone up to date."

"I can make it brief," Dave began. "The parish council appreciates the staff. They believe we do fine work, but in fact, they don't know how we're being compensated compared to others in this diocese or to those around us. At the top? In the middle? At the bottom? While they do know a lot about personnel matters, they've never looked closely at compensation in this parish. They simply want to make sure they're taking good care of us. That's what the report's about. I can't say it any more plainly."

Dave looked around the table, hands extended, inviting questions, folding them in front of himself when there weren't any. "Now let's let Joe explain what his concern is."

The pastor's eyes were moist with rage. He gritted his teeth and shuddered, struggling to compose himself.

"There's two issues here," he argued, fighting the urge to bark. "One is salaries. Face it. You'll never get rich working for the Church. We haven't got the money. You know it. I know it."

"Joe, tell me something," Dave interrupted. "What would the parish finance committee say about all of this? Bob Talbot is liaison to that committee. Can you explain to me why he didn't comment on this last night?"

"The finance committee will support me on this, Dave, don't worry about that. We talk about parish finances every time we meet and between meetings, too. The biggest concern is always payroll and benefits for staff."

He held up two fingers. "But let me go on to my second point. You know, don't you, staff, what's really at stake here?" He waited a moment, pretending he expected an answer to the question. They knew he didn't want one.

"The issue is about control of the Church," he continued. "We can't just let everything go to pot because volunteers want to do their thing in the Church. They don't have the education and the full picture. They start. They stop. They're not like you and me." He waved his arms to include everybody. "We're here for the long haul, pastor and staff. We've got to pull together—*together!* There are movements and kooks out there that threaten our very foundations. We've got to keep the horses in the barn or..."

"Joe, Joe, for God's sake, stop it," Clarice insisted, halfway out of her seat with indignation. "Just *stop* it. That's a terrible image—horses and barns." She put fisted hands on the table, balancing herself. "We've got to have more trust in the people, Joe. If Jim Jensen is empowered properly, he is no threat to your authority, nor to the Church nor to God nor to anyone nor anything else."

It was tipping, tipping out of his control, Joe thought, blanching.

They can say what they want. I know what has to be done. A parish is the responsibility of the pastor. He's the guy on the line. The bishop doesn't call Clarice Morgan or Jim Jensen or anybody else when there's trouble. Oh, no! He calls Joe Burns and it's Joe they nail, him they screw. That's why a priest has to keep the wraps on —first and foremost.

"Jim Jensen is a threat," the pastor repeated. "To the whole parish." Clarice sank back into her chair, shaking her head.

"We've got to keep moving ahead, but we have to remember at the same time it's important to hold things back at times."

"Joe, it's not..."

"Don't argue with me, Clarice," Joe demanded, rapping the table. "I expect you all to rally around me on this. Jim Jensen is going to ruin this fine parish. People talk about him. He has no conscience. It's your jobs and your ministry that are at stake. When we run out of money, you lose your jobs. It's that simple."

"I hear people talking, too," Clarice responded, "and most of the comments I hear about Jim Jensen are good. They like him. They think he's on track with Vatican II."

"Enough!" The pastor stood abruptly. "I've got phone calls to make." He left the room in a huff.

The staff exchanged glances. There was nothing more to say, nothing any of them hadn't said before. They got up and went back to work.

"So... this is a staff meeting," Gary said, walking to the door with Dave.

"We'll talk about it," Dave muttered.

"Let's, but I'm not sure I'll be here very long. This place is nuts."

CHAPTER 12

Wednesday, November 8

4:40 p.m.

C hilling gusts of wind staggered Joe as he hurried along the north side of the church to enter through the main doors on Fourth Street. Out of sight of the school, he turned back to face the sun. It was low in the sky but full and visible from where he stood, painting scattered clouds in shades of pink and purple. He lifted his face to the sight and stood motionless until a car door slammed in the school parking lot, claiming his attention.

Following the neatly shoveled walk to the front of the church, he climbed the fourteen steps to the entrance, entered the vestibule, and paused, admiring the play of the late afternoon light on the sacred space before him. Eventually, inevitably, his eyes were drawn to the altar that Ted and Bob had helped him get down from the night before. He stiffened against a flush of embarrassment. It was a mistake, that's all. Done unconsciously. Harmless. He would make no apologies, no explanations. None were needed.

Out of the corner of his eye Joe caught sight of a man sitting in the back of the church. He looked closer. It was Peter Featherstone, an Ojibwe Indian who'd moved from Hibbing the previous year to live with his daughter and her family.

The day he registered in the parish, Peter and Joe had talked for an hour and a half, more than twice the time the pastor normally spent getting to know new parishioners. Among other things, they discovered they were born on the same day, but ten years apart, Joe in 1931on the farm in Stearns County, Peter a decade earlier on the Fond du Lac Reservation just west of Duluth.

They'd had a number of intriguing conversations since then. Joe discovered that, in Hibbing on Minnesota's Iron Range, Peter had worked for the same mining company until, after thirty years, a back injury forced his early retirement at age fifty-three. Then, as a hobby over a period of eleven years, he took classes at night and on weekends at a nearby college. He completed his high school requirements and then registered for art classes and history courses, wrote poetry and studied world literature and some geology—always and only what interested him.

Joe made his way over to Peter and slid into the pew to sit next to him. He nodded toward the slim volume on the bench between them. "Still doing it, I see."

"Always will, Father."

Joe picked up the book, rubbed his thumbs respectfully over the cover and flipped through the pages. Thin and worn, they were marked lightly in places at the margins. He remembered the day Peter had first explained what the volume was and what it meant to him.

ᕈᕈᕈᕈᕈᕈᕈᕈᕈᕈᕈᕈᕈᕈᕈ

Several years after a first marriage on the Reservation ended in divorce, Peter had married Running Waters LaCouture. She had taught in small-town schools on the Iron Range until she settled in Hibbing, where Peter had moved and where she and Peter met while volunteering for the food shelf at Blessed Sacrament Catholic Church. They were together until she died of cancer the month after their silver wedding anniversary. Peter was forever grateful to her for giving him the incentive to get the high school diploma, which led to his passion for continued schooling.

"The second woman was from heaven," Peter told Joe. "I tell you, Father, she was my life. I called her my *Nibi*—my moving, fresh water— in Ojibwe and that's what she was. Fresh water that moved my spirit."

On the day they found out that Running Waters had terminal cancer, Peter stumbled into the back pew of their church to pray. There he found a Bible someone had left behind and, opening it to the middle, he found the book of Psalms. "There it was, Father, waiting. Meant for me."

The Psalms painted splendid pictures that fit his native heart, he explained. A pathway. A lamp for his feet. A tree close by a river. Solid rock. A fortress. Eagle's wings to fly, to protect.

He'd known kids who drowned in abandoned iron ore pits on the Range. The Psalms assured him he was safe from the pit. As God protected his own eyes, the Psalms promised, so would God keep Peter safe. Like a deer, Peter would be sure-footed and unharmed.

"The Psalms?" the pastor had questioned, trying to hide his surprise. "You pray the Psalms," he declared finally, prepared to believe it.

"Since that day, Father, I've prayed the Psalms because I found the Spirit-God, my first God, there—the one I had known growing up, at my side, in the natural world. "

Peter shrugged, paused, and shrugged again, fumbling for words.

"The native ways, Father," he said finally. He'd hesitated again, passing a hand over the day-old growth on his face. "I have to say honestly, Father, that I've found my native prayer better—maybe I should say *more helpful* – than what I had to learn at the church—the required prayers and all those answers to questions to make first Communion and later, for Confirmation. I first learned to pray from the many experiences my people had with the Spirit, over many generations. Then I discovered, by accident, that many of the Psalms pray what my people prayed.

"It was my only prayer book after that," he'd informed Joe. "One day I bought this thin volume that has just Psalms in it. Every time, before I finish, I put a kiss on the cover. It's my only prayer book. So now you know the story, Father."

ら゚ら゚ら゚ら゚ら゚ら゚ら゚ら゚ら゚ら゚ら゚ら゚ら゚ら゚ら゚ら゚

Joe set the book carefully back on the bench. "Thank you, Peter, for the painting you made for the staff room. It's beautiful."

Peter shrugged modestly and pushed a large hand back over black hair that ended in a short ponytail. The diminishing light somehow illumined the lines and the life etched on his face. "You're welcome, Father. I took up painting some time ago. After Running Waters. I'm working on two other pieces, both of them western skies, late afternoon, at different times of the year. I love coming to the church late afternoons, Father, this time of year especially. The quiet of winter and the light inside the church help me pray."

"I like it here in late afternoon, too, Peter. Pray for your pastor, won't you, please?"

"Of course, Father."

"Which Psalm will you pray for me today?"

"What would you like, Father? What would fit today?"

"Give me a couple of minutes to think about that. I've got a lot on my mind this afternoon."

Peter waited, gazing at the far wall of the church, where stained glass glowed, lit by the one star that shaped the earth and all its wonders. *What would a priest think if I said it out loud —what I'm thinking?* He held the light and the colors—the reds, the yellows—a moment longer. *Why not? Go ahead,* he urged himself. *Say it.*

"They talk today, Father, about this explosion—the Big Bang, they call it. They say it created the universe."

"Yes. The Big Bang, Peter—a theory commonly accepted in science today."

"Have you ever thought, Father, that perhaps God, say, simply gave himself over completely—*exploded* himself maybe—and in this mighty and creative way got the universe started—and that it is still unfolding in the wonders we find all around us every day—up above, in the heavens and all around us, right here on earth?

"Are you asking me whether I think God may have *blown himself up* somehow, maybe, to create the universe?"

"I like to think about it that way, Father. Some creation, I'd say! Maybe God *is everything* in a way we can't say, except maybe in poetry."

For a moment, Joe Burns pondered the large man at his side. *Six-*

three, or four, like me, and must go two-sixty—a gentle giant, really, the more you get to know him. Where's he going with this?

"I've never thought about it that way, Peter. Go on."

"I find him unfolding in the wind, Father. Easy on my face in summer, blowing me along in winter. He's the sun, riding the sky, running the course everyday. He is the face of a child, the plate of food I lift in thanks at table, the water that falls on my head in the shower. I find God all over, unfolding everywhere, revealing more and more, like when I let the sun or the afternoon sky talk to me. Father Joe, I hear him in the song of a bird or the voice of a cricket. I listen to him, I see him. Everywhere. I smell him, touch him, I hear his melody."

Joe nodded, encouraging him to continue.

"They say it's location, Father. The perfect place, the right distance between the sun and the earth is what made it work — the right distance to vary the seasons and make so many different kinds of life, including our own at one point. All of it is God, living his life, doing the things he does.

"Native people find God close by, Father. I look on a bearded iris or deep down into a tulip and I find God's path crossing mine. Native people look in front of themselves or on either side and they find the creator. All my grandparents, back beyond a time any of us can remember, were certain that anyone who gives himself over to nature will find God. My first lesson of every day comes from the world around me, Father, starting on either hand, at either side."

Joe nodded again. "Go on."

"There's nothing more to say, Father Joe. I will pray a psalm for you yet today."

"Well, thank you, Peter. That will help. It's hard being a priest today."

"Is that right, Father? I suppose so."

Joe grabbed Peter's hand to squeeze it and bid him goodbye, and then got up from the pew to make his intended, one-man stately procession to the sanctuary.

As he made a profound, unhurried bow toward the altar, a verse from the Psalm he prayed at Mass the previous morning came to mind. "Hold my hand," he came up whispering. He mouthed the words again as he sat down in one of the padded chairs at the side of the sanctuary. *Hold me by the hand*, he prayed in his heart, eyeing the vaulted sanctuary above.

Disappointed, Joe? a presence he heard as the voice of God came back. *You're disappointed, right? Things aren't what you expected.*

Unnerved, the pastor didn't answer. He looked upward again, instead, folding his arms, thinking, praying.

"Right," he whispered finally, admitting it. His fingers danced over his chest. He rubbed it lightly, coaxing out the discontent.

Tell me, he prayed in his heart. *What happened to this Church of yours?* He stretched his long legs, bumping the padded kneeler in front of him. *Yes, at times I've had mixed feelings about the Council, Vatican II. I don't mind saying so, like this, privately, where it's safe. It seemed so right, so easy, so* natural *at the start. But think about it. A whole generation of Catholic kids don't know their prayers. Parents don't go to Mass. Confession as we knew it? Gone. Kids can't name the Sacraments. A whole generation of churchgoers—lost.*

Maybe, maybe not. You think, perhaps, you got fooled by Vatican II? Sacked, maybe?

Sacked? No. Disappointed? I'd have to think about it. Some days, yes. Maybe.

It was a Pentecost, Joe. Another one. They aren't easy, Pentecosts.

The light in the church changed slightly. Joe looked toward the vestibule. Peter was pushing open the heavy front door of the church, on his way home. It closed quietly.

"People want too much," the priest continued, now half out loud. "What they want is either not permitted or we haven't got the skills to give them. Did you hear that Clarice woman? In the staff meeting? Fussing over an *agenda*?"

Yes, I heard Clarice.

Luis Alvarez entered the church from the side door to lock up for the night. He noticed the pastor in the dim light, took a few steps to get closer and apologized for disturbing him.

"No problem, Luis. I was about to leave. Go ahead, lock up and I'll leave by the sacristy."

As the maintenance manager's footsteps faded, the pastor sat back, sucked in a breath, held it, and then let it pop from his cheeks. The presence wasn't speaking at the moment. His chin fell to his chest.

Deep Water, he prayed, recalling another Psalm. *Wash me. Take me.*

Joe sat in the sanctuary, arms folded, eyes shut, pressing inward, holding himself until the last trace of light left the sanctuary. Then he returned to the rectory and prepared his supper, a bowl of tomato soup from the can. Leaning on the stove, staring into the pan as he waited for the soup to heat, he considered the holidays ahead. *A lot to do, and more this year than usual, with another parish council mess.*

The holidays could help release the pressure, he decided. He'd see Sister Janine and catch up with Dave, but next week would be soon enough. Right now, what he needed most was some time, a break. He ate the soup quickly and headed upstairs for bed. A full night of sleep would give him the break and restart him for the crises he knew he would have to face in the days ahead.

CHAPTER 13

Monday, November 13

9:00 a.m.

J oe was getting into his car outside the local hardware store where he had just purchased a new windshield ice scraper. Charlie Beckins tapped his car horn lightly as he passed behind Joe's car and parked several spots farther down.

Charlie was an active parent leader in St. Mary's Boy Scout troop and a volunteer coach for kids in the Mapleton youth basketball programs. His wife Mary had been a teacher in the religious education program from the time they registered in the parish eight years earlier. Their children, three-year-old Suzie and eight-year-old Peter, were delightful youngsters.

Never in a hurry, this Charlie, Joe mused, admiring him as he waited and watched Charlie approach in his sheepskin coat, jeans and a green stocking cap. *Intent and self-assured, but never a rigid person. Satisfied with life as it is—a soft smile on his face every time you see him.*

"Good morning, Father." Charlie stuck out his hand and shook Joe's. "Can you believe it?" Charlie asked. "I came here over the weekend and now I'm here again."

"You forgot something?"

"Ice melt, of all things. Amazing what a guy can forget even when his driveway looks like a skating rink."

"You've got a lot on your mind, Charlie—family and your work with the traveling you have to do. It would be easy to forget things."

"I'm better than Jim Jensen, at least," Charlie laughed. "I ran into him here Saturday. Seems back in August he brought in a hedge trimmer for sharpening and forgot to come back to pick it up. The store called and told him they were going to sell it soon if he didn't get in here for it. That brought him here in a hurry."

Joe's mouth had gone dry at the mention of Jim Jensen's name, and he could feel the skin on his face tightening. Charlie didn't seem to have noticed. Joe wet his lips, pushing his tongue to the corners of his mouth.

"There was a parish council meeting the other night, Jim said?" Charlie's question was innocent. "A hard one?"

"They're all hard, Charlie," Joe replied. He searched Charlie's face for clues to how much Jim had yapped about the meeting. *What about the altar? Cripes! Don't need any more of that! It's over! Forget it.*

"I'm sure they are hard, Father. I wouldn't want your job." He examined the older man. Joe's face was frozen—as if it would crack if he moved a muscle. Who was living there, in that stiff body, he wondered.

"You do great work, Father Joe." He was glad to tell the priest that—figuring he probably didn't hear it as often as he should. Charlie had heard the talk. People—certain people—said Joe Burns was abusive—a manipulator. *Sure, but that gets exaggerated. In church, things ought to be better—cut the bickering and get along.* "And that was a great sermon yesterday, too."

"Thank you, Charlie. You always say that."

"I mean it, Father, I do. You always give me something to think about.

Joe grinned, warmed by the younger man's affirmations. "Those are kind words, Charlie, thank you. They make me eager for the holidays in spite of the extra workload they bring. I'm looking forward to them."

"My favorite time of year, Father. Next to deer hunting, that is," he added, pretending contrition. "I have a few chores to do for Mary, but then I'm heading north to hunt my deer." He had told Joe several years ago about this annual event taken as a week of vacation—how much it meant to him to get together with his brother and a childhood friend, how much he enjoyed the time outdoors, whether or not anyone bagged a deer.

"Have a great time," Joe said sincerely. *Charlie's one of the good ones— true and sincere every time we talk.* "And travel safely. I want to hear all about your adventure up north."

ৰ্চৰ্চৰ্চৰ্চৰ্চৰ্চৰ্চৰ্চৰ্চৰ্চৰ্চৰ্চৰ্চ

The next morning Joe was relaxing in the recliner in his study after breakfast. The phone rang, disturbing his composure.

"Father Joe, this is Jack Gilmore." Gilmore-Gerhardy Funeral Home did most of the burials for parishioners at St. Mary's—two a month on average. "This is a tough one, Father Joe. Charlie Beckins was killed in a hunting accident late yesterday afternoon."

The pastor snapped the recliner forward. "Oh God, Jack, not Charlie," he begged, stuttering the name.

"I'm afraid so, Joe. I just finished making arrangements with Mary here in the office. She's not doing well, as you might imagine."

Joe struggled to focus on the details of a funeral, any funeral: Mass, ten o'clock, probably Friday; wake on Thursday. "Okay. I'll visit with her and call you later."

Stunned, the pastor hung up the phone and fell back into the recliner. This kind of news wearied a man. He recalled a summer Sunday at the door of the church, greeting Charlie and his beautiful family—the next generation of faithful Catholics; up to date, current with Vatican II. And he'd talked with Charlie just a day ago!

Joe forced himself forward and out of the chair. He had to visit Mary and the children. He called the office to tell Betty the news and let her know that he'd be gone for awhile.

Eight-year-old Peter, his eyes red and teary, answered the door a moment after Joe touched the bell. The pastor hugged the boy warmly and went to Mary, who was seated on the sofa in the living room, friends from the neighborhood on either side. One stood to make room for him.

"Mary, for godssake, Mary. God bless you, Mary," the pastor said as he squeezed in beside her. "I am so sorry. So sorry for you. And for Charlie. And for the children."

He hardly recognized her. Normally a woman with a gracious, wide-open smile and a can-do bearing, she was bereft, the usual sparkle in her eyes replaced by tears. She leaned onto his shoulder, sobbing without regard for appearances. Joe put his arm around her, pulling her to himself and then, squeezing with both arms, he rocked her gently. "Mary, Jesus loves you. Trust him. Trust him, Mary."

"Father, how could this happen?" she sobbed, her voice thick and muffled. "Why Charlie, Father? Why Charlie? He was so good. The kids, Father. What are we going to do? Why did it have to be Charlie?" Sobs shook her body until she fell silent in Joe's arms.

"Jesus loves you, Mary. He cares for you. He's got Charlie now. Somehow, it's all in his hands. I don't understand it any more than you do and I don't know what's next, but at a time like this we don't need to. We just have to say 'Okay' and 'Let it be.' Try to say, 'Let it be,' Mary."

They sat without moving. The pastor continued his gentle press. Five minutes passed. Joe Burns was in his own world. *This is where a priest belongs,* he thought, *holding a woman who needs Jesus, a sorrowing woman, one a priest is* meant *to help.*

Mary moved a finger, then a hand, and opened her eyes. The pastor lightened his embrace and pulled his head away from hers.

"Trust Jesus, Mary. We don't know what these things are about when they first happen."

"Have you talked with Jack Gilmore?" Mary asked, wiping at her eyes. The neighbor on Mary's right offered her tissues.

"Yes, Jack called me. I am already planning the Mass for you and Charlie. I'll call later today to see how you're doing and to talk a little bit about the funeral. Will that be okay? Or would you rather wait until tomorrow? Whatever is best for you."

"I don't know just now. I can't think."

The pastor pressed her hand again. "It's fine, it's all right. I understand," he said. "I'll call back later. You'll be okay till then?"

Mary assured him weakly, almost inaudibly, that she would.

He got up from the sofa, pulled Peter to himself for a firm hug and bent over to kiss Suzie on the cheek, then excused himself.

Joe sat quietly in his car before turning the key in the ignition. He had reached into Mary's soul, he just knew it. He felt it, felt her let go, felt the Spirit of God taking over in her. He thought he might even have seen the beginning of peace in her tearful eyes as he left the house. Jesus had comforted the sorrowing.

His chest expanded. He felt like a priest, the way a priest *should* feel. This was why he had become one in the first place. He started the car and headed back to the rectory.

ᏋᏋᏋᏋᏋᏋᏋᏋᏋᏋᏋᏋᏋᏋ

At the Mass of Christian Burial for Charlie Beckins on Friday, Joe found eyes glued to him from all over the church as he spoke during the homily about the pain and breakup of human life.

"My friends, when we are faced with the numbing pain of something like the death of Charlie Beckins, we cannot afford to hold on to anything except for Jesus. Grief and personal loss can make you feel like you're standing at the edge of a cliff, looking down a hundred miles. With every sorrow we share in the death of Christ. The passing of Charlie Beckins is a time like that."

From her seat in the first row of the crowded parish church, Mary looked over at the pastor. He was standing center aisle to preach from the floor of the assembly, rather than from the pulpit in the sanctuary. He paced in front of the first pews, then took a few steps into the center aisle and back, reflecting, reaching into his soul on behalf of his people, walking among them. He was a shadow just beyond Mary's tears.

"We know for sure, however, that just on the other side of the grave and our sorrow there lies a resurrection to some kind of new life. In the meantime, people, you just hold on. There aren't many answers at times like this. Mostly there are questions. God has some answers. Jesus does. But really, from our side? There are only questions."

Mary Beckins reached for the hands of her children, sitting on either side of her.

"So go ahead now. Ask the questions you want to, people. It's all right. You can talk to your God. You can question him. In your own voice. Go ahead. Do it. Right now." The Spirit of God had a hold on Joe Burns, doing a work of mercy.

"That's it. Tell God how you feel. How you loved Charlie. How you care about Mary. And Peter. And Suzie. Tell him. Ask him. Question him. Go ahead now. He wants to be your friend. One on one with the Lord now."

Joe's spirit soared, as he remembered his own family, his mom and dad, brother and sisters, his grandparents. How good, how central his family was for him. And men like Charlie, women like Mary. Children like theirs. Family is the hope of the future, the heart of the Church! It rushed over him now, what he did for others as a priest, for single parents, too, people divorced, betrayed, unemployed, overtaken by a sudden death. These called to his heart. This was where he was best. *This is your life, Joseph John Burns. Press on.* "I saw Charlie at the hardware store on Monday morning, just before he left to go hunting. 'It's not the deer so much any more, Father,' he told me once. 'It's the quiet, the stillness in the woods. I pray, Father. It's easy to pray in the woods,' he said."

The pastor looked out over his flock. He shivered. "Well, Charlie, you are at home. At peace now forever. Face to face with the Lord."

He paused and then continued. "Let's be thankful for the time Charlie spent with us, my people. They were good times. For Charlie and for us. That's a good man there, Charlie Beckins. God bless him and God bless you all today."

In the sacristy after Mass, Joe thanked the altar servers. "It's a great thing to be a priest, boys. You should think about it. It's a great life to live. God blesses his priests. Remember that. Trust in God, boys. He'll never let you down."

After the burial in the cemetery, Joe invited Mary's family and friends back to the church basement for lunch, prepared by the men and women of St. Mary's Funeral Guild. On the way out of the lunchroom he stopped to speak with Sister Janine Rowan, present for the funeral Mass as the parish pastoral minister.

He still had to bring her up to date on the staff meeting she had missed, he reminded her. It had already been more than a week. "I could do it tomorrow morning, sister. Or what about this evening?"

"Tonight's fine," Janine replied, deciding she just wanted it over with. They agreed to meet in the rectory at 7:30.

CHAPTER 14

Friday, November 17

4:30 p.m.

L ater that afternoon, after resting from the funeral, the pastor
called Dave Hanratty. He said he hoped, despite the hour, especially on a Friday, that he'd be available for their customary conversation about the parish council meeting, postponed now for more
than a week.

"That'll be fine, Joe. I have about half an hour, maybe forty minutes,
but then I have to pick up my daughter from practice. Basketball, you
know."

When Joe arrived five minutes later at Dave's office, the only light
on in the room was a single gooseneck lamp bent low over his desk. "No,
leave it," Joe said when Dave offered to add some light from the ceiling
or from the table lamps in the corner, an area he had arranged for soli-
tary reading or for special conversations like the one he was expecting
momentarily. The pastor sat down instead on one of the straight back
chairs in front of the desk. He leaned forward, fingers of both hands
splayed on his thighs, elbows out sharply, pressing forward.

"Dave, I have appreciated the support you've given me here at St. Mary's from the first month you were on the job. We haven't always been in agreement on some things, but when you do disagree with me, even at staff meetings, you never do so in a way that is unprofessional or hurtful. I always feel safe with you, Dave. What is it, ten years now that you've been here?"

"It'll be ten next summer. Thanks for the compliment."

Dave remembered well that first month with Joe. A group of parishioners had been concerned once again about the workload expected of the one priest assigned to their parish. They had asked the parish council and the pastor to petition the archbishop, this time for an ordained deacon if he did not have a priest available.

Vatican II had encouraged reestablishing the practice of ordaining married men to the diaconate, a venerable tradition from the earliest days of the Church. Deacons were ordained to preach, to baptize, to conduct funerals and even to preside at weddings, thereby freeing priests to do more of the daily pastoral ministry expressly theirs and for which there were fewer and fewer of them available.

Joe agreed to consider the matter of asking the archbishop for a deacon and, in spite of some reservations he had about it, consented to the public meetings that parish council members wanted. During that time and independent of the deacon proposal, he hired Dave Hanratty as director of parish volunteers.

One day the pastor sought Dave's perspective on the question of ordaining married men to be deacons. The two men discovered that their views on the matter were very similar. They both believed that properly trained and committed lay baptized and confirmed Christians could just as effectively do the work planned for ordained deacons.

Dave learned that Joe was of the opinion that having married deacons in the Catholic Church was simply a strategy, an ineffective one at best, to forestall the day when married men would be ordained to full priesthood—an idea Dave supported completely. In addition, it concerned Joe that ordination to the diaconate was not open to women, whether married or not. In his opinion, this was first of all an injustice to women who might discover themselves called to Holy Orders and secondly a fateful failure to make use of the gifts that women had for ministry. Therefore it was a grave injustice to the people in the pews.

Dave never used the term "a shortage of vocations" with Joe. The so-called shortage of priests was, he believed, more the result of a scarcity of insight and wisdom. Forced celibacy was not a reasonable requirement for priesthood and, in fact, was a leftover from practices begun a thousand years earlier.

Dave's thinking supported the pastor's position on the diaconate, and within thirty days, Joe decided on his own to discontinue parish council consideration of the proposal for a deacon. The council vice-chair resigned immediately, as did two others of the twelve parishioners elected to the council in those days.

The pastor's action was a singular disappointment to Dave, done summarily as it was, and he told the pastor as much. Dave found the decision arbitrary at that point and at odds with a more basic principle of empowering lay members to actually make decisions in a Catholic parish when they are able and skilled to do so.

The most significant thing about the event for Joe Burns, however, was the realization that he had on staff a highly competent colleague who would speak his mind and respectfully take a differing position on important matters. It was the beginning of what he considered a solid relationship with Dave Hanratty.

෨෨෨෨෨෨෨෨෨෨෨෨෨෨෨

The pastor leaned forward onto Dave's desk now, clasping one hand on top of the other. "There's not a time I can recall that I haven't been able to count on you, Dave."

"What's this about, Joe?"

"I'm not trying to be coy or deceptive. You know what it's about. You were at the council meeting last week."

Dave lifted a hand, prepared to speak. Before he could do so, the pastor continued. "We've seen it many times, haven't we." It wasn't a question. "Most of the time when there's a parish ruckus it quiets down. Usually. But there's a different feel to this one."

Dave lifted his hand again. The pastor stopped.

"Joe, you shouldn't be in this mess. You asked for that report. You should have at least considered it and then replied after having done so. To simply reject it was not right, Joe. And not smart."

"So then, what? Fake it? Act as if I'm going to consider the proposal and then come back to reject it anyway? I'd much rather say it straight up. No money, folks. Forget it."

"Joe, please, there is no proposal to spend more money. This is a report. A *report*, Joe."

Dave debated suggesting that there might be a connection between Joe's behavior and the oftentimes-heated response of parishioners. Timing was key in a matter like this, however, and at the moment the timing seemed bad. He waited.

"You can't always afford to be completely honest in public, Dave," Joe continued. "They'll hand you your head. There's too many publics out there, too many people to satisfy."

"Joe, what if you were to face this potential slugfest with the parish council with open and honest discussion of the report they brought you? Why wouldn't that work for you?" He let Joe Burns think about it, sitting back in his chair and waiting.

"Most priests would like to be more honest, Dave. I certainly would like to, but it won't work. A priest is first of all a shepherd. The people come first. You need to protect them so that they get the truth. Small bites is a good rule."

"Look, Joe, the Church has been preaching the message for twenty centuries. Many people today are finding the package irrelevant; they're leaving the Church behind. There is no safety in hiding or in being anything less than completely truthful with them, not if we hope to hold onto searching people as interested believers."

"You've always spoken honestly, Dave. Priests can't always do that. There's more at stake when priests and bishops speak."

It was a compliment, somehow, Dave figured and a signal to proceed.

"Not once, Joe, have I been shaken by any change that is occurring in the Church. No theory, no new idea, no fresh insight has ever threatened me. Everything I have studied and considered has deepened my faith, made me more devout and prayerful and made my relationship with Christ and all things divine stronger and deeper."

The pastor raised a hand, palm flat facing Dave, inviting him to take a breath so he could say something himself.

"Just one more thing, Joe, and I'll be done. This matter that became so ugly at the parish council meeting is crucial. We need to partner with people, not fight with them for control."

"Let me be direct, Dave. Very few people in the parish find this a matter of any concern whatsoever. And I am going to crush those few people who do and who are making it an issue for others. Regardless of how pure they believe their intentions are, I'm not going to let them upset other people and take away my place as pastor. It isn't right."

The pastor got up and went to the windows. Arms folded, he began to pace. Dave made no effort to follow his movements behind him. Finally, Joe returned to the front of the desk, making room by sliding one of the chairs aside, and leaned fully onto the desk. Raising his head and lifting his eyebrows, he was literally face to face with his director of volunteers.

"Who's going to hold it all together, Dave? Where's the glue? A parish council of volunteers? That's a joke. You need the regulars, guys who are going to be here tomorrow and the next day. And your priests and a strong staff give you that. Here's what I want, Dave. I want people to line up and support me on this matter with Jim and Megan."

"I am willing to cooperate, Joe, but frankly, I get nervous when I hear you talking like this. What is it you're asking?

"You're a leader in this parish. You're recognized as such. Jim Jensen is not. Megan Roberts is not. These two, and a few others, are divisive. You have a chance to really make a difference at St. Mary's. We need to get people lined up for support. I need you to help me do what's right here."

"How do you define that? 'Lining up.'"

"I'm not completely sure yet. It may mean that Jim has to resign."

"That would be a mistake, Joe. Jim is not the problem. I suggest you think more about this, a lot more. It's a weak move."

"I have to take action on this. The parish expects it." Joe straightened up. "As I've said, I've always felt safe with you, Dave. I ask you to keep this discussion confidential."

It was past time for Dave to pick up his daughter. He moved the papers he had been working on to the side and slid back from the desk.

"Think about it, Dave. That's all I'm asking for now, but I assure you, I am going to fight this. There's some real loonies out there, even breaking bread and calling it Eucharist—nuns and other women, breaking bread! That won't work, bypassing Christ's priests to be priests themselves. It's nuts."

"I have to go, Joe. I'm late for my daughter." Dave grabbed his coat from the hook in the corner, threw a quick goodbye over his shoulder, and left the room.

The pastor sat in near dark for several minutes, turned off Dave's desk lamp and went to the rectory. He needed to prepare. Sister Janine would be at the door in two hours and she could be a handful.

CHAPTER 15

Friday, November 17

7:30 p.m.

"Come on in, sister. Just what we needed, hey?" Shaking the snow from her red parka and hanging it on the coat tree, Joe welcomed Sister Janine Rowan to the rectory. "I appreciate it that you're on time for our appointment on a night like this."

"They say eight to ten inches before this storm is over," the nun replied. She fluffed large snowflakes from the bangs she wore and cleared her glasses with a handkerchief. Sister Janine was dressed in a dark brown pants suit. She hadn't worn a religious habit in twenty-five years and, truth be told, no longer owned one.

He showed the nun to one of two rooms in the rectory used for conferencing and counseling. To set the right tone for this important meeting, Joe had lit at their lowest setting the lamp on the desk and a floor lamp in the corner. They seated themselves in two oak chairs he had placed in advance in front of the desk, facing each other. A white votive candle in front of a polished cherry wood statue of the Virgin Mary flickered on a small table at the window.

"Thanks for taking the time, sister. I know you're busy."

"I'm sorry I couldn't be present for the staff meeting, Father Joe. You know how I am about canceling visitation to the nursing homes. The residents expect us on certain days, and I had volunteers scheduled to go with me."

"You do good work, sister. The parish appreciates it."

"Joe, isn't there something we could do to plan these staff meetings in advance?"

"We need so few, sister. I hate to plan them. Besides, they seldom accomplish much anyway, so I don't put a lot of work into them. I suppose you've heard about the agenda for the meeting?"

Sister Janine frowned and looked past the priest to the Virgin on the table and then out at the large, damp snowflakes gliding past the window. *Here we go. Please don't drag this out, Joe.*

"I've heard there wasn't one."

"Is that what they're saying? Tell me, Janine, why is that always such an issue? We're there—there must be a reason. That's the agenda!"

"I think they want to know they're using their time well."

"They should be so concerned the rest of the time! In this case, the staff meeting was about Jim Jensen and the murderous challenge he issued to me as pastor during the parish council meeting the previous evening."

"I've heard about it."

"Sister, this man could be the ruin of us. You know how it can be with people like Jim. They want to take control of the Church and that's why I called the staff meeting—to clear the air, to answer questions and to get staff support as I deal with this unruly, ferocious chairman."

She fingered a distinctive silver crucifix and chain that hung around her neck. "I know about the brutal fight at the council meeting, Joe."

"No fight, Janine. I simply walked out of the meeting because Jim got nasty and no one challenged him, except for Ted and that only made it worse. Jim's type wants to run the show and I'm not going to put up with that any more. And that's why I am taking time with you this evening."

The nun turned in her chair, trying to relax.

"You've been in religious life now for how long, Janine?"

"I professed my first vows as a Franciscan nun back in 1955, Father Joe. It's coming up on thirty-five years."

"That's a long time and they've been tough years. He put his arm onto the desk and drummed his fingers. "It's a quandary, isn't it, sister? How do we keep Church reform going and yet slow it down or stop it when it takes a wrong turn?" He shook his head. "Some people are just plain nutty and that's why I need so much support at certain times—and why I need it now."

"I can't help you on such matters, Joe. You hired me to visit the sick and help the poor and find shelter for those who need it. That's what I do. In any given period, there are hundreds of people who look to this parish for help, even from outside our boundaries because we've always been so generous. So many, in fact, that I can't keep up with the need."

"As I said before and have told you often, sister, you do fine work."

"Thank you, but it means I don't have time to get involved in a lot of discussion. This parish spends too much time talking to itself."

"Tell me about it!"

"I don't want to get all tied up with meetings and conflict. I don't have time for that."

"Time isn't the issue, Janine. Solidarity is what counts now. Very few members of the parish trust Jim Jensen."

"From what I can tell, many people *do* trust Jim."

"That's not so, sister. I've called to arrange some time with him to clear the air, but he's out of town on business. I will do so soon. It's pretty clear to me that he's at the center of the problems in this parish. I'm tempted to ask him to resign."

"I can't say this any more directly, Joe. Don't try to arrange for Jim's resignation. It will backfire. You need to find a way to work successfully with him because of the support he has—on the council and generally in the parish. People respect him as an effective leader who communicates clearly and well."

"Regardless, sister, I need to have your support, and there may be times when I'll need it publicly. As a religious, you have a special role to play. People look to you. I'm depending on you for leadership on the parish staff."

"Dave is your staff leader, Joe. Clearly."

"Yes, Dave does a fine job and I count on him. But you are different, Janine. In a battle that would become public over Jim, the people of the parish would flock around you and trust you as a nun. They regard you *so* highly for the work you do."

"I appreciate the trust you put in me, Joe, but here's the situation. I'm here as a pastoral minister. I support people through the rough times of their lives. As long as you let me continue doing that kind of work, I am fine. I'm tired of all the parish controversy, however. If I have to get involved in that, then I'll go some place else."

"No, no, don't do that, Janine. I want you here. You are very valuable to this parish."

"That's the condition, Joe. Leave me free to do my work."

"Absolutely. There may be times when I need you to speak up, however."

"I'll do my best, Joe. As time passes, however, I'll have to decide what I am able to do. I can't promise more than that."

"Fine, Sister Janine. I know I can count on you."

"I'll have to decide for myself how that will play out, Joe.

They rose and stepped into the hallway. Joe helped the nun put on her coat. "Good night, sister. God bless you." After watching to make sure she made it safely down the rectory's sometimes slippery steps, the pastor shut the door and locked it, extinguished the lights and the candle in the room they had used, and walked the hallway to his study. Kicking off his shoes, he settled back into the recliner.

It's been a good week, he thought, ticking off the relevant events—the funeral for Charlie Beckins. A good talk with Dave, and now with Sister Janine. *Next week? A breeze. Ushers' meeting Monday. Tuesday, Women's Auxiliary. No agendas. No arguments. What's to argue?*

It'd be an easy week, he decided, at least by comparison. On Thursday, Thanksgiving, he would lay out a course that he was confident would free him from the circus.

CHAPTER 16

Thursday, November 23

9:00 a.m.

"Now what?" Jim Jensen whispered to Peg. She shrugged, but she, too, sensed that something was up. Joe Burns had a cocksure air about him as he took the pulpit for the 9:00 Mass on Thanksgiving morning.

Sitting near the front of the church, a child on either side, Mary Beckins watched the pastor too. Such a presence, she thought. How has he done God's service all these years? Such a pitiable contrast with herself, a week and a half after Charlie's death, still not knowing if she could make it through another day without him.

Esther Clemenceau had been observing priests at St. Mary's from her seat in the third row, directly in front of the pulpit, for nearly seventy-five years. A short woman and somewhat corpulent, yet she was robust for her age. Esther thought Joe Burns the best of the lot, the most courageous, and pastor at a time when it was hardest to be a priest. *Take care of him, Lord Jesus,* she prayed. *And all of your fine priests.*

"Good morning, everyone, and happy Thanksgiving Day to each of you," the pastor began his homily. "I know that you all have important things planned for this afternoon and some of you will be traveling yet today to be with family. Don't worry. I won't keep you long. I think you will find what I have to say important, however, and exciting."

Peg Jensen elbowed Jim. She couldn't help but grin, but covered it with her hand. The pastor appeared to be rebounding—up to something.

"I'm taking this occasion to announce to you that in just a year and a half we'll give thanks to God in a very big way, a *special* way, at St. Mary's. And well we should!"

"Many of you know, but for those who don't or who may have forgotten, I'll remind you that on June 1 of 1991 we will mark the seventy-fifth anniversary of the founding of St. Mary's as a parish. It was on that date in 1916 that the great John Ireland, archbishop of St. Paul, established the parish of St. Mary's and named Father Guy Leclercq as the first pastor, way out here in what was just farmland north of the Twin Cities. Imagine! This will be our Diamond Jubilee! We'll be seventy-five years old at St. Mary's in just a year and a half! We've come a long way, haven't we?"

Mary pulled Suzie closer to her side. Eighteen months seemed a long way off. Too long, really, to think about when you couldn't wait for the end of the day you were enduring at the moment. She couldn't help but admire the pastor's energy and the idea of a jubilee celebration, but the day at hand was the only one she could bear.

"The diamond jubilee of the parish will also mark my twentieth year as pastor here," he continued. "I know you are very proud of your parish, and rightly so, and I'm proud and happy to be a part of it with you. By that time, twenty of my thirty-five years as a priest will have been spent in one parish! And so today, Thanksgiving Day, I'd like to express my deep gratitude—to you, God, and to you, the good people of St. Mary's. And, of course, to Archbishop Meuncher for his support and continued confidence in me as pastor."

There were bullheaded people in the parish, Esther had heard—and she had reason to consider it the truth—who were out to get this man. *The whole world's gone crazy,* she thought. *They're perverse, these people. What do they want from a priest? Here I am, almost ninety, and I've seen every kind of priest God ever made. This one's the best, no question. What he's been through at St. Mary's takes a saint. That's a priest!* She bobbed her head, sure of it, and smoothed her silvered hair.

The pastor scanned the faces of those nearby in front of him and back to those in the far corners of the church. Reaction was mixed. More heads down than up. Less support, perhaps, than he had hoped for. He carried on.

"God has been good to St. Mary's for these three-quarters of a century. He has sent you good priests. Those of you who go back to the very early years of this parish remember those fine men. What a special day it will be in June of '91 when we remember and offer thanks for all of them."

Peg folded her arms tightly against her chest. *Seventy-five years of priests, he says? What about the people and the families that have been here that long? Who would ever begin the story of a parish church with its priests!*

Esther nodded. *We've been lucky with our priests. Just a country church to start, mom and pop and other folks twisted arms to get someone assigned out here. Thank God they came. People should be thankful.*

"And we can't forget the dozens and dozens of Franciscan nuns who served this parish for more than fifty years before we were forced to close the school in 1973. Great ladies they were, women who gave their lives for God and for the people, especially the children of this parish. God bless them. God bless them, every one."

Peg tilted her head back for a better view. *Who was this harebrain who talked about a new and reformed Catholic Church, but didn't seem to understand any of it—claiming Vatican II as his personal reformation, yet suggesting that a parish church was first of all about its priests and nuns? How could he?* Jim, fidgeting beside her, wasn't having an easy time with that, either, she noticed. He was spreading his fingers, stretching, flexing them, in and out, back and forth.

The pastor's words made Esther think of Sister Mary of the Blessed Sacrament, the first grade teacher at St. Mary's for forty-one years. *Thank you, Jesus, for all of them, special as they were in their religious habits—that white cord gathering heavy brown cloth at the waist. Today you can't even tell who's a nun and who isn't. They should dress the way they used to. Those were nuns.*

As he scanned the congregation again, side to side, front to back, Joe still couldn't determine exactly where he was at with his people this Thanksgiving morning. He still found eyes that were not looking at him, arms that were folded, fingers checking wallets or digging through purses. The church was half-full and people were scattered throughout—a good metaphor, he decided, for their gaps in understanding and lack of interest in the important matter at hand. He pushed on.

"And of course we mustn't forget the wonderful new role played by lay people. My helpers in ministry."

Jim grabbed for the bench on either side of his legs and rocked forward and back twice, then again, studying the pattern in the carpeted floor at his feet. Peggy covered the hand nearest to her, calming him.

"I know that the people of this parish will want to commemorate these events in a big way. So very shortly, after the first of the new year, I am going to appoint a committee to begin working on the celebration. I'll have more to say about this at the Christmas party for the lay leadership of the parish. You'll get plenty of information then and afterwards as plans develop."

The pastor looked out over his people. He still couldn't detect much reaction. Even so, life felt good this morning, and he somehow found himself in control again, confident that he was handling well the pressures of the parish and of being a priest these days.

"Thank you, my people, for everything. Be thankful to God today for this parish and for all the good things that have happened here over the years. We'll plan how best to celebrate our jubilee and move together into our next twenty-five years. I'm happy to be here to do it with you."

The Mass completed, the pastor greeted departing parishioners at the main doors to the church. Up close—shaking hands, patting children on the head—he sensed more support than he had observed from the pulpit. Truly, there was much to be grateful for.

Mary exited the church by the side door, pausing as she took holy water to recall how Father Joe had reached into her soul the day Charlie died. And realizing that, for today, she was thankful. She hadn't known that a priest would put his arms around you and hold you like that, as he did. *There's* a priest who knew how to say things. Even for a hunting accident. Bless the man.

"Indeed, God has been good in blessing this parish with fine priests," Esther said to her friend Rose Reilly, as they left the church together after the crowd. "We must double our prayers for vocations." Rose nodded in agreement.

"What a jerk," Jim mumbled to Peggy. He unlocked and opened the car door for her at the passenger side, then slid the van door open for the kids.

"My thoughts exactly," she replied, sliding in. She twisted to make sure everybody was buckled in and then fastened her own seat belt. There was much to be thankful for, to be sure, but everything argued for the bumpy road that lay ahead.

CHAPTER 17

Sunday, November 26

5:00 p.m.

Joe Burns squeezed Audrey's hand as he slid into his chair at the table reserved for them at Jack's Roadside Steak House outside Prescott, Wisconsin. He and Audrey Welch met at Jack's for dinner the last Sunday of every month—except in December, when they postponed it for a week or two. They'd been doing so for almost eleven years, missing only once, the day Joe's mother died in 1984.

Audrey clasped his hand between hers. "You look tired, Joe."

Joe studied his friend in return. At fifty-four, Audrey was five years younger than he. She perfectly fit his image of an attractive woman with her full-breasted, full-bodied five-foot, nine-inch frame and head of silvering black hair. A silk scarf and handcrafted silver earrings enhanced the fine cut of the blue suit she was wearing, further highlighting her beauty. He couldn't claim a similar elegance, but he was wearing his best pair of gray wool trousers and a new navy blazer over a light gray shirt and no Roman collar.

The final Sunday was the best day in any month for Joe Burns.

Audrey Welch was the reason, and he made no excuses for it. He relished their monthly get-togethers at Jack's, which refreshed his soul in a way few other things in his life did. A steakhouse with a low, slanted roof, tucked into a grove of trees, out of the way, just off a country road. Inside, white linen tablecloths, red linen napkins, and red candles, a stone fireplace with Christmas garland, soft light, intimate dining and—best of all—conversation with a significant friend.

Joe slipped his hand free to pull his chair closer to the table. "Tired? Yes, I'm tired," he confessed. "Exhausted, in fact, but I *am* getting back on track. I'll tell you about it." He reached over to pat her hand. "It's really good to be here, Audrey. Thank you, as usual." He signaled for the waiter and they ordered cocktails.

꩜꩜꩜꩜꩜꩜꩜꩜꩜꩜꩜꩜꩜꩜꩜

Joe and Audrey met in 1978 at a one-day seminar in downtown Minneapolis titled "Managing for Results: Effective Supervision." Seated next to each other in the morning, they ended up making easy conversation during breaks and lunch. Discovering that neither of them had a commitment for the evening, they decided to dine together at the hotel in which the seminar was being held. When they exchanged phone numbers after dessert, Joe gave Audrey the private line for his study in the rectory.

Over the next six weeks, they talked by phone several times, sorting out issues raised by the seminar. Not prepared at the outset to reveal that he was an ordained priest, Joe concocted a story about a manufacturing business that he'd inherited from his father. Whenever she asked about his own experience or business situations he was facing, he redirected the focus to her work as superintendent of schools in Hudson, a position she'd taken recently after twelve years as a teacher and ten as the school principal at two different sites. She noticed that Joe seemed evasive, but postponed inquiring about it.

Eventually, Audrey asked whether they could meet over dinner and talk further. They met at Jack's, a place not far from her home—and a safe distance, Joe thought, from the eyes of his parish. Before they finished that evening, Joe disclosed to her that he was a priest.

Audrey replied that she was glad to know, because whatever he was, the fiction he had been spinning about a manufacturing business had raised some serious concerns for her and she had been preparing herself to ask pointed questions about it. If the story were not true...well, she said, she wasn't going to invest any more time and further talk about matters that weren't real. His being a priest was not an issue. In fact, it made the prospect of further conversation even more interesting for her, as long as she could be sure he was, in fact, a priest and not playing make-believe again.

That evening Joe also told her about some of the circumstances that had led him to the management seminar in the first place, detailing issues at St. Mary's and even the names of some of those with whom he was at odds at the time. Audrey's lighter take on life provided the perfect tonic and, best of all for Joe, a good laugh or two. It extended dinner and dessert that evening by more than an hour.

It was never difficult, during the dinners that followed, for Joe and Audrey to decide what to talk about. Her lifetime passion for gardening rekindled in him an interest he had always had in flowers and gardens.

"It's a great pastime, Joe, but it's best to be *in* the garden, doing the work yourself, with your hands," she said. She even went so far as to suggest that a hobby like gardening could even make a person a healthier— and maybe more effective—pastor.

He enjoyed the quip but, despite Audrey's urgings, he never took up gardening himself. It did lead, however, to improved landscaping on the property at St. Mary's after he instructed Luis to plant more chrysanthemums, keeping the grounds colorful, depending on weather, up until Thanksgiving.

At other times they talked about their mutual interest in history, in Joe's case, Minnesota history and, in particular, the successful immigration and farm programs sponsored by the archbishop hero of his—a story he relished telling Audrey.

More often than not, they talked about what they were reading— from pop psychology books, especially those on body language and the games that adults play, to Audrey's favorite, Anne Morrow Lindbergh's short and artful volume, *The Gift from the Sea.*

Another night they spent most of dinner talking about celibacy as a mandatory requirement for priests in the Catholic Church. Joe told her that celibacy was the only way he could bring all that he had and all he could be to the work of the priesthood. It was a personal requirement for him. Audrey, he learned, had passed up several opportunities to marry in order to dedicate herself to the education of children, her consuming passion. Being single and celibate gave her a freedom she cherished for her life's commitment and she would not trade that freedom. Freely, they were celibates.

A lifelong Catholic, Audrey liked the changes instituted by Vatican II and, in fact, thought they had been long overdue. She had never gotten involved in church committees or projects, however, despite having been recruited frequently. Believing her work to be a generous offering to the social fabric of the world, she reserved evenings and weekends for herself.

That didn't prevent her from stepping into theological and pastoral waters with Joe at dinner each month, offering him a heart that listened well and a voice for helpful feedback. In a way, she took that as her contribution to the reform of the Church, besides her weekly worship and an envelope offering.

As their relationship grew increasingly comfortable, Joe grew more expansive on the issues and difficulties that he had faced in the past as well as new ones as they occurred. People couldn't get it straight in their heads, he told her, that it was circumstances alone that had forced the closing of the school. That he couldn't reasonably be expected, as the only priest serving the parish, to achieve the results that he desperately wanted for a growing parish like St. Mary's. Staff and program expense grew every year and the parish council was no help—quite the contrary, in fact. It was increasingly strident—vocal and unruly—in the way they worked for him.

Joe brought some of his deepest and most personal and desperate concerns as a priest to the table and found Audrey not only a good listener but at the same time a compassionate, straight-talking friend who considered herself his equal and one not accustomed to mincing words with people she cared about.

For Joe Burns, his friendship with Audrey Welch had graced his life inestimably from the beginning. They did not correspond between dinner engagements and rarely spoke by phone. One Sunday in May, Audrey had showed him the large garden she had planted in daffodils. On another occasion she called Joe to tell him her father had passed away suddenly. Joe drove to Milwaukee for the funeral.

It was a platonic relationship, rooted in Joe's commitment to celibacy and Audrey's dedication to elementary school education. For the pastor, dinner with Audrey Welch the last Sunday of each month was a chance to get his wits back—a secluded evening to refresh his soul, like a week on retreat.

౿౿౿౿౿౿౿౿౿౿౿౿౿౿౿

The waiter delivered their cocktails, a Brandy Manhattan for the pastor and a Whiskey Sour for Audrey. "I'll let you study the menu, shall I, and be back in a few minutes?" Joe nodded; they viewed the menu briefly and continued talking.

"You said you're tired but also back on track. What's that about?"

As they sipped their drinks, Joe related in detail the events of the parish council meeting almost three weeks earlier. The names were familiar to Audrey, as was the story line. She could hear the voices and visualize the gestures and the posturing. As he continued, Audrey saw the rage in Joe's eyes and in his agitated hand and leg movements. He talked for almost half an hour—pausing only when the waiter returned to take their orders—and in the end the result was what Audrey was expecting.

The waiter arrived now with their dinners. He placed broiled walleye pike in front of Audrey. "Enjoy it, ma'am." He turned to Joe. "Filet mignon, sir, medium rare. Would you care for steak sauce with that?"

"No, I'm sure this will be fine."

"May I bring you both another cocktail?" They nodded and began eating. The waiter returned promptly with their drinks.

"So," Audrey said with a smile, testing and feeling her way. "What about that hobby? Wouldn't it help in these situations to have something you could do to be kind to yourself? It would be good for you, Joe."

He released a heavy sigh. Audrey drew it to his attention. "See, just the thought of it relieves some pressure." She smiled again. "As crazy as it may sound, Joe, for some busy people a break from their work has to be *scheduled*. Think about it. Wouldn't a bit of time for yourself on a scheduled, regular basis make your problems with Jim Jensen, your parish council, and everything else feel different?"

Joe fingered the fresh drink, adjusting the glass on the table, moving it forward, then back, left, then right. "Yes, it could be helpful," he allowed.

"What's most important for me right now, however, is to schedule some time with Jim to straighten things out with him. I have to be proactive on this. Problems with people like this simply do not go away by themselves. Unfortunately, I'm not the only one dealing with crazy situations like this. Overcoming lunatics like Jim goes with the territory of being a priest today."

Audrey studied the man in front of her as they ate. At last she said, "Joe, the Catholic Church is probably going to survive its current problems. And you know what? It will probably do so even without Joe Burns."

"Imagine that!" The pastor wiped his lips, breaking into a hearty grin as he looked over his napkin to find Audrey smiling at him.

"You work hard, Joe, but can you imagine how much more effective you would be if you could let go and lighten up a bit? It seems to me that priests often cause their own most difficult problems." She sipped her cocktail, then chased the ice around inside her glass with a tiny plastic straw.

Joe cut a large bite from his steak and then sipped generously from his drink. "My dear," he said, trying to begin lightly. "This is an historic time in the Catholic Church—maybe the greatest period in five hundred years—since Martin Luther, really. It's an important time to be a priest, Audrey. There's so much at stake."

"I understand, Joe. There are cycles that occur in educational systems as well and some are even historic. That doesn't mean I'm going to make one of them my own personal crusade."

"This isn't a crusade, Audrey. And I'm not a crusader. This is just my work. It's what I bargained for a long time ago when I began studies for the priesthood."

Audrey leaned forward and pinned her eyes to Joe's. "What I am saying, my friend, is that it often feels like you *are* crusading when you talk. That's all I want to say. In my own work I can't afford to act as if the whole universe circles around either my favorite ideas for education or the dark and pessimistic predictions about failure in our schools. I have to remain steady and realize I can't do everything. Sure I worry some at times, but things don't possess me the way they seem to possess you, Joe."

He had to think about that. He watched as the waiter used a poker to raise sparks and a flame in the fireplace on the other side of the room. "Fire's going out," he said.

"What's that?"

"The fire—in the fireplace—it was going out. One of the waiters just stoked it up." He looked at Audrey. "Why do you suppose it never angers me, doesn't even bother me in the least when you challenge me like this?"

"Could be the messenger," Audrey smiled, sliding her fork under a final bite of walleye. "Or the way it's said. Sometimes the wrapping is as important as what's in the package, Joe. Commitment and being right aren't the only important things. You've got to reach the listener. It's possible to always be right and never be heard." She pushed her plate to one side. As Joe finished his steak, they continued conversing graciously for some time, enjoying the warm, holiday ambience of the restaurant.

"Dessert tonight, folks?" They asked for coffee only. The waiter delivered it after clearing the dishes from their table.

Joe looked at his watch. The time had passed quickly. It always did, the last Sunday of the month. Audrey's words were always measured, considered, careful. Nobody likes to be lectured and she doesn't do it. He'd come to trust her as a kindred soul. He could depend on that now.

"Audrey, I am committed a hundred percent to the Church—as you are to education. One is your package, the other one is mine. How the packages are wrapped, how a person says things, the externals, those are secondary."

"I agree with only part of that. We need sharp, dedicated priests, Joe, but you guys have to be smarter about how to get your message across. You're losing the world. You won't be able to take it with a hammer and a pickaxe. You have to make it something that people want to have, to own as theirs. You cannot force the Church on the world."

They sipped their coffee.

"This has been harder than usual for you today," Audrey said finally. "Your honesty and your courage are admirable qualities, Joe, but they have gotten you into trouble at your parish over the years. And then it gets you down when people don't appreciate you."

"The work does get me down at times, I admit it. But the worst is not the work. You're right. It's the lack of appreciation. That's what kills a guy."

"I find you open and honest, Joe. That's refreshing. People in your church may not see it that way. It's hard for me to say, never having been a member of your parish. There must be something, though, that gets in the way; it causes problems so often. You need to share yourself better— what's going on inside you. It makes for a beautiful person."

"Sounds like something my staff would say. Be 'vulnerable.' *This* week, that is. Next week, it's something else. Be this. Be that. Beejeebers. I'm tired of it."

"I'm sure you are. I need to be totally honest with you. It's important for both of us. I can support you personally, but at the same time I don't want to enable you or encourage you to continue wearing yourself out. A person can't be effective that way, not in the long run."

They sat again in silence. Audrey watched Joe ponder the evening and everything that had been said. At length he looked up, reached toward her and squeezed her hand when she put it into his. "I appreciate that," he said. "It's been good again. I love this place and this table by the window where they seat us. Thanks for listening and for speaking honestly with me, as usual."

"Of course," Audrey said. They split the bill, paying cash. They walked slowly to their cars. Joe gave Audrey a pat on the back, rubbing just slightly, got into his car and waved as he pulled out of the parking lot onto the country road. In the rear view mirror, he saw the taillights on Audrey's car disappearing to the east.

Driving west to Minnesota and another month at St. Mary's, it dawned on him. He'd forgotten to tell Audrey about his plans to celebrate the diamond jubilee of the parish and, of course, his own twenty years as its pastor — somehow helping him to start some things over and thereby save himself again.

It was just as well, he thought. He wouldn't trade the evening or a single word that was said. He flipped on the radio, just in time for the hourly weather report. The forecast was for below-zero temperatures most of the week, he noted. It was time for some ice fishing. Time to call Ken Halpin.

CHAPTER 18

Monday, November 27

7:30 a.m.

Dave Hanratty picked up his phone messages while he waited for his two-cup coffee maker to deliver the first one of the day. There were nine messages, four from Jim Jensen. The most recent one was time-marked an hour earlier. "It's nice to feel wanted," Dave joked when Jim picked up. "But four calls?"

Jim chuckled back. "It's harassment, right? I tried two or three times on Friday, thinking you might be working."

"Not quite. After Mass on Thanksgiving we all piled into the car and left for Fargo to spend the weekend with Carolyn's folks. We got back last night about nine-thirty."

"I was out of town myself on business for ten days before Thanksgiving."

"So I heard."

"I need someone to bring me up to speed. What's happened in the last couple of weeks?"

"Well, let's see." Dave paused to straighten papers in a folder on his desk. "A long weekend in Fargo will do this to you," he breathed into the phone, meaning he'd been away from it all for four days himself and he had to get refocused. He mentioned Charlie Beckins' funeral and Joe's fine homily, his own conversation with Clarice the morning after the council meeting and the staff meeting that same afternoon. "Oh, and then maybe most important of all, what he announced at the Mass on Thanksgiving."

"I was there. I heard it."

"So you know the plan. Celebrate the parish diamond jubilee."

"He hopes that'll distract us."

"I agree."

"So how'd the staff meeting go?"

"He walked out. Clarice was pressuring him for an agenda."

"Two days, two meetings; he walks out of both. How long before we do something about this, Dave? When I got back from my trip last Wednesday, I had a message that he wants to meet next Monday evening in the rectory—to straighten things out, to have a meeting of minds, make some peace—all his words."

"So... you going to do it?"

"Of course, though I don't have much hope for peace or a meeting of minds. If I don't come out of there with some indication that things are going to be different, then I'm going to call on the parish council to agree on some action to resolve these issues."

"Good luck on that."

"Problem is, this man acts as if he were the student of everything modern—work teams, theories of behavior and motivation, personnel policies, reformed liturgy. All of it, in theory. But when it comes to putting into practice a fresh theology of the Church, for example, he can't even get started. That's the predicament."

"Agreed, Jim. He loses his nerve on the really big issues."

"That, and more. And I do agree with Sheila. Start in the market place. There's not a whole lot of difference between marketing a business and marketing a parish church. The problems may be different. The goal is the same."

"Agreed, Jim."

"Thanks for bringing me up to date. Wish me luck for when I see your boss."

CHAPTER 19

Thursday, November 30

11:30 a.m.

For six years Joe Burns and Ken Halpin had considered it a sacred rite of sorts to go ice fishing during the first week that freezing temperatures made it safe to go out onto area lakes. With the mercury already below zero on Monday and a statewide prediction for three or four more days of the same, the two priests had agreed earlier in the week to hold Thursday open for their first outing of the winter.

Ken called early in the day to be sure Joe was still able to go.

"You bet. It's a great day for it. Cold, sunny and bright."

"And you're bringing the lunch."

"Right. You're getting the bait."

"Okay, then. See you at Bald Eagle about 11:30."

Joe left the rectory at 11:00, bundled in a heavy forest green parka and a wool stocking cap. Beneath the parka he wore a wool shirt, buttoned at the top. Wide suspenders held up a heavy pair of tan pants. Like canvas to the touch, they covered sweat pants that in turn were layered over long underwear. His feet were encased in thick wool socks and tucked into dark brown moon boots.

From a cabinet in the garage he grabbed two durable plastic milk cases, the strainer they'd use to clear ice and slush from the fishing holes, a small plastic box with extra hooks, line and sinkers, and a folding knife. He brought hot coffee in a thermos and two roast beef sandwiches, dill pickle spears and half a dozen brownies in a zippered thermal container that would keep their lunch from freezing.

Just inside the trunk he placed the heavy, treasured, five-foot ice chisel his father had left to him as a monument to the several hundred hours the two of them had spent on Minnesota lakes in winter. Next to the chisel he placed his fishing pole, fashioned from the shaft of a broken hockey stick. Two nails, a third of the way from either end of the stick, served to hold, unwind, and rewind fishing line. A sharpened third nail, on one end, enabled a fisherman to stab the pole into the ice when he didn't want to hold it.

༒ ༒ ༒ ༒ ༒ ༒ ༒ ༒ ༒ ༒ ༒ ༒ ༒ ༒ ༒

The trunk of his car lifted open, Joe was waiting in the parking lot that offered public access to Bald Eagle Lake when Ken arrived and pulled in beside him. Ken tugged on a red plastic sled to remove it from the trunk of his car and loaded onto it two plastic milk cases that matched Joe's, his ice-fishing pole and the pail of minnows. Joe added the gear he'd brought and slammed his trunk shut. "Ready, set, go," he said. A gust of wind clipped them across the face. Zippering up their parkas tight to their throats, they turned into the wind and began walking toward the spot they normally fished, a quarter mile out onto the lake.

The ice snapped and groaned under them, continuing to thicken and expand even as they walked upon it. Ken eyed their progress, looking for the line that extended out from the small marina on one shore to the point where it intersected a similar line from the huge oak tree on the north shore. "This is about it, correct?"

Joe agreed and began pulling the load from the sled. He took the ice chisel and chopped two eight-inch holes eight feet apart—close enough to talk. Ken scooped ice out with the strainer and in a few minutes they were fishing.

They did so in silence and inside five minutes Joe pulled up a tiny perch, removed it from the hook and slipped the fish back into the water without comment. A bit later a small crappie shook itself off Ken's hook and onto the ice. It squirmed, jumped twice and disappeared back into the icy water. Joe didn't notice. He was lost in thought.

"Managers," he said finally.

"What did you say?" Ken asked, summoned from his own thoughts. "Sorry, I didn't hear you."

"They expect us to be *managers*. What do we know about managing, for cripessake?"

"You've got something there, Joe. We have to do it, but you're right, we don't get much training for it. A guy has to find it for himself."

"I used to run good meetings. *Good* ones. Now they want a *productive* meeting and they expect you to measure *how* productive it was, compared to others. There have to be minutes and written agendas—everything done by the latest lousy book. A fellow gets rated on how he delegates and shares authority. It's not enough to just get the job done anymore." He huffed, steam billowing around his head. "Things take too long that way."

Joe pulled in his line, checked the bait, then dropped it onto the ice near his foot, reflecting. *Administration used to mean paying bills, seeing to repairs, and meeting with the two trustees to decide things. Simple! Today there's stuff like copyright law—you used to just copy music if you wanted it. And employment law—you don't own your staff anymore, because the law and the Chancery hold you hostage, protecting employees who aren't even doing the job; fire someone and you end up in court. Equal opportunity. Safety in the workplace. Equity. The buzzwords.*

"I need a minnow, Ken. My guy's dead here." He got up, fished a replacement from the pail, and returned to his seat. Ten minutes later he stabbed his fishing stick into the ice and stood up.

"Ready for lunch?"

"It's why we come, isn't it?"

"You bet. Heavy horse radish on roast beef," Joe announced. "Here's some pickles. There's brownies, too, but only after your plate is clean." He laughed. "Coffee? I'll pour." He brought it to Ken in a large white mug marked with a Minnesota Twins emblem. "Black's okay, right?"

"Always."

They opened their sandwiches and had lunch, for the most part talking and chewing, but occasionally taking a peek at the open fishing holes.

"I was happy to be a priest," Joe continued, "but today they expect you to be a community organizer, a member of the school board, an advocate for affordable housing, drug programs, schools and jobs. No thanks! That's not me. I'm just a priest. No one in a million years could do everything they want. It's too much."

"Yes, you're right, Joe," Ken said finally, exhaling visibly in the cold. "It *is* too much. And so a guy has to choose what he can do well and then let others do the rest. You know what? They're right about delegating matters to others. Call it managing or whatever you want to. You've got to let other people do some things. They do it for themselves, not the pastor, remember. It's *their* church." Joe bit further into his sandwich, took a swig of coffee and then another bite.

Another long silence ensued, during which Ken reflected on his own convictions and how he had arrived at them. The two men stared into the holes in the ice in front of them until Ken continued.

"It's all about perspective, Joe. I try to have a sense of humor about things. I probably use that in my work more than anything else."

"It gets to a point where things aren't humorous any more."

"You remember Mozart, right?"

"I can't do it that way, Ken. If I simply wait for things to happen in my parish these days, I'll get creamed." He reminded Ken about the most recent parish council meeting. "I'm not waiting around to get run over by a steam roller. That's not what being a parish priest is about. We've got to be out front. The more I think about your Mozart idea, the more it doesn't sound right."

"Joe, I simply insist with myself that I keep the big picture as clear as I can. People need time, time to change, time to embrace it all. Meanwhile I can't let myself get all bent out of shape over it. It's not really in my hands. It's not really my work. You know whose it is."

"Easier said than done, my friend. They come after you with a pitch fork."

"It's not a war, Joe. We have to keep working at this reform of the Church, but we've also got to keep in mind that the really crucial issues, even in today's Church, are few in number. Not many that a guy would want to die for. I don't have to have an answer for everything. I let ideas sit and stew for a while."

"What are the few issues you would die for?"

"What would I die for?" Ken responded. "What comes to mind? Well, to start with, I'd say more lay leadership in the Church."

"What else?"

"Election, not appointment, of bishops in some way—by priests and the people."

"And?"

"Certainly a married clergy. Women as well as men."

"That's all?" Joe said, chortling. He opened the container of brownies he'd brought.

Ken took one and continued, "Joe, every time I let the people of the parish make a decision, I believe we're making progress. It's important that the people do things. Frankly, I don't believe that God needs the official Church as we've known it. And I don't worry about loyalty to the Church when I say that. Honestly, Joe, do you think that God the almighty needs the Catholic Church to save people? It's *one* way, *one* Church among many, and yes, a fine one. I'm involved in it and I'm giving a good piece of my life to help create conditions for people to find their God there. But the Church is just a vehicle, Joe—and one that has a big time interest in preserving itself, as does any institution."

Joe could find no response for Ken's priceless honesty. He stood and faced into a wind that had lessened from the gusts of earlier in the afternoon, then humped his back, bending, stretching, bobbing for his toes before finally pouring Ken coffee for the brownie.

"Not much fishing going on here," Ken commented.

"That's for sure. I don't think I've even got bait down there." At that moment the bobber on Joe's line went down with a snap. He hurried to set his cup down, spilling half in the process. Hand over hand he pulled the line up until a crappie that appeared to go a pound or so came out of the hole in the ice, shook itself in the frigid air, and fell back into the water. "Damn! That could have been somebody's supper."

"Or part of it, anyway," Ken agreed. He put the thermos on the crate as his own bobber disappeared. He pulled up his line to find the hook stripped clean. "There went the rest of your fish fry."

"Time to get serious here," Joe responded. Ken got up for a minnow and gave one to Joe. They re-baited, scraped the sides of the ice holes with the metal scoop, cleared the slush and dropped their lines into the water.

"Balance is so important, Joe," Ken said after a bit, staring at his motionless bobber. "I work only so many hours a week. I have friends and interests outside the priesthood. I make certain I do enough reading and have enough quiet time to keep some perspective. It keeps a person laughing—or smiling at least—with all the work and stress we have in this Church today."

"You're a good man, Ken. I admire you."

"I set clear goals for my work, Joe, ambitious goals. But I don't take my goals or myself too seriously. When I do, somehow it becomes all about me, and then it gets ugly. I start trying to force things. I've stepped on people to get God's work done. Think about that! Stepping on someone to get God's work done!"

They fished for another half hour without much conversation beyond, "Slide me the minnow pail, would you?" and "More coffee?" By 3:30 they were ready to leave. Joe loaded the equipment onto the sled and Ken added the four plastic crates. "You ready?" Ken asked.

"Yep," Joe said as he grabbed the rope. They began the trek off the lake and back to their cars.

CHAPTER 20

Sunday, December 3

9:00 p.m.

T he weekend had passed uneventfully for the pastor. He had presided at all three parish Masses, as was his custom, and after the last one he threw his black wool overcoat onto his shoulders and hurried from the sacristy back to the rectory. Honoring a sudden impulse to sit outside on the porch, he unfolded a lawn chair stored there. He drove his fists deep into the pockets of the coat, stretched out his long legs, and tried to trace the origins of the uneasiness that was gripping him. It could be his scheduled meeting with Jim Jensen on Monday, he decided. Had to be. Eyes closed, he sat out for twenty minutes in the thirty-degree weather.

That afternoon he had lain down for a nap, a luxury Joe Burns allowed himself every month or so on Sundays. He awoke after two and a half hours and splashed water on his face in the bathroom, recalling he'd had a dream that it was the last Sunday of the month and that he'd be dining with Audrey Welch. Later he went for a long walk and stopped on the way back in Fairview Park, three blocks from the rectory. He took in the last signs of light for the day from an elevation overlooking the park athletic fields. A thought about Jim Jensen broke his meditation.

He had spent the evening catching up on his reading, marking three articles from a theology journal to read at another time. He went upstairs and got into his pajamas and decided to begin a book Ken Halpin had recommended. He couldn't quite remember the title—something about a green dragon—and it took a trip to the study downstairs and back before he found it finally, resting on the shelf inside the nightstand.

He sat on the edge of his bed flipping pages, ready now to read the book. He turned back the covers, maneuvered into bed and arranged a pillow behind him to sit back against the bedstead. A green dragon, for cripesssake! He opened the book. Contents: primary revelation, cosmos, epiphanies of the earth, end of the fireball. He flipped to page twenty-five. Some character, a youth, was asking, "Why do you say, teacher, that the universe is a green dragon?"

He'd done enough for one day. A dragon only reminded him of the appointment he had in less than twenty-four hours. He pressed the switch on the lamp, pulled up the covers, and turned onto his side to sleep.

☙☙☙☙☙☙☙☙☙☙☙☙☙☙☙

At a minute before seven on Monday evening, Jim Jensen stepped onto the back porch of the rectory, the door the pastor had asked him to come to. Just as Jim was about to press the doorbell a second time, Joe opened the door and escorted him through the kitchen and down the hall to his study.

A blinking red light there signaled a message on the answering machine. Joe waved Jim to the leather chair that faced his recliner and then hit the playback button. The message turned out to be nothing urgent. He made a note about it, straightened the crucifix and letter opener on his desk, and then plopped himself into his own chair, flipping out the footrest.

Fixing Jim with his gaze, the pastor began. "I'm sorry that this whole affair has gotten so out of control, Jim. We can't go on like this. At least, *I* cannot. How are we going to resolve things?"

"What have you thought of, Joe?"

"You know what it's like, Jim—being a priest, I mean. I'm thinking that maybe, somehow, two folks like you and I, we could work at this together."

"Go on."

"Used to be, when the priest said something, people would listen. At least *that* much."

"It's different today, Joe. The expectations they gave you in the seminary and the teaching they offered—the training you got—isn't that helpful today. You're aware of that, I'm sure."

"No, Jim, I'm not, " Joe said, stiffening slightly. "Frankly, I don't believe it. Sure, I had to relearn some of my theology after Vatican II. It was a lot of work, but I did it. I believe in Vatican II, but I will not accept the idea that everything before that was entirely useless."

Jim folded his hands and drummed the tips of his fingers together. It was always hard to believe that Joe Burns had really bought into Vatican II, that he had integrated it into his life. It was time to ask outright. "Really, Joe? You believe in Vatican II? You *own* it? And it owns *you?*"

The pastor laughed snidely, hissing several times through his nose. "What's that?" he said, his face stiff. "Now let's not get started here."

Jim lifted his hand to object. Joe talked over it. "Yes, sir, I do believe in the Vatican Council and, yes, I have taken it into my heart," he declared. "That should be clear to you."

Jim squirmed in his chair.

"I don't *like* it all," the pastor continued. "I don't get it all *done*, but I accept it. You bet." God knows, he'd tried—right from the beginning. Hired a staff when the sisters left, empowered a planning committee, formed the parish council, wrote policy manuals—everything. "I've made this a new kind of Catholic parish, right from the start. Don't talk to me about Vatican II."

"People give you credit for that," Jim answered. "But remember... "

"But remember nothing, Jim. If people would just give a person credit, we wouldn't be having these problems. There's no authority given to the pastor. No respect."

"Joe, you know the same things I do about authority and leadership. There's no leadership unless people consent to being led."

"I cannot accept that, Jim. Authority comes from God, not from the people. There's no way you can say it the other way around. Look, I don't want to make an argument of this. I invited you here to talk this out."

His fingers twitched. He rubbed his hands together and then slid them back and forth over his trousers.

Jim ran his eyes over the bookshelves on the wall to his right. *The Documents of Vatican II.* Hans Kung, *Infallibile? An Inquiry.* Schillebeeckx, *Christ, the Sacrament of the Encounter with God.* Rahner, O'Brien, Raymond Brown. Another entire shelf held books on psychology and personal growth. *Born to Win. Games People Play. The Seasons of a Man's Life.*

He sighed, eyeing the other side of the room. *Hard to figure—he reads the best, yet so little evidence of it.*

"Joe, tell me something, will you, please? What happened there on the altar that night? After the council meeting, when we came to the church. What were you doing there?"

Joe glanced at Jim, then at the portraits of the two popes on the far wall. "That's where I find Jesus," he said quietly. "I go there at wit's end, when there's no place else."

"You were up on the altar, Joe. *On* the altar. Lying there, curled like a child in the womb. What was going on?"

"I was praying."

"Praying."

"Something wrong with that?"

"There *is* something peculiar about it, wouldn't you agree? Lying on the altar?" Jim underlined each word.

"Peculiar? Why do you call it that? That's a putdown." Joe dropped the footrest, pulling the recliner sharply to its upright position. "Call it unusual or special or something," he said, jabbing his finger at Jim, trying not to lose control of himself and of the evening. "But to say it's peculiar is hostile. I don't like it."

Jim wondered again, as he often had since it happened, just how unconscious the pastor had been throughout that whole business on the altar. He'd been in a thousand scrapes before, but clearly the stakes were higher than normal that particular evening. Would Joe have concluded that he had to decisively win the argument that night? Hence, the altar stunt?

"It's like climbing up on the cross," Jim declared. "Making a martyr of yourself."

"Nobody likes a martyr, Jim, least of all me. I'm just telling you that when I feel the way I did that night, I go to Jesus. So I got up on the altar.

Peculiar? I don't think so. Martyr? No. And really, I don't care." He sat forward in the recliner. "I'd like to get back to where we started a while ago. I think we can work this out, Jim. You and I."

"I'm not so sure about that." Jim twisted his shoulders, trying to relax. "I would like to, but you and I have some fundamental differences. The biggest one is the way we understand the Church. Today, priests are servants, Joe, or they're nothing. You yourself have preached that for twenty years, and it's right. Your priesthood alone doesn't put you in a higher state than lay people or make you better or right about everything."

"That's the theory. In practice, though? The priest is still special."

"That you have to *earn*, Joe. What you did at the last council meeting, trying to take charge of the meeting and bullying people the way you did, that won't work anymore."

"Aw, Jim, for cripessake! Don't use that word. I'm not a bully. I can tell you about lots of guys like me, good priests, who just don't stand for it." He struck his knuckles on the arm of the recliner and leaned towards Jim, his face twisted. "They get the people they *want* on their council, *mister*. Most priests don't hand over any real authority at all. Or haven't you noticed?"

Jim leaned forward, too, arms splayed on the arms of his chair. "Those priests, they're dinosaurs," he sneered, face taut, eyes burning. "Those days are gone. And don't call me mister. You know I don't like it."

"Don't tell *me* I'm a dinosaur." Joe stabbed the air again. "Ever. We're a lot more modern here than most parishes. We measure up well, mister, and you know it."

Jim bit his tongue, fighting for control.

"Not all the ideas have worked, of course. Our success was often our greatest problem. We had elections, for example. We gave people a voice. It doesn't work. Look at us."

"So, tell me, Joe... why do you think it doesn't work? That would interest me."

"Let me tell you... I don't care what your interest is. Your interest is not that important. My interest, as pastor, is to keep things in line at St. Mary's. That's what counts."

Seeing the fatigue on Joe's face, Jim made an effort to relent a little. "Why won't you accept help when it's offered? What about just letting go a little more?"

"Let go? Let go, you say! You don't get it, do you? As pastor, I *can't* let go. I have to be at my post. *You* can let go. I cannot. My calling is different."

"Spit it out, Joe. Is it that I left the priesthood and you have not? Is that the issue?"

"Take it any way you want to, mister. You're the one who's got to answer for it. I'm glad I don't have to. Excuse me a minute. I've got to go to the bathroom." Joe got out of his chair and hurried across the hallway.

It's turning ugly. Jim reminded himself how important it was to relax as Joe became more intense. He looked around the room. *Everything in perfect order.* Desktop clear, end tables set beside the chairs, dusted and polished. Books and bookcases everywhere. Magazines and journals piled neatly on the floor near the recliner. He turned in his chair to view the corner behind him. A six-inch candle etched with colorful sacramental symbols centered a round table and three oak chairs positioned there, secure in the view of the popes on the wall above. *With whom does this man meet and talk at that table? When does the candle shed light on parish work? Who reads the books in this room?*

Joe re-entered the study. "People have lost their faith." He plopped back into his chair and kicked out the footrest again. "The only thing some of them want to do is to keep on fixing things. Fixing *me*, changing *me*, telling me what do." Joe leaned back, studying the ceiling. "If people would just cooperate, things could work and we'd all be better off."

"Tell me honestly. You'd be just fine if St. Mary's didn't have a parish council, wouldn't you." It was not a question.

"No sir, I would not. We need a council, but it has to work with the pastor. It's like the pope with the bishops. If you're a bishop and you're not in union with the pope, then you're not in the ballgame. That's standard, Jim, and you know it. It's standard. And until we agree on that, we can't agree on anything. As pastor I'm in charge here. But, yes, of course we need a council."

"Doesn't seem that way. Seems like all you want is for people to stand aside or rubberstamp whatever it is you want to do."

"We've done fine around here," the priest said, tapping the arm of his chair. "I've been one of the new breed of priests in this diocese, right from the start. I'm all *for* Vatican II. I like it. But there's more to the Church than Vatican II. Things are getting out of hand. We've got to keep things within reason. And who's going to do that, Jim? Laymen?"

"Why not?"

"People are stupid, Jim. You know that."

"Whatever are you talking about? That's nonsense. I won't sit still for it."

"C'mon, man, you know how it is. People don't have the background. They don't follow through."

"We're not getting any place here." Jim moved to get out of his chair. "Let's quit for tonight and start fresh another day. Where are we at on this?"

"Here's where we're at. I want you to resign. We're not getting any place with you on this council, especially as chairman."

Jim's face contorted before his jaw dropped. He tried to cover it with a dry chuckle, sliding back in the chair and going through the motions of listening while he grabbed a moment to think.

"Look, Jim, there's no need for you to be embarrassed by any of this. We'll explain it to people. You can even take the pulpit. Tell them it's your work, maybe. You know... your consulting firm is doing well, you're busy. You've done a *good* job on some things; people will be grateful. You've got only six months left as chair anyway. Sheila can take over. It's the good of the parish that counts, of course. You want that, too."

"That's nuts. Forget it."

"Now wait just a damn minute. I won't stand for *that* either."

"You're missing the point. It doesn't make any difference that my term as chair is up in June; it doesn't mean I'm done. I'm in this for the long haul. This is my *church*, Joe."

"That's enough, Jim. Stop it. *Now!*"

"I'm going to make a difference, chairman or not."

"So resign if it doesn't make any difference."

"What in God's name are you talking about?" Jim flared. "I didn't say it makes no difference," he continued, almost shouting now. "I said it makes no difference whether I am *chairman* or not. It's still my parish. You can't get rid of me."

"Listen to me. You're a good man, Jim, but it's not working. I can move this council forward. You're an obstacle for me, however."

"You really have no idea what this is about, do you?" Jim shook his head. "You are not going to treat people like this any longer. Not in *this* parish."

The pastor's face soured. "There's nothing wrong with the way I run this parish."

"That's the problem, Joe. You don't *run* this parish. It's not *yours*. It's not yours to *run*."

"I'm the one responsible to the bishop and to God for this parish. Not you, Jim. Not any damn council or any fool lay person," he spluttered. "I'm in charge here."

Jim jabbed at the bookcases beside them and glared at the pastor. "All that *reading*! All that *learning*!" Jim pushed himself up and towered over Joe, still in his chair. "All that *posing* as the freethinking, post-Vatican II, liberated priest! It's a lot of bullshit," he snarled. "Posing, always *posing*. Pretending to be something you are not, instead of the hopeless, arrogant demagogue that you really are."

The pastor stood, bumping against Jim as he did so. Jim retreated a step and continued, nearly poking Joe in the chest.

"Joe, I will not let you off the hook for what you have done to people here for twenty years. You have *destroyed* people in this parish. You have debased and humiliated them, staff and parishioners alike. I will not let that happen again. I will have sympathy for a sick man—which is what I believe you are, Joe—but I will also have truth and justice. You're crazy if you think we're going to put up with this any more."

Bristling, the pastor stepped away from where he was pinned, between Jim and the recliner. "I've done my best in this place for almost twenty years," he fumed, throwing up his hands, proclaiming his innocence. "How can you argue with success, Jim? I think you're the one who's out of line here. And *you're* the fool, the one who's crazy, if you think I'm going to stand for *this*."

"It's not about success on your terms," Jim fired back. "I'm going to give it to you straight, Joe. This is about abuse." Jim folded his arms. "You treat people badly. It's as simple as that. But they're no longer afraid of you and your power, and they don't believe that breaking your rules and laws will bring God's disfavor on them. You, and a lot of men like you, are running on empty."

The pastor stepped back, boiling, as Jim continued.

"You profess one thing about the new, reformed Catholic Church, and then you act in a totally different way. We're not going to take that any more. We're going ahead. Moving in a new direction. We know you were born into a priesthood which is dear to you, but we think you've put that honor ahead of God and conversion and justice and treating people decently."

"Enough!" Hands on his hips, Joe rose to the balls of his feet, then settled back down, again and again.

"It's about that, priest. About abuse, plain and simple. It shows up in a million ways, in the pain, the wasted resources, the wasted effort and wasted people who live and work with you in this parish community. It's the focus of the struggle in this parish today and of the evil that's been at work here for twenty years."

"Jim, I won't stand for your insults anymore," Joe stammered, barely subduing his fury. "I can't."

"Neither can I," Jim retorted. Grabbing his coat, he stomped out of the pastor's study and the rectory.

ॐॐॐॐॐॐॐॐॐॐॐॐॐॐ

Jim phoned the Chancery Office the next morning, asking for an appointment. The archbishop had a policy, well publicized, of listening directly to the voices of the people in a parish when that was requested. He was going to test that. His call was transferred to the archbishop's secretary, who had his calendar in front of her.

"May I ask what this is about?"

"I'd like to talk as soon as possible with Archbishop Meuncher about a grave situation at St. Mary's in Mapleton, something I'm sure he'll want to know about."

"The soonest the archbishop can be available for this kind of appointment, with the holidays and all, is the first week of January, Mr. Jensen. Would Thursday, January 4, at 9:00 a.m. work for you?"

Jim marked his calendar, thanking the secretary for making time for him and for St. Mary's.

"These appointments allow for twenty minutes with the archbishop, thirty at most," she continued. "Will anyone else from St. Mary's be coming with you, Mr. Jensen?"

"Just me," Jim replied. Twenty minutes? He'd make it work. He hung up the phone, confident that the direct approach would get the results he wanted; it usually did.

Little did Jim know, Harry Droesch had been at the desk of the archbishop's secretary as she took his call.

CHAPTER 21

Tuesday, December 5

5:20 p.m.

Joe was in his study, eyes closed, Evening Prayer completed, when the phone rang.

"I'm thinking you'd want to know this," Harry Droesch said without ceremony.

"Good afternoon, Father Droesch," Joe singsonged, injecting a bit of levity to balance the gravity he sensed on the other end of the line.

"Your chairman, Mr. Jensen."

"Yes. Jim Jensen. What about him?"

"Mr. Jensen has a one-on-one appointment with the archbishop early in January."

"What's this?"

"I was at the Chancery Office this morning, outside the arch's office, waiting for my ten o'clock appointment with him. The secretary, what's her name again? Marilyn?"

"Yes. Marilyn."

"Well, I'd stepped over to Marilyn's desk and I'm joshing with her a bit when she takes a call from a Jim Jensen."

"Mine?"

"Hold on a minute, let me finish. From Marilyn's face I can tell the tone on the other end. This guy has 'concerns' that he wants to discuss with the archbishop. She said she could schedule him the first week of January."

"But there must be other Jim Jensens."

"Oh, this is your guy alright. She confirmed his parish when she was taking his information. Unless you've got two Jim Jensens at St. Mary's, this is your troublemaker and he's on with the archbishop for the fourth of January, nine a.m."

"For cripessake! I had a knockdown brawl with him here just last night. The man is intransigent. I told him I want his resignation."

"I thought you'd want to know. This guy is up to no good. You need to take care of this, Joe. You can't win with a man going around you to the archbishop like this."

Joe slapped the arm of his chair. The sharp crack startled Mindy, who scurried down the hall, her fur raised. "Hold a minute, will you, Harry?"

Joe pitched the receiver into the recliner and stomped to the door of the study, then back to the triple window behind the desk. He stood there for a moment, fists posted at his hips, glowering through sheer curtains into the suppertime darkness, before retrieving the phone from the chair. "You still there, Harry?"

"Yes, of course, Joe."

"Let me get this straight. You're telling me that the chairman of a parish council in this diocese is going behind a pastor's back to talk with the archbishop."

"Believe it. How long are you going to put up with this?"

"I told you. I asked him to resign, very clearly, last night. He refused."

"Of course. You've got to fire this type. Get rid of him."

"He thinks the chairman is in charge. He wants to run the parish. I told him he can't. Not here anyway."

"Right, Joe. Stick to that. These guys'll destroy you if you don't watch out."

Joe breathed heavily into the phone.

"Get out of this mess, Burnsy. There's gotta be someone else who can chair your council."

"Could be. I've told you about this gal Sheila. She's vice-chair, next in line. She'd be good, a sharp woman. I plan to meet with her soon."

"Do it sooner. Could she help you get rid of this guy?"

"She's a smart lady; she'll play ball, I think. She wants things to work."

"Just be careful. Like I always tell you, this ship isn't run by consensus. Over here, we meet, but I hold the roof on really tight. They've finally gotten the message: 'We'll work together, sure, but I'm in charge, boys.'"

"You know how to play hardball, Harry."

"Whatever. I'm in charge. After all, when the axe comes down, whose neck does it fall on? Harry's. That means Harry is in charge. It can't be any other way."

"They're squeezing us from every side, Harry. People push forward, bishops hold you back. Left wants it faster, right wants to slow down. You can't win."

"This is not why I became a priest. I wanted to help people save their immortal souls. That's *all*. The people need God's grace. That's what I'm about as a priest; that hasn't changed. It's about grace and saving people's souls. If I wanted to be a manager, I would have become one. I'm not a manager, Joe, I'm a priest."

"Me, too, Harry, but we can't let go of Vatican II. This guy I've got is killing me. Killing the *parish*, I should say. Still, you've got to have a parish council. I don't think a pastor can get by without one today. "

"Sure, but you don't have to like it. As I told you, it's my parish, so I make the rules: 'Play it my way, folks. I'm glad to listen, but stay out of center ring.'"

"It's just this damn chairman; he's a *mule*."

"Former priest, right?"

"He is."

"They're all over and they're angry, Joe. They gave it up and they're mad as hell. I don't give 'em anything to do here. Keep 'em clear of any responsibility. They take over."

"You help me keep my feet on the ground, Harry. I take the liberal side on things, as you know, but you help keep me practical. I appreciate that."

"Liberal is a nutsy idea, Joe; you don't want to be there. It isn't going anyplace. There'll be another Council or something soon and Rome will reverse all this stuff. They aren't going to stand for it; not in Christ's Church."

"I appreciate your heart, Harry, and your honest advice. Thanks for alerting me to this Jensen thing."

"Of course, Joe. Anytime. Well, good luck with it. Have a good night."

Joe hung up the phone. He stood for a while, his head bowed, weary of it all. He trudged to the kitchen to prepare his dinner, knowing he had to nail Jim with a deadline.

CHAPTER 22

Friday, December 8

9:50 a.m.

Most of the parishioners who attended the nine o'clock Holy Day Mass had left the church when Joe came upon Peter Featherstone sitting in his customary place at the back of the church, the book of Psalms open on his lap. The pastor slid into the pew beside him.

"You're looking well today, Father."

"Yes, I'm fine, Peter. I love this feast day, the Immaculate Conception."

"The Virgin Mary. Yes, Father."

"So tell me, Peter. I see your prayer book open there," he commented, leaning over to see the page. "I tell you, Peter, I admire the way you pray—more than I can say."

"Well... thank you, Father Joe. It's just my way, you know. And it's nice of you to say that—nice to be appreciated. Thank you."

"Do you ever find yourself feeling *not* appreciated, Peter?"

"I suppose so. That's easy for an Indian, you know."

"Yes, I would think so."

"You must enjoy your work, Father. Helping people the way you do."

"Not all the time, my friend." He looked at Peter and then over his shoulder, as if someone could be listening. "You look surprised, Peter. Maybe you think you shouldn't be hearing that from a priest."

"That's up to you, Father." Peter maneuvered in the pew and grimaced. Joe reached for him. "It's my back, Father. Years of working on the Iron Range, you know. Sometimes I just move wrong. It'll be all right. Go ahead."

"You're sure, Peter? That looked very painful."

He continued after receiving another assurance from Peter. "Let me just say that it's got to do with people and with how hard some of them make it for priests today."

"You say so and I have to believe you, but it still sounds like the best job in the world—to me anyway."

"Not exactly. In fact, far from it."

"Paradox, Father Joe."

"Paradox?"

"Yes, it's a paradox. I've guessed that you have the best job in the world, being a priest, but you tell me that's not necessarily so. I think to myself, how can that be? For me, it's a paradox."

"Peter, tell me something, will you? Where do you get all this? You have such an incredible vocabulary and such a healthy take on life. Tell me something about a paradox in your life that has really touched you."

"The wheat and the weeds."

"No, I don't mean parable, like the stories of Jesus in the Gospels. I said *paradox*, the same word you used a moment ago."

"Yes, I know, Father. The way I see it, many times they're the same thing, parable and paradox. Losing all that time to find a lost coin? Leave the sheep to find just one? Strange divine counsel, but it works. Hard to figure why things turn out the way they often do. The message, for me anyway, is always the same. You can't figure God's ways. You have to be ready for what comes—even a paradox."

An older couple who remained after Mass for private adoration before the tabernacle passed in the center aisle on their way out of the church. The pastor glanced quickly toward them, signaled good day, and returned his gaze to Peter's face.

"Life is that way, isn't it, Father?" Peter continued. "You can't figure it for sure. Why would anyone in charge of a field let the weeds grow with the wheat? It doesn't add up very well. It's baffling. That's why it's divine."

Peter leaned deeply to his right, then made a gentle circle with his upper torso and rolled his shoulders. "Sorry, Father. I get stiff."

"Sometimes a person has to pull the weeds, Peter. Many times you have to take action—you can't just let things be the way they are. Look at your own people, Peter. If they had not fought for justice, they would have none today."

"I suppose people hear stories in different ways, Father. Those who always take action could easily not pay attention to the parable about the wheat and the weeds. Still, the story stands." Peter rubbed a hand over his face, slid it down over his cheeks and paused to steal a quick look at the pastor. "Action people may not want to wait for results in the Creator's own time, but can they afford to *ignore* the story?"

The church floor creaked at a point beyond the center aisle. Joe looked around but saw no one. He looked back at Peter, who was waiting for him with his eyes. "Why do you watch me so closely, Peter? Every time I look at your face, I find you looking back at me."

"I'm listening, Father Joe. You have a lot to say."

"Thank you. I wish more people felt that way; life would be easier."

"It helps to listen."

"The wheat and the weeds story is not my favorite."

"I understand that, Father. You're a busy and active man."

"A priest has to be that way today."

"I find there's more than one way to do most things and two points of view on everything. Pull the weeds or wait? Both ways can be good. We don't honor the other person's way often enough. That was the problem a hundred years ago in the West; my people and your people. We didn't honor each other. That's the human way and you pay a price to pay for it."

"I'll have to think about that."

"It takes a lot of thought Father."

"I want you to pray for me, Peter. Your pastor needs some help."

"Sure, Father Joe. I pray a good part of every day. No problem to speak to God about you."

"Thank you. We should talk more, Peter."

"Any time, Father."

As he got up from the pew, Joe Burns pressed Peter's hand. He walked slowly down the side aisle and into the sanctuary. There he dropped onto the padded kneeler. *Peter is right,* he prayed.

How's that? the Presence questioned.

You must know! People pick their parables, the ones they like. Me? I'm a man of action. Weeds get in the way and, worse, they choke other plants —the ones you want, plants that belong. There's no place for weeds—no more than for moneychangers in the Temple, a thing you might recognize. They were out of place. Desecrators. Unfit. Bad pennies. You tossed them. And so it is with weeds.

The pastor listened. Hearing no answer, he left the church to get his breakfast.

CHAPTER 23

Sunday, December 10

11:15 a.m.

T he mist and fog that had prevailed since noon Saturday turned
to light rain and snow overnight and laid down a sheet of ice
that by Sunday morning was half an inch thick. It covered the
lower half of the state of Minnesota and two of its neighbors,
Wisconsin, east to Eau Claire, and Iowa, as far south as Des Moines.

Radio stations advised no travel for Sunday. Nonetheless a couple
dozen St. Mary's parishioners braved the colossal ice storm to attend the
8:00 Mass. There were another several dozen at 10:30. At both Masses
Joe named them brave worshippers and extended the invitation to gather closer to each other in the front pews, suggesting that they might find
new meaning in the Mass by sitting closer to the altar table. Most did as
he wished and the front seven pews were dotted with hearty but hag-
gard-looking faithful. At the 10:30 Mass Jim Jensen took a seat away
from the center aisle, at the far end of the second pew.

Joe decided to forego his prepared homily for a few words simply
spoken as he walked back and forth in front of the first row of pews and

back a half dozen rows into the center aisle. He invited questions and commentary on the readings from Scripture by those sufficiently confident to do so.

The Mass was over in forty minutes. The pastor thanked parishioners for having come to church under difficult conditions and encouraged them to go slowly on the way home. "God love you all and be safe." He gave the final blessing and turned for the sacristy.

There he quickly pulled off the vestments from Mass and left them in a pile on the vesting cabinet. He threw his overcoat onto his shoulders but didn't bother with buttons before he hurried out the door. The ice underfoot forced him to waddle over the long stretch of sidewalk along the cedar fence that separated the schoolyard and parking lot from the backyard of the rectory. As he inched his way, he looked up every other step to check the path in front of him. He kept the wool coat pinched shut at the collar and twice tried unsuccessfully to keep the rest of it closed.

Halfway to the parking lot he caught up with Charles Constable, a former member of the parish council, and his wife. Charles had completed two terms as chairman of the parish council ten years earlier. He grabbed a slat in the fence to steady himself as he turned to greet the pastor, at the same time extending an arm for his wife to hold. "We'll be there, Father." They'd obviously received the invitation for the annual Christmas gathering in the rectory for current and former parish leaders. "Wednesday, the twenty-seventh. Right?"

"Right. I want you to help prepare for our diamond jubilee, too. I presume you heard about the plans."

"Of course, Father. Be careful there. Don't hurt yourself on this ice."

"I'm alright, just in a bit of a hurry." He flipped the fingers of one hand several times, signaling he was rushed and needed to get by. Charles and his wife stepped aside, their backs to the fence, holding onto it for balance as Joe passed. "Yes, the Christmas party. We'll have the usual good time, I'm sure." With leather soles on his shoes, Joe slipped and would have fallen, had he not caught the fence with one hand.

He continued inching his way along, finally arriving at the six cement stairs that descended to the parking lot. Two charter members of the Ushers' Club stood there.

"Easy there, Father Joe. It's icy," one said.

"You're the only pastor we've got," said the other, thinking the pastor might smile or say something. "Take care, Father. We need you," he added.

The two men could have been ice statues. The pastor's mind was locked on the ice underfoot—and his mission.

He grabbed the handrail and, to save a precious second or two, bent over it to see past a row of wintering lilac bushes heavy with ice. "Hold on a minute, will you, Jim?" he yelled out. "I've got to speak with you." He carefully descended the last four steps and made his way, stepping gingerly again, toward the spot where Jim waited for him. "Hold on a minute," he repeated, drawing close. He puffed a sigh of relief when he finally stood across from Jim, looking at him over the roof of his car.

Jim pulled his gloved hands from the side pockets of the parka he was wearing and rested his arms on top of the car. "Yes, Joe. What is it?"

Joe extended his hands onto the roof of the car as well, then withdrew them quickly, stung by the ice.

"Bad ice today," Jim said. "It's amazing anyone came for Mass."

"These are good people," the pastor replied, rubbing his bare hands. "Some of them get here no matter what. They're amazing. Jim, I wanted to talk with you about something."

Jim pulled his arms off the car and looked down at his unzipped overshoes, then stared at Joe again across the roof of the car.

"I've been meaning to follow up with you on our conversation in the rectory on Monday," Joe continued.

"Follow up?"

"Yes, we've got to bring this conflict and this bickering to an end. It's going to take us a while to get some of these things figured out, and by *us* I mean the whole Church. We don't know how to do parish councils yet, Jim. It isn't working this way."

"Parish councils will never be perfect, Joe, but we've come a long way in twenty-five years."

"Won't work, Jim. We've tried. Things are out of control—all over, not just at St. Mary's. Priests don't know how to handle it. The people don't either and that's for sure. They keep forgetting some important things."

"Like what?"

"Like who, at the end of the day, is responsible for it all."

"The way I learned it, we're *all* responsible. The parish belongs to the people, Joe. You work here. You work for the people."

Joe rested his bare, clenched fist squarely on top of the car. "You're nuts, Jim. Now listen to me. Your problem is power. You're an angry man, you lost what you had and now you want it back, but without all the responsibilities that go with being a priest. You want the cake. You don't want to bake it. I won't accept that."

"Joe, you're missing the point. I do have power—all I need. It's not the type of power you're thinking of, perhaps, but I do have it because I am a baptized Christian adult. I don't want to be a priest. I *do* want a new kind of Church. You can't take away the sacrament and what it made me. That's my power."

"It's not just here, at St. Mary's, Jim. I hear it from priests all over. We've got to get the horses back in the barn. We've got to control the pace of change. It's gone crazy."

"They're out of the barn, Joe. And they aren't going back into it. It's too late. There's too many horses out. You need to run with us, Joe."

"*Run* with you? You've got to be kidding me. You have no idea where you're *going*. You're just *running*. You and your so-called new-church people are out of control, just running." He put his hand back into his coat pocket. "You've lost your way. All of you." He shrugged his shoulders and pulled the collar of his coat tight around his neck.

Jim folded his arms and glanced at the street and then back at Joe. He squinted. "Joe, look at us here. Talking across the roof of a car. It could be an ocean or a universe. We're in entirely different places—worlds apart. I don't know how to get this together either, but we can't go back to the church we grew up in."

"We cannot possibly solve this problem. I told you what I want. I'm telling you again. I want your resignation. I'm surprised I haven't gotten it by now."

"You're kidding, right?" Jim looked straight at Joe, who returned the look steadily.

"Kidding? Kidding, Jim? Of course not. This is dead serious. The good of the Church is my concern. I never kid about that—can't afford to. I'm committed to the Church in ways you haven't even dreamed of."

"You talk the new theology, but you just don't get it, Joe. You cannot just ask for my resignation and think it will be given. It doesn't work that way anymore."

"We'll see what works and who works for whom here, Jensen."

"You are employed by this parish, Joe Burns. You do not own it."

"I guarantee you, you are not in charge here, mister. I am giving you this week to find a way to explain this to the parish and save face. If I don't have your resignation on my desk in a week, I'll take the necessary steps to fire you. Kaboom! You'll never sit on this parish council again. You're through, mister."

"No, Joe. It's over for priests like you."

Joe glowered across the car at Jim. He banged the icy roof of the car with the flat of his hand. Saying nothing more, he turned to make his way back to the rectory.

That afternoon Jim Jensen began calling parish council members to schedule a meeting without the pastor. He'd been considering the move since the homily Joe delivered at Thanksgiving, Jim's first clue that the diamond jubilee celebration was a convenient strategy—a diversion, a distraction from matters the pastor could no longer control. The meeting would be at his house.

CHAPTER 24

Sunday, December 10

9:00 p.m.

It took Jim most of Sunday afternoon and part of the evening to finally reach every member of the parish council and explain his intention to them. He described the confrontation that he'd had with Joe in the rectory the previous Monday and then told them about the added hostility in the parking lot that morning after the last Mass, including a second demand that he resign as chairman. Believing that the parish council was at a crossroads with the pastor, and hoping he could persuade the members about the importance of confronting him and addressing the current impasse, he was calling for a meeting at his home, without the pastor, on Thursday at 7:30.

"If we don't meet this week, we won't do so until after the holidays," he told them. "That won't be soon enough because I have arranged to meet with the archbishop on the fourth of January to bring the issues at St. Mary's to his attention. We need to discuss how best to use the twenty minutes I'll have with him."

Ted Kroenig couldn't see any urgency and told Jim he should cancel the appointment with the archbishop. The next scheduled council meeting in January would be soon enough, he said, to continue the discussions and, in any event, he probably would not attend a parish council meeting without the pastor present.

The problem was larger than Joe Burns alone, Bob Talbot thought. He said he believed that a parish council, any council, should challenge dysfunctional leadership by a pastor, any pastor. He'd be there.

Megan Roberts considered the meeting urgent. Joe Burns was a laboratory in what it meant to be an ineffective and abusive priest, she said. The meeting should take place as soon as possible.

Rosa Perez and Tom Andrews both expressed concerns about being fair to a pastor who had given twenty years of his life to the people of St. Mary's. Rosa, however, made the same point she had at the council meeting—people should not tolerate unacceptable behavior from anyone, not even a priest.

Priest bashing would serve no purpose, Sheila Martinson said. As she saw it, however, the latest developments were part of a larger malaise that was beginning to overtake the Church as a whole and the council should address those issues at St. Mary's.

Dave Hanratty would have liked to be present because he thought the issues were important, but he said he should not do so since he was not actually a member of the council and was present only to help Joe evaluate meetings afterwards.

In the end, every member agreed that matters were spinning out of control and that they needed to attend to the latest conflict. Ted even conceded, if reluctantly, that the pastor's unilateral, repeated request for Jim's resignation might not be right. And so, in this case, he would attend.

Rosa, Tom, and Megan said nothing to Jim about his unauthorized appointment with the archbishop. Bob, Sheila, and especially Ted questioned it, however, and Jim had to agree with them—it had been done unilaterally. He considered it exploratory, however, and given the urgency of the matter, he told them, he had believed it important to get at least *something,* a first step, underway on behalf of the parish.

๛๛๛๛๛๛๛๛๛๛๛๛๛๛

For the meeting on Thursday evening Peggy Jensen prepared two trays filled with a variety of crackers, cheeses and meats, a plate of peeled shrimp and another with Jim's favorite, small filets of pickled herring. Jim placed them on a low, glass-topped table in front of the fireplace at one end of the first floor family room.

He returned to the kitchen for tall glasses and two ice buckets. Pecking him on the lips, Peggy reminded him that there was soda already cold in the refrigerator and more ice in the freezer if he needed it. She'd be upstairs helping the kids with their homework and keeping them out from underfoot, but available if he needed anything.

"Thanks, sweetheart. Have a good time," Jim said distractedly.

Back in the family room, he sat on the sofa and stared into the fireplace, his eyes fixed on two smoldering logs, placed there an hour earlier. Tension seeped from his forehead to the back of his neck, creating a dull ache, as he pondered a parade of faces from his years at St. Mary's. *Faithful people, all of them; from good families and hard workers. And well-intentioned, yes, but people who often checked their nerve and their brain at the door when they came for a church meeting.*

The doorbell rang at 7:15. It was Tom Andrews. By half past the hour everyone was present, seated, and sampling the refreshments. Bob, Rosa, and Megan took the sofa. Sheila and Ted sat beside each other on the love seat. Jim took one of the two wingback chairs, offering the other to Tom, who said he was comfortable where he was, having opted for the large stuffed pillows on the floor.

Jim called the meeting to order, offered a prayer and began.

"I'll be brief, folks. You know why we're here. Change is painful. An organization can't remain unchanged when the world is moving in new directions, however—not if it wants to be healthy and relevant. That's true for churches, too. I believe that responsible leaders in a parish today have to take up-to-date, sometimes difficult positions on important issues. And in the Catholic Church since 1965, that means the reforms called for by Vatican II. We are here tonight for the good of the parish."

"I just don't see what's so difficult about this situation, Jim, or so different," Ted declared. "Most churches are struggling with the same things we are. You find it all over. I assure you, we're doing fine here at St. Mary's."

"And I remind *you*, Ted," Megan said, "that some members of this council and many, many longtime members of this parish are *not* so sure about that."

"I just want to be clear about where I stand," Ted replied. "I'm loyal to our priest. I always will be. As I told you on the phone, Jim, there'll be no lynching a priest on my watch. You can go to the bishop if you want to but I don't think it's right or fair. Anyway, you'd be wasting your time."

"It's not a question of loyalty to the pastor, Ted," Sheila maintained. "The council has a responsibility to the parish in matters like this."

"A lot of people don't know about all the things that are going on in the Church," Ted argued. "Me? I've been around here forty years and on this council for most of them—seems so anyway. People hear this criticism of the pastor, or worse, of all priests, and they jump on the bandwagon, complaining about anything and everything that suits their fancy. Young people hear it and they don't know what to think. How will they ever end up loyal to the Church? I want my grandchildren to be able to be members of the Catholic Church."

"That's the point," Megan said. "I'd like that for my children and my grandchildren, too, but I don't think the Catholic Church will survive like this, in its current form, with the frightening behavior and poor leadership of priests like Joe Burns. How could that be what God wants or intends for people?"

"It's the Church of Christ, who is the Son of God, the second person of the Blessed Trinity, for cripessake!" Ted snarled. "The true Church will survive, Megan. Mark that in your little book."

Jim called the discussion back to the purpose of the meeting—to develop a plan that would resolve the stalemate with the pastor. He wanted to begin, he said, by making a confession of sorts. He swallowed hard.

"I have a habit of speaking strongly and authoritatively most of the time," he said. "I know that and I think about it often. I know it can adversely affect the outcomes of things I try to accomplish. I know that has been true in my relationship with Joe."

He stared at his hands, noting a couple murmurs of surprise.

"In the first years of seminary I was exposed to the same kind of education and training Joe got. I must admit to you—and frankly I'm embarrassed to say it—that I believe I could have become the kind of priest I find Joe to be. Vatican II saved me. It freed me up to think differently and more creatively about the priesthood and the Church. It led to significant changes in my life and my thinking. I never looked back.

"I know that I don't always say things in the best way. I know that I can be just as dogmatic about Vatican II as Joe is about his way of seeing and doing things. Peggy helps me work at this.

"That said, I am committed to the reform of the Church and of this parish in particular, come what may. This is where I live, so this is where I make the best and most informed contribution to change that I can. What I contribute is not always done perfectly, though. I admit that."

"I don't know," Ted quipped. "Where's that coming from? Is that you, Jim? I must say, I appreciate hearing it—and the way you said it." Others nodded, agreeing. "But that doesn't mean that you should expect my opinion or my feelings about all this and our pastor to change."

And so it went, for another hour: It's been hard on priests. The triangle; the circle. No alibis, just be thankful. There's a shortage of priests. Making excuses; making it work. The priest's world got tipped on its ear. That's crap; they lost their nerve. Hot buttons, values, benefits. He's all priest. That's true. That's nuts.

Options surfaced: Everyone should see the archbishop, not just the chairman. They should write him a letter with parish signatures—a petition. Pickets at Mass. Alert the press. Everyone could resign.

In the end, no one option had gained favor and no one had the energy either to challenge or to discuss Jim's appointment with the archbishop—except for Ted. He reproached him for having taken the step unilaterally—the same thing, exactly, that Jim had so brutally and so often accused the pastor of doing.

Finally, it was quiet in the Jensen family room.

"I've got a proposal," Bob said at last.

"Let's hear it," said Jim.

"Let's go with Sheila's sense on this. What would most easily get Joe's attention? I'll use the word. Benefit. What would benefit him the most? The man is exhausted. Maybe there's a way for him to name a single, prized value he would welcome from this mess we're in."

"It's a waste of time," Megan said. "There's never been any two-way talking with this guy."

"Negotiation with a person like this won't work," Jim contended. "That's why I scheduled a visit with the archbishop, as a backup to this meeting here tonight."

"We need to go back at it again," Bob argued.

Ted agreed. "Let's find out what Father Joe really needs—his *benefits*, as you call it, Sheila. I'm for it."

Despite Megan and Jim's reservations, the group decided that Sheila should call to schedule a special meeting of the council with the pastor. The purpose of the meeting would be to agree on a single place to begin, with one benefit, without using the word, that each side is asking for and that the other might provide—and so make a start toward settling this standoff with him.

The meeting adjourned quickly. Saying little, Jim stood at the door, patting each council member on the back as they left. As soon as the last car left the driveway, Peggy came downstairs.

"So. How'd it go?" she asked as she kissed Jim on the cheek, then on the lips.

"I'm not sure, frankly. They want to meet with him and trade horses."

Peggy let it rest. Grabbing his hand, she tugged him toward the family room so they could clean up.

🙟🙟🙟🙟🙟🙟🙟🙟🙟🙟🙟🙟🙟🙟

"I don't think so," Joe Burns said the next morning when Sheila called him from her office. "I suppose I could meet with the rest of the council if necessary or with you alone, as long as Jim is not a part of it. I've told Jim to resign and I haven't changed my mind about that. There's no reason to include him."

"Can we talk about this, please, Father Joe? The council met last night..."

"What's this? The parish council met without its pastor?" he scowled. "I've also heard that Jim is seeing the archbishop in January—about all *this*, presumably. How could these two things ever happen, Sheila? There is no parish council without the pastor. Everyone knows that."

"Yes, we met last night. We did so because we want to reach a workable solution with you."

"Where? Where did you meet without me?"

"At Jim's home."

"Jim's house. What time?"

"Why is that important, Joe? The meeting was scheduled for 7:30 and we met for a couple of hours."

"Two hours, for cripessake! Tell me, who was there?"

"The whole council was present, Joe."

"I'm surprised that you would go along with this, Sheila." He choked. "Tell me Bob Talbot wasn't there."

"Of course he was, Joe. I told you, everyone was there."

"This meeting changes everything, Sheila. This has to stop. I will not stand for it."

"We met for the good of the parish."

"That's not possible if the people aren't in union with their pastor. The priest heads the parish church." Adamant, he raised his voice. "And I could never sit down with a man I have asked with good reason to resign."

"Joe, listen please. We can…"

His tone softened. "Here's what I suggest, Sheila. What if just you and I meet together? I've always been able to talk comfortably with you. I can be reasonable and I can be collaborative, no matter what crazies like Jim Jensen may say. So let's you and I meet and just begin talking about things. If there is a problem, we'll fix it."

"Joe, listen to me. I will not proceed without our chairman. Jim is a dedicated man, a member of this parish who believes in many of the same things you do. Nobody on the council believes you should try to force Jim's resignation. And furthermore, in a showdown of some kind in this parish, if it ever came to that, I believe many people would support Jim. This is about more than the one incident at the last council meeting. You know all the stories and bad feelings stored in the minds and the hearts of many of the people in this parish. Stirring those memories to life again would not be all that hard to do and you could have a sizeable and public revolt on your hands, an embarrassment for everybody. And so Jim really has to be included in working out the solution to this impasse."

"I'm telling you, Sheila, there's no impasse because Jim is no longer a part of this."

"That won't work for me, Joe. The council supports this proposed meeting with you. They truly want to find out what will serve you best, but we can't bypass our elected chairman."

"No way. Call me when Jim is out of the picture. In the meantime, I'm moving ahead." The pastor hung up the phone.

Sheila wondered if the last bridge had finally been crossed. Perhaps finding a new parish was the only solution for her personally.

Later that morning, she phoned Jim and reported that the pastor wanted to meet with her alone. "He says he won't sit down with you under any circumstances, Jim. It's his position that you are no longer a member of the parish council and therefore can play no part in solving the current deadlock or planning the future."

"It's what I expected, frankly, and as much as I hate the idea, I think you should meet with him and do the best you can. I'll call the council to explain."

"It's not that simple," Sheila replied. "I told him not an hour ago that you had to be included or else. I need to think about it and also talk with my husband. We may have to make some decisions about whether we'll remain parishioners at St. Mary's and under what conditions."

⤳⤳⤳⤳⤳⤳⤳⤳⤳⤳⤳⤳⤳⤳⤳⤳

The next morning Sheila reached the pastor by phone. "Okay, I'll go along with this, Joe, and meet one on one with you to talk about the situation. At the same time we can also plan the agenda for the parish council meeting in January. You need to know in advance, however, that in the end I will not, under any condition, be part of a parish council meeting that excludes an active, able chairman. Do not, under any circumstances, try to force me into that position."

"That'll be fine, Sheila. We'll do the agenda for January and then talk about this other issue, too?"

It didn't seem a question. They agreed to meet in the rectory about 8:30, after Mass, the morning after the Christmas party.

"A blessed and merry Christmas to you and the family," Joe said. "I'll see you at the annual Christmas party, won't I?"

She confirmed it, without sentiment.

CHAPTER 25

Sunday, December 17

4:30 p.m.

Joe had hardly slept since Friday and hadn't been able to eat all weekend. What sleep he had gotten was restless, stolen as he sprawled in the recliner in his study. He didn't preach at weekend Masses even though Advent was his favorite liturgical season. Instead, he'd asked parishioners to ponder the Scripture readings on their own at home. After the last Mass, he didn't go to the doors of the church to greet members—normally a personal highlight of his weekend—and instead went directly to the sacristy and then to the rectory where he spent the afternoon thinking and pacing; twice attempting to eat a little something, then throwing it out; trying to nap and finding himself not able to, then staring out at the yard from the kitchen window and dozing off. Such was the despondency that had afflicted him since he'd learned that the parish council had met at Jim Jensen's house without him.

At one point he had a mind to call Ken Halpin, but thought better of it because he hadn't warmed up in the least to Ken's Mozart idea. So far it had only helped unravel him.

He went to the church to sit in the sanctuary and the fading light of day that he loved. He peered out over the empty pews, along the stained glass windows that graced the west wall of the church and finally to the vault above where he was seated. He took in the silence.

"We seldom vote at St. Rita's—almost never—and on really important matters, not at all." It was Ken's voice coming back at him from a year earlier—on the lake—fishing. *"There's seldom a vote because we talk about everything long enough that everybody at the table can live with a decision we make. There's no pressure to hurry. We do things temporarily—provisionally. That gives us room to be flexible."*

He studied the fading light that remained. He had to admit it. Ken does some fine things.

What in particular? Where do you want to start?

He wasn't sure he wanted to talk with the Presence at the moment and delayed several minutes before he asked, *So what was your question? Where do I want to start, you ask? Let me tell you. I want some relief—some peace and quiet.*

So? What can you do about that?

So, this is no life.

No life, you say?

I'm too tired to even stand up at the end of most days. Worst of all is this parish council idea of yours.

What's that you're saying?

I go from the altar to meeting after meeting and then repeat it all, over and over, trying to help your lay people find their place in the Church. It's not working for me. I like the altar. That's what I signed up for.

No one said it was going to be easy. Things are changing.

Tell me about it! Look at us. It's been brutal, in case you haven't noticed.

I've seen it all. And I've been with you, trying to get through to you.

Joe thought about that, got up and left the church for the rectory and his bedroom. He lit a lamp on the small table that held the picture of himself with his parents on ordination day. He went to the bathroom and studied himself in the mirror, then stepped back and lowered his head, leaning on the sink. He made himself look again and held a sigh, considering the image there.

I said I've been trying to get through to you.

I have people I can't handle. They're unmanageable.
You can learn from Ken Halpin.

Shaking his head slightly, the pastor wondered. He got into his pajamas, turned off the lamp and crawled into bed. It was 7:00. He reminded himself that he had to call the archbishop first thing in the morning. A shoulder twitched. He turned onto his side and slept through the night twitching, enough on two occasions to wake him.

CHAPTER 26

Monday, December 18

8:30 a.m.

The pastor had been up since well before sunrise and in the kitchen for an hour, fixing and eating breakfast and watching sunlight begin to gradually illuminate shapes in the garden. There being no 8:00 Mass at St. Mary's on Mondays, he thought he might be able to get a call through to Archbishop Meuncher right at 8:30, before he left for an appointment or closed the door to his office for a scheduled meeting. Joe put his coffee cup, half-full, into the sink and went to the phone in his study. The receptionist put his call through immediately.

"Good morning, Joe," the archbishop answered cheerily. "How was the weekend at St. Mary's? Try to convince me there's a liturgical season better than Advent! I love it, as I know you do. What's on your mind this morning?"

"I'm glad I reached you, archbishop. I won't take more than a couple of minutes of your time." He notified the archbishop of the events that had taken place at the parish council meeting in November and what he termed the subsequent hullabaloo.

"Now, on top of it all, I've discovered that the chairman of the council, a guy named Jim Jensen, has scheduled an appointment with you the first week of January."

"That's right," the archbishop said. "Now that you mention it, I do remember seeing an appointment scheduled for someone from St. Mary's, but I don't recall the name at the moment. You know my policy, Joe. I make time for as many people from the parishes as I can. It's so important for the archbishop to listen to people in the pews when the opportunity presents itself."

"I'm calling because I have concerns about Mr. Jensen's intentions and what he's up to."

"Parish councils can be difficult, Joe. What's going on?"

"Basically it's just a few people."

"That's often the case, isn't it." It was a declaration. "That's why I keep on listening. Usually the tension can be diffused."

"In this case, Walter, I have reason to believe that a small group here wants me replaced as pastor and that that's what Jim is going to propose to you. The parish council met privately, without me, last Thursday evening. I can't imagine it was for any purpose other than to consider that step and make plans for it."

"That I don't like, Joe, but you know that I do like to find ways to keep sincere and energetic people working for the Church. How could we best use Jim's energy and leadership skills there in your parish? You've told me before he's a former priest. That could help you, Joe."

"No help there, archbishop. He's destructive—a lone-ranger type, looking for power and image for himself."

"Whatever the case, you are the pastor at St. Mary's, Joe. I have no plans for any change. My issue is different. Wouldn't it be fine if you could discover how to use the talents and the faith of a man like Jim Jensen to improve your parish?"

"I don't see how that's possible. Jim doesn't have a shred of good will toward me nor does he have any practical way to go about helping the parish."

"In any event, I assure you again, Joe, that I will not bow to any pressure to remove a pastor. But know also that I believe that if we take these things to prayer we sometimes find the most unexpected solutions. I'd ask you to do that and see what happens."

Joe wished the archbishop good luck with the chairman in January and the conversation ended. *A good man, the archbishop,* Joe reflected as he hung up the phone. *Not practical, though. In this matter, anyway.*

Picking up the phone again, he called Betty Halvorsen in her office at the school building. "Tell everyone, please, there'll be a staff meeting today. Call them right away, at home if need be. Three o'clock."

༒༒༒༒༒༒༒༒༒༒༒༒༒༒༒

"Why are these meetings scheduled with so much advance notice?" Clarice Morgan groused to Dave Hanratty as they entered the staff room.

"Beats me," Dave breathed as he took a Mountain Dew from the counter before joining Clarice, Gary Pirot, and Betty Halvorsen at the table. Lorraine Larsen and Sister Janine followed shortly and then Luis Alvarez, who had been checking on a furnace problem in the rectory. Joe Burns sat erect at the head of the table, arms folded, studying staff members as they entered. As soon as Luis was seated, he began the meeting.

"Thank you for being on time and for coming on short notice on the first day of what I know is a very busy week. I wanted you to know where I stand on the parish council situation." He rose and began to pace across the room and back. "Usually things settle down a bit if you give people time to think matters over. I regret to inform you, however, that Jim Jensen has scheduled a meeting in early January to talk with Archbishop Meuncher about his devilish, dangerous ideas."

Staff sat dumbfounded. *Devilish? Dangerous?* They stirred in their chairs nervously and cleared their throats. Setting a mechanical pencil on the table, Clarice caught Lorraine's eye and aimed the implement, torpedo-like, at the pastor. Dave snapped open the Mountain Dew. Clarice slid back from the table.

Joe, seated and quiet now, waited until each member of the staff eventually looked at him. Clarice met his eyes coldly.

"I don't like what's going on in this parish," the pastor continued. "Frankly, I don't like Jim Jensen either." He paused. "I have to confess that." He waited again. "But we've always been able to work things out at St. Mary's when there were conflicts. Until this man became chairman, that is." He slapped his hand on the table. "He has scheduled a meeting for himself with the archbishop and there's no reason for that."

"Tell me, Joe, has anyone asked Jim his reason for wanting the meeting?" Clarice asked. "It doesn't necessarily mean he's up to no good."

"It's not necessary to ask that, Clarice. Everyone knows Mr. Jensen's concerns," the pastor snarled.

"I *don't* know, in fact. I can only guess it's about the parish council—power issues, maybe."

"Listen, lady. There is no *power* on a parish council. Don't forget it."

Clarice met his stare. "Joe, they do have power. Maybe not the kind you are talking about. But they obviously have some kind of power if you are threatened by them."

Joe's impulse again, as on many occasions, was to fire the woman—on the spot—for insubordination. He knew that would be no solution for the bigger issue at hand, however. "Do *not—ever—*suggest that I have been *threatened* by these people, Clarice, much less by Jim Jensen. You know that parish councils are purely for consultation. They're no threat to me. Now let's move on."

Sister Janine sat with her head lowered, as did Luis. Lorraine doodled on a paper pad. Stealing a glance at Joe, Gary got up for a Pepsi. When the can hissed open, the pastor's head snapped toward the handsome youth worker, his eyes watering coldly. He re-fixed his glare on Clarice, who glanced at Dave, then stared back at Joe.

"Let's move on," the pastor repeated, pausing just long enough for Gary to slip back to his seat. "The council needs to understand several essential matters." He ticked them off on his fingers. "One, they do not have any power in a Catholic parish. Two, the priest is in charge. Three, Jim Jensen has to be removed. He is an obstacle to the effectiveness of our parish council. And four, the archbishop supports me on this. I spoke with him this morning."

He glared at the staff. "Now I need you all to understand this and to help me resolve this matter. That's one of the things you're here for, part of the reason we pay you."

Softening her tone enough for the pastor to notice and listen, Clarice appealed to logic. "You asked for a report, Joe, and they produced it. You refused to even read it. The council didn't like that. Then, I've heard, you asked the chairman to resign. And he went to the archbishop." She spread her hands. "I ask you, Joe. What did you expect? This was completely predictable, wasn't it?"

"A pastor can't treat a parish council this way. Not today," Dave asserted, supporting Clarice. "I have said that to you privately, Joe, so it should come as no surprise when I say it to you now." He paused, choosing his words carefully. "A person can't hang his hat on Vatican II one day, Joe, and then behave the next as though he's never heard of it."

The pastor surveyed the faces around the table. They were carefully neutral and non-commital. His jaw tightened. "As I said before, people, I expect staff support in ending this power play by Jensen. Apparently you need more time to get this sorted out. We can talk all afternoon—till midnight, if you want to—but I know you'll see my point eventually."

"Joe, this staff does not seem ready to just line up and salute. I think you can see that," Dave stated cautiously.

"This meeting is over," the pastor declared. And, Dave, I'll see you in my office in ten minutes, please." Joe Burns left the room.

       ನಾನಾನಾನಾನಾನಾನಾನಾನಾನಾ

There were messages on Dave's answering machine, but he called his wife instead of checking them. "I'll be here with Joe for awhile," he said. Carolyn murmured sympathetically. "So I'll be late getting home. Go ahead with dinner."

He knocked on the door next to his. The pastor was waiting for him, staring out the window, arms folded. "Tough meeting, Dave," he said, without turning around. "We have a war on our hands." Joe sat down in the black high-back swivel chair behind his desk and motioned Dave to take a chair in front.

"You have hooked some people on a very sensitive point, Joe. Empowerment of the laity is a no-trade item for a lot of people today and you're messing with it."

"I've been working on this parish council fiasco for six weeks now, my friend."

"*Friend?* Doesn't sound friendly, Joe."

"Don't interrupt. I've been explaining and then explaining again. They don't get it."

"Six weeks of talking, Joe. How many of listening? Do you think you've really heard anyone?"

"You're not with me on this, are you? You're agreeing with these people."

"I'm asking you a fair question, Joe. Do you think you've *heard* these people? You asked a group of trusted laypeople for a report. Then you told them you wouldn't even read it, didn't need it, or even want it. You pissed on their work."

"Enough! I don't like what's going on here or your tone of voice." The pastor scrubbed his face with both hands, then looked up. "You're wrong on this one, Dave. I respect you because you tell the truth as you see it. I appreciate that and I know that I'm not always right. This time, however, I am."

"You're not getting it, Joe. For years you've talked about empowering people and now, once more, you're trying to take power away from them, dishonoring them. That's not going to fly in the Catholic Church nowadays—perhaps never again."

"No, Dave. *You* are missing it. You know your stuff, but you're missing what's going on in this case. You know these parish councils are a mixed blessing."

"A mixed blessing?"

"You bet. Very mixed. Good ideas, but things get out of control so easily."

"Joe, listen to me..."

"No, Dave, *you* listen. There's more at stake in this matter than usual. When the people are right, it's okay. But when they're not, you can't give them any room to go in the wrong direction. They need guidance, Dave."

"Joe, I'm sorry, but this simply won't work anymore."

"It has to, Dave. It *will*. Christ will not forsake his Church or his priests. I need your support on this. We can take care of this. Agreed?"

Dave Hanratty did not answer.

"It'll take some time, Dave, but we *will* get this right."

Dave got up and left the office without a word. Nor did he look back.

CHAPTER 27

Wednesday, December 27

6:00 p.m.

The festive Masses that marked the feast of Christmas every year at St. Mary's had left the pastor moved—and confident that, with a little bit of nudging, the normal course of events would prevail and the peace on earth proclaimed at the scene of Jesus' birth would come again soon to St. Mary's and to his own life as a priest. At the door after each Mass, he pulled aside certain individuals, encouraging them to attend the Christmas Party for Parish Leaders.

Every year, on a weekday evening between Christmas and New Year's Day, the pastor turned the entire first floor of the rectory over to this event. The party was the centerpiece of his strategic plan to shape the parish. Members of the current parish council and the staff received invitations, as did their spouses. He also invited the past members of every parish council convened during his tenure as pastor. Spouses rarely attended and turnout by former members was optional, but for current members of the council and for staff he made it clear that the event was a command performance. In all, there were usually forty to fifty in attendance.

Joe examined the rectory as the time approached for the guests to arrive. A large dining room separated by large oak doors from a spacious living room filled the first floor at the rear of the house, together with the huge kitchen and pantry. These rooms to the rear of the rectory were ordinarily private and separated from the public areas to the front by an oversized oak door with large glass oval, etched elegantly with symbols of the Virgin Mary, patroness of the parish. Beyond the oak door, in addition to the first floor study for the pastor, there were private counseling rooms, the tiny bathroom, unused office space and a reception area near the front door.

For years, the Women's Auxiliary had taken on the party as a special project for the pastor, making arrangements for catering, baking and otherwise preparing the desserts and decorating the rectory with help from Luis and his maintenance staff. Elegant boughs of fresh pine decorated every doorframe and, in fact, traced the main lines of the magnificent oak woodwork throughout the house.

Six card tables, sprinkled around the first floor and topped with festive red and green linens, offered guests a choice of red or white wine and a variety of hors d'oeuvres. The ornately carved, built-in oak buffet in the formal dining room was overflowing with cakes, custards and other holiday desserts. A narrow six-foot serving table nearby held sugar cookies cut in Christmas season shapes with red and green sprinkles.

Joe always prepared his Christmas party message with the same care he paid to the refreshments and decorations. Parish leaders were rarely able to guess what he was going to address. Some valued it for the personal, sometimes daring and revealing look it gave them into their pastor. For others it only signaled the beginning of more wrangling and struggle over yet another of Joe's projects that would make St. Mary's the ideal post-Vatican II Catholic parish community.

᨞᨞᨞᨞᨞᨞᨞᨞᨞᨞᨞᨞᨞᨞᨞᨞

"Hello, everyone. I hope you're all having a good time," Joe Burns said as he sidled into the crowded kitchen. "Charles Constable! It's nice to see you here," the pastor said to his longtime friend who resembled him in stature. Ten years earlier Charles had completed two terms on the parish council, the last two years as chairman. Joe pulled a small tray of fresh vegetables and dill dip from the refrigerator and passed it quickly through the kitchen. He pretended to not see Jim there, for the sake of the party avoiding the nasty issue between them, and smiled at Charles a second time without saying a word and then disappeared into the hallway, tray above his head, waiter-like.

As he twisted his way down the central hallway and back, offering the tray, encouraging guests to enjoy what had been prepared, he bumped into Ted Kroenig. Pulling him into one of the counseling rooms just off the hallway, he asked about the meeting that Jim had held at his home just before Christmas.

"They're crazy, Father," Ted said quietly, checking to be sure they were not within hearing range of anyone. "It'll come to nothing, as usual. I wouldn't worry about it."

"I appreciate your support," the pastor said, reaching to pat Ted on the shoulder, then to shake his hand. "You're a fair and decent man, Ted."

Returning to the kitchen for another tray of hors d'oeuvres, Joe crossed into the living room and approached Bob Talbot. Aiming for a light-hearted air, he offered more of the prepared dip to go with the tiny carrots Bob had on his plate. "The calories don't count when the dip's on veggies, after all," Joe quipped.

At Bob's chuckle, the pastor checked first to each side, then behind himself and finally asked, "I was surprised about the meeting at Jim's house. Do we need to talk about this?"

"I know you must be concerned, Joe. And yes, we should talk about it. I'm leaving for Jamaica with Jeannie first thing in the morning, however, so do you think it could wait until we get back? Let me just say to you—there have been situations like this before at St. Mary's and undoubtedly there will be more. Never fear. We'll get through this as we have the ones in the past."

"That'll be fine," Joe said. He offered Bob the tray again, exchanged some pleasantries, and then excused himself, stepping quickly into the bathroom off the hallway to freshen up.

He splashed handfuls of water on his face, dried it, and studied himself in the mirror, gripping the edge of the basin. *I did it,* he decided. *And well.* Disappointed one day, in a stew the next, it had been all he could handle to not confront Bob and Ted earlier. He'd postponed it deliberately—wisely, he concluded—to catch them at a time when the matter could be brought up with some class, not bitterly. Everything was under control. He returned to his guests.

At 7:00 the pastor took his place at the head of the dining room table, his back to the classic built-in buffet and called the festivities to order. Guests seated themselves at the table on the high back, formal dining room chairs, squeezed four at a time into the large sofas in the adjoining living room, or found folding chairs. Others stood or leaned against a wall. Several knelt or sat at a spot on the floor from where they could see the pastor. Some listened from the kitchen just across the hall from the dining room. Ted Kroenig and Charles Constable each took a station, hands behind their back, in front of one of the open oak doors to the living room. Jim Jensen was standing next to Dave Hanratty at the far end of the living room. He smiled and tapped Dave on the elbow. "Guards," he whispered. Dave smiled, forgoing further comment as the pastor began to speak.

"This is number nineteen, folks. Imagine that! The nineteenth Christmas party for our parish leaders. How many of you can remember that first one, just six months after I was named your pastor? Or even remember *anything* about your parish back then, after all these years?" He chuckled and looked for hands. A few were raised. Leaning forward slightly, Joe braced his hands on the table, balancing himself. He surveyed the leaders of his flock, looking down the table, stretching his neck to include those outside the room, around the corner in the hallway and in the living room, trying for eye contact with as many as possible.

Straightening up, he lifted his hands and held them in front of his stomach, palms upward. He studied them. He was sure of it—they'd been caring hands, over the years.

"I've been thinking about our years together," he began. "I'd like to review them with you in some detail on this occasion, Christmas of 1989, the last of the decade. It will take some time, so I ask your indulgence and patience."

He spoke deliberately, trying to give perspective and include humor where he could as he recalled numerous events and many stories after nearly twenty years at St. Mary's. There had been good times, marked by gratitude and celebration—and bad times, too, he confessed, made difficult by discord and conflict. At times, polite laughter and nervous chuckles had circled through both rooms and the hallway. At one point there was uncommon shuffling everywhere and someone bumped a floor ashtray in the living room, tipping it over.

He finally looked at his watch. He'd been talking for forty minutes, he saw. His face had soured, he feared, as he recounted some of the struggles and losses connected with Vatican II. His jaw worked furiously as he pushed back the thought of that godawful council meeting. He compelled himself to not look Jim's way. He dug deep, fearful of losing control, losing face. Could he lose the evening and the party as well? He pressed on, forcing a grin.

"Be that as it may, we're going to celebrate it all. You'll remember that at Thanksgiving I promised you a committee to begin the planning for a seventy-fifth anniversary of the founding of this grand parish. Our diamond jubilee! Imagine that! And for me, twenty years as your pastor."

It wasn't working. He felt a darkness inside him, sure now it was also on his face. Something told him to quit. Duty was calling, however, his duty to share his best thinking with his flock. He'd be doing it for Jesus; he forged ahead.

"Every priest is called by God to be the principal teacher for his parish. Used to be a priest preached a sermon on Sunday at Mass, visited the parish grade school once a week to check up on catechism answers, and sometimes organized mid-week discussion groups for adults."

He asked someone, anyone, to bring him a glass of water.

He felt himself sweating and slightly dizzy as he looked over his leaders. *Were* they leaders? Did they have what it took in the Church today? He swayed or thought he did. Had he? *Careful now. Keep going.*

"Well, I've rambled on a bit this evening, haven't I? But I just want you to know, as I recall nineteen Christmas parties with you, that we've come a long way. I just want to remind you on this occasion that to be a teacher is one of a pastor's main responsibilities. Jesus, of course, was the true teacher, but he commissioned his apostles and his priests to teach the people in his place."

The glass of water arrived. He grabbed it and drank half, sipped again and placed it on the table, away from where he might bump it. He proceeded.

"And we take that very seriously." He reached for the back of his neck to massage it, pressing with his knuckles, kneading the tightness there, rolling his head, trying to loosen up, to free himself from this loss of control, this pit in which he now found himself.

Even so, he upped the intensity another notch, trying to convey exactly how important the ministry of faith formation was, how well they'd done it and his part in it as pastor. "The pastor is ultimately respon-sible for the faith of his people. He is the final authority in his parish, under the bishop, on what gets taught and what practices to foster. As bishops must be in union with the pope in what they teach, so also a parish must be in union with its pastor." His voice hardened. "That includes a *parish council*."

Finally! Joe Burns had tiptoed around the elephant all night and guests had been dreading a Christmas party confrontation. Most had heard about the blow-up at the last council meeting, though opinion varied somewhat about the reasons for it or what should be done. But at last—the words they had been anticipating!

Ted rescued him from the awkward silence that followed. "Here's to you, Father," he said, lifting the empty glass he had been holding, raising it first to Joe and then to those in the room. "It's been rough for you, for all priests. God bless you, Father Joe, for all you have done for us."

The pastor smiled weakly. *You could always count on Ted. Would anybody else help? Tom Andrews there? No—shaky, like jello on a spoon. They're all too timid. Most of them anyway.*

"Well, that's enough for tonight," the priest said, thankful for Ted, ready to bring his remarks to a close. "I've said enough for one night. Just know that we've gotten good results at St. Mary's over the years. But I must remind you that it has always been done and it *must* continue to be done through a combination of the people and the pastor—working *together*. And that means the parish council, too, has to be in union with the pas-tor. We've always done it that way here and that's what will keep us suc-cessful."

He could stop now, Joe decided. He had gotten enough—some—nods, which he took for approval. He tried to grin. "Let's keep the party going. God bless you," he said and stepped away from the table, motioning with his arms for folks to resume talking with each other. People were get-ting up and beginning to move around. Whatever it was that had a hold on him had let go.

Sheila Martinson was on the far side of the living room, chatting with two former members of the council. As Joe approached, they moved away. "Thanks for the party, Father," one said. "'Nite, Father. Always a pleasure," said the other.

"Working the crowd, hey, Sheila?" the pastor asked, searching her eyes for a report on what had turned out be a tiring, long address.

"I make my living by working crowds and listening, Joe," she responded lightly.

"Yes, you do, and you're good at it. Very good." He was sincere. He looked around the room and found himself alone with Sheila. "I'm bushed. That was all pretty serious, hey?"

"Yes, it was. Heavy stuff."

"It *is* serious, Sheila."

"Let's give it a rest for tonight. We meet after Mass tomorrow to prepare the agenda for the January meeting and do some follow-up on the last one—specifically, finding a solution for the ugly situation still between us, Christmas party or no."

Guests leaving and thanking the pastor for another holiday party interrupted them. The pastor left the living room to see his guests out the back door to the parking lot.

Jim entered the room, taking the pastor's place. "So! Tomorrow morning," he said, reaching for the last triangle of sliced Swiss on a plate balanced on the arm of one of the sofas.

"Yes, tomorrow," Sheila said. "I'm sticking to the central issue, the report he requested and then wouldn't review or even consider. That's where this started and it's still the symbol for what has to change—not only in this parish, but all over—in the Church as a whole."

"Some people don't consider this important. You're right. It's symbolic. Symptomatic."

"It's time to take it on."

"Agreed." Scooping up their coats, they left the rectory by the front door and took the path alongside the rectory that led back to the parking lot.

CHAPTER 28

Thursday, December 28

8:30 a.m.

Sheila Martinson sat in her car, waiting for Joe to emerge from the sacristy after the 8:00 Mass. When he did so ten minutes later, she met him half way to the rectory and walked behind him as he made his way carefully over the light snow that had fallen overnight. He escorted her through the back porch and suggested they sit at the table in the kitchen. "Sorry I am late," he said, explaining that he had to hear a lady's confession after Mass. "You've got to take those when they come, you know?"

"Sure, Father. No problem. I like your kitchen."

"No kidding! I can't believe you haven't seen it before. I guess we've always met in my study down the hall or over in the school. Yes, I love to sit here for the peace and quiet I find in the morning. It's easy to pray here, especially when the sun comes streaming in like this. He pulled coffee from the cabinet above the counter. "Decaf, right?"

"That's what I prefer, yes, but whatever you have will be fine."

The pastor started the coffee maker and sat opposite Sheila, squinting as he looked out the window. He adjusted the blinds slightly and began without ceremony.

"We're in a bad spot, Sheila. Before you ask, I have to agree with you—at the January meeting we have to at least acknowledge the report that has become such an issue with our former chairman. That's about it, however. I'd like you to let me handle the meeting after that."

"Father Joe, it's no longer as simple as just accepting the report on salary administration and then perhaps apologizing to the parish council." She saw his jaw muscles jump. "There's the report that should be accepted, yes, but the whole matter has flared into a significant conflict over the way things get done in the parish. It doesn't help that the problem is wider than what's happening at St. Mary's, in the opinion of many anyway. Some people see what's occurring here as an example of a fundamental issue in the Catholic Church, an issue over the relationship between clergy and laity."

Joe eyed the brewing coffee, then directed his gaze to Sheila. It was time to take control of things.

"As I said, I'll be glad to accept the report. I'll even apologize." His tone grew firmer. "But, as I suggested at the last meeting, there are developments in the Church at large that are scaring me and many other priests as well. There are some things we simply cannot let happen." He leaned forward, an earnest expression on his face. "It's about what we call the Deposit of Faith, Sheila. God has given his Church certain things that are right and eternal. A lot of the deposit is under attack today. Priests and parish leaders have to be ever careful and vigilant to preserve the deposit. That's why I am so concerned about this insurgency at St. Mary's."

"As I understand it, Joe, this deposit consists of all of the truths entrusted by Christ to the Apostles. What part of the deposit is involved in this report from the parish council?" Sheila asked, believing that the pastor could not possibly maintain that it was any threat to those truths.

"No, no, it's about power, raw power, Sheila. Some people in the Church want it desperately and can't have it. That makes them loony."

"If you're thinking of Jim Jensen when you say that, I have to say I think you're wrong about Jim. That's just a personal observation, for whatever it's worth. I agree with you, however, that power and control are issues here."

"It's also about genuine concern for the Church, Sheila. Jesus gave it to us and it's a full-time job. You can't have laypeople taking care of the

Deposit of Faith. Nothing against you; I don't lack confidence in you personally. It's just not a part-time job." He peeked at the coffee pot; it had finished brewing.

Sheila waited for the pastor's eyes to track back to her. "You've been preaching for years, Father Joe, about the significance of baptism. You've always said God gives people the gifts that will benefit the Church. Why get in the way of that now? You've got a good thing going."

"There's a time for everything," the pastor rebutted. "Yes, a lot of things in the Church have to be changed, but there are forces in the world today that are going to ruin the Church."

"I consider all that movement to be God's *spirit* in the world," Sheila replied. "The Holy Spirit, if you will."

"That's the dilemma. Imagine how confused ordinary people are. What's from God and what isn't?"

"I'd say, Joe, that most people *like* what they have been seeing in the Catholic Church for the last twenty-five years."

"I'll say it again, this is not a Church of volunteers. You can't run it in your spare time."

"What about just not *running* it? Why does it have to be *run?* You've said all along that it's about community, about personal ownership of the message and commitment to it. And stewardship of our gifts."

"The gift beyond every other gift is the Deposit of Faith."

Sheila shook her head. "I hear the way you're talking this morning and I can't believe it's the same person who speaks on other occasions."

"No, I'm the same, Sheila. I don't change." He rose. "It's ready." He brought the cups to the table, then sugar and whole milk from the refrigerator. While they doctored their coffee, he switched topics.

"I must say, I was very disappointed to hear about the meeting that Jim held at his home a couple of weeks ago. I want you to know that I consider it a mistake for you to have participated in it. That kind of meeting will never get a parish anyplace."

Sheila sipped her coffee, studying the pastor. "That meeting should tell you how serious things are. I was present with good reason."

The pastor waved away her reply. "I don't want to make an issue of this or even talk about it. It's in the past. The council will come around; they always do."

Sheila's face grew serious. She looked at the pastor and waited for him to set his cup down. "Joe, I'd like to say something to you; I would like you simply to listen until I have finished. Okay?"

She waited until it was clear that the pastor was prepared to sit back and listen. "Okay, shoot," he said.

"Thank you." She looked at the man, measuring him. "This is not the first time we've had severe conflict at St. Mary's, Joe."

"It's not that severe," he shot back impulsively. "It comes and goes. We take it as it comes."

Sheila held her hand up, a cop in traffic. "You were going to listen."

"You can't completely control conflict. Jesus had it with the Jews. Paul and Peter fought like hell about some things."

"It's important that you listen, Joe. This won't take long."

"Fine," the pastor said, sliding back in his chair, but impatient now. "Go for it."

"No matter how severe you think the conflict is this time or how frequently it has occurred in the past, the fact is, Joe, that many people in the parish believe there has been a clear *pattern* of conflict, often severe, for many years. I have to tell you, I share that conviction." She leaned back, studying his face. "What about changing the dance?"

"Dance?"

"Yes. What about a new dance step? A different starting point, a different strategy, if you will. What if, instead of beginning with the Deposit of Faith, we began with what people want from their parish church?"

"This is your benefits speech. Save it. I've heard it before. People don't come to church for benefits. They come to be saved."

"You may be surprised, Joe." The pastor moved to get up. She put a hand out, signaling that she wasn't finished. He sat back. "Let's start there. I call it a 'benefit.' Whatever you call it, if you begin the way I am suggesting—with a different, open mindset—there will be an enormous difference in how people receive your message."

"This is not *my* message. It's God's revealed message. That's what I mean by the Deposit of Faith." He tapped the tabletop lightly with his finger. "There's a word that might help here. This stuff is *revealed*, Sheila. You can't change it. Do any dance you want to."

"There must be other places to begin. God is not bound by this deposit, is he?"

"Of course he is," the pastor asserted, surprised that Sheila would even ask. "It would take us too far afield to explain right now, but trust me on this. Human beings, churchmen, did not create the deposit. It comes from God. That's what the Church is for; it keeps the deposit safe."

They were stuck and Sheila knew it. The man was a giant earth-mover when he wanted to be—defining and shaping a landscape, using power and tools that only he had at his disposal. "Let's move on then. Maybe we can talk about the deposit idea another day."

"I'd like that," Joe responded. "You're an intelligent woman, easy to talk to—and not bitter about priests, like some in the Church. You bring something to the parish that I've found in very few other women over the years. I appreciate, too, that you seem to recognize the bad spot I'm in at the moment, yet I don't sense the same pressure from you that I get from others."

"Let's talk about the agenda for our meeting in January," she replied.

"I'm going to ask you to not worry about the agenda this time," he answered. "Let me take care of it."

"You must know I cannot do that, Father Joe. Not *worry*, that is. The council—and I would include many members in the parish who have heard about this conflict and are following it—the council, I say, is extremely tense about this whole matter. I'm sure you noticed there was something different about things at the last meeting."

"That's just one person, maybe two. The others will be fine."

"That's not true. The teaching and the learning in the last twenty-five years has made a difference in what people believe and how they live their faith. There's a determination this time to hold the line with you on this issue."

Joe Burns began to review his position for her again. She cut him off.

"Excuse me, Joe, but that's not what we need to pay attention to here. What I am saying to you is that the parish council is extremely anxious— I'd say desperate—to resolve this standoff. I've never seen it this ugly around here. You need to negotiate very carefully. It is not going to go away."

"I have to compliment you on your tenacity, Sheila, and on your firm beliefs and principles. I appreciate all that. My life is all about principle." He toughened his tone and repeated his assertion. "You need to trust me on the agenda for January."

"The members of the council are trusting *me* on this matter, Joe. For years you have set the agenda with the vice-chair in advance of council meetings. This is not the time to change that practice."

"Sheila, I know there's been some tension over this report, but let me make it clear again that, number one, most people in the parish don't give a hoot about it and, number two, a parish council must be in union with its pastor. There's no room in the Roman Catholic Church," he continued, "for loose cannons or for cowboy-like, gun-slinging parish councils. Let me take care of the agenda for January, will you? Please?"

"Is it that you want *no* agenda or that you want your *own* agenda?"

"I don't want a commitment to any agenda, not at this point anyway. Frankly, I'm not sure just exactly how I want to handle this yet. I wanted to keep our appointment for this morning, though, so that we could talk." Unwilling to meet her eyes at the moment, he picked up the coffee pot and offered her another cup. She held up a hand to say she'd had plenty and glanced out the window.

"Pretty," she said, dryly, uninterested. She took a deep breath.

"I really appreciate your view on things," the priest interjected, pouring a half-cup for himself. "Though it may not seem that way sometimes. I like the way you say things, even though on occasion I may not agree with you. I'm sorry. I just can't subscribe to a marketing approach for a parish church; the whole notion really burns me." He made a concerted effort to unclench his jaws and form a smile.

When Sheila finally looked at him, he leaned forward, arms folded, elbows on the table.

"Three things, Sheila. The first you already know, but I want to be clear about it again—there'll be no special meeting with the parish council. That's not going to happen. Secondly, the normal night for parish council meetings falls on the second of January. That's too soon after the holidays for most of the council; Bob Talbot, for instance, won't be back from his trip to Jamaica. I'll be away myself on a private retreat—a bit of a break—for most of the following week. So we'll have to postpone the meeting. It'll be on the sixteenth, the third Tuesday of the month this time. Please be sure the council knows about the change in date. And, finally, I will bring the agenda for the meeting."

She opened her mouth to speak. "Oh, and I may have already told you this, Sheila, but I'll say it again. The archbishop has assured me that I have his support in the face of any mutiny that people like Jim Jensen and Megan Roberts might try to cook up. Be sure the council knows that, too."

Sheila looked at him wearily. "These aren't wise decisions, Joe. None of these are an appropriate way to treat a committed, responsible parish council." She pushed back from the kitchen table. "I'll call Jim and let him know your plans."

"Not that it matters. He'd stand in the way, no matter what was planned by those in charge."

"I don't think you're hearing Jim correctly."

"I'll get your coat. Leave the cups and stuff. I'll clean up."

After Joe helped her slip into her coat, Sheila examined several books stacked on a small table near the back door. "Three on human behavior! You're taking psychology in your spare time, Joe?"

"I used to read a lot on the subject," he replied. "There's so much to learn."

"Yes, there is," she said, marveling again at her pastor's inability to convert laudable instinct into useful action. Adjusting the coat on her shoulders, she walked to her car.

ॐॐॐॐॐॐॐॐॐॐॐॐॐॐॐॐ

There had been a brief recorded message from Jim Jensen when Sheila got to her office midmorning. "Results?"

They played phone tag until late in the afternoon. "It's not what we agreed on," Sheila said when Jim finally reached her at her desk. "No special meeting and no agenda for January."

"So... no meeting."

"A meeting, yes. No agenda."

"No agenda or Joe's own agenda?"

"I asked him the same question. It will be his own, of course. One more thing. It'll be on the third Tuesday, the sixteenth."

"And why's that?"

Sheila explained. "I gave it my best shot, Jim, but there was no place to go with any of it. I'm not sure there are any solutions for this parish."

"With this pastor."

"Right. He's convinced, I think, that I will agree to chair the council next year. That's what he's holding out for."

"That's crap. Things are going to come to a head long before that."

"Right. He has to finish this year first—and you're chairman until June. That means finding an acceptable solution to this mess. If he can't accomplish that, well, then he can have the job next year—and the parish, too. I won't be party to any more of this."

CHAPTER 29

Thursday, January 4, 1990

9:00 a.m.

Archbishop Walter Meuncher appeared from behind an oversized mahogany door almost before Jim Jensen was able to take a seat in the reception area.

The archbishop was wearing a finely tailored black clerical suit with a soft v-neck charcoal sweater. Almost seventy, with a head of full, silver hair and a slight bulge that betrayed his fondness for a good rib eye steak, he was the picture of a man at peace with himself and his forty-two years of priesthood.

"Good morning, Jim. It's good to meet you," the archbishop said, bringing Jim in close with his handshake, so near that Jim could feel the back of his hand pressing against the archbishop's stomach.

Jim found himself taken in by the archbishop's warm, apparently genuine welcome. "I'm extremely happy that you called and that we're able to meet today. Happy New Year, by the way."

"Thank you, archbishop," Jim replied. "I appreciate your making time for me. And for the people of St. Mary's, really, which is why I'm here," he added, eyeing the archbishop further to gauge his genuine pleasure at the visit and his company.

The archbishop led him past the hospitality area and down a long, red-carpeted hallway to the large room that served as his office, part of a three-story brick mansion on Summit Avenue built in the 1880s by a logging and fur-trapping baron.

"Come on in," the archbishop said as they entered. "We've got a little more time than the twenty or thirty minutes we originally scheduled. My nine-thirty appointment got cancelled. Here, have a seat." He showed Jim to a corner that contained four comfortably upholstered chairs, clustered around a glass-top coffee table.

"We've got plenty of time then. That's great," Jim said as he settled into one of the chairs.

The archbishop offered coffee. "Or tea, perhaps?"

"Coffee will be fine. Thanks."

"I'll get it," the archbishop said, leaving the room.

While he was gone, Jim admired the space, paneled in well-cared-for mahogany. There was another, smaller area set apart in one corner with bookcases on both walls, a leather recliner and a small television set on a moveable cart nearby. The archbishop's reading and study area, Jim figured. On the opposite end of the room was a tabletop display of some kind. He got up and, moving closer, discovered that it was the model for a proposed regional Catholic school. Hands in his pockets, he studied it briefly and then returned to his chair.

He was reaching to examine a book on the table in front of him when the archbishop returned, carrying a tray with a pot of coffee, two Minnesota Twins coffee mugs and the packets necessary for doctoring the coffee. He poured a cup for Jim and then one for himself, then closed the door so they wouldn't be interrupted. He sat in the chair at Jim's right.

"So, Jim, I understand you used to be a priest," the archbishop began.

"Yes, sir, I was. Ordained in 1967 for the diocese of St. Cloud. I left the priesthood five years later. It was a good decision."

"So. It worked for you. I'm glad. I enjoy talking with former priests. Do you mind if I pick your brain a little?"

"Go ahead."

"We're struggling mightily with this whole issue, as you well know—

celibacy, the shortage of priests, and so on." The archbishop paused. "Some studies say things are getting better—more men entering the seminary, but I don't know. It depends on how you read the numbers, I suppose."

He studied Jim for a moment. "I don't know whether you follow this much or even care about it, but some bishops are starting to lose some sleep over this. The very first hurdle has little to do with celibacy or with a shortage of priests. It has to do with differences of opinion among us bishops and our inability to talk about this, even with each other, even privately. You might not believe that."

"Oh, I do, archbishop. I do."

"The situation is only going to get worse, I'm afraid."

"There must be some bishop, someplace, thinking about using former priests, isn't there?" Jim tested.

"Frankly?" The archbishop stroked his face, deliberating. "You won't quote me, will you?" He grinned. "Yes, honestly, I'd have to say there are some who might consider using former priests like you."

"Would you do so, Archbishop Meuncher?" Jim smiled at the archbishop.

"Would you be *interested*, Jim? Frankly, personally, I would have no objection. The pope says no, however, so that's the way it is. In any case, other issues are now part of the discussion. Celibacy for one thing, but it's moved beyond that, as you know."

"Women!"

"Yes, there are powerful forces looking for women to be ordained."

"How do you feel about that, may I ask?"

"I have to be careful how I say this, but I believe the Church will eventually change both the celibacy and the gender requirement for ordination. And not just because there is a growing shortage of priests. I think we may finally come to admit that we're using half the talent God gave us when we ordain only men, Jim. We can't move ahead of the Church in Rome, however. When the time is right, the Holy Father will make the change in a way that will re-introduce the idea and the practice of having a married clergy. Eventually that will include women. That's my opinion. I think it's coming, but the Church isn't ready for it. The people aren't ready."

He really believes that? He wanted to ask, but waited a moment and instead answered the question the archbishop had posed earlier.

"Would *I* be interested, as a former priest? I don't know, honestly. A lot would depend on how my wife and our four children would look at it. I could be interested, but it would be a family decision. Actually, I haven't given it much thought. According to what I read, it's not going to happen, not any time soon. The pope isn't budging, is he? On anything."

The archbishop sipped his coffee and then smiled broadly. "So, Jim, what's on your mind today?

Jim thought about softening his message in light of the archbishop's warm welcome and his surprising candor about important Church issues. He decided against it. "Well, Archbishop Meuncher, you've probably heard a certain amount about it already. To put it mildly, we have an ineffective—or worse—pastor at St. Mary's. I'm here to ask for a change."

"Father Burns. Go ahead."

Jim considered a number of words that fit the situation—abusive, righteous, controlling, unmitigated brute, among others—but discarded them, for the moment at least.

"Let me speak candidly," he continued. "Joe Burns has done well in some respects. St. Mary's is a fine parish; he deserves some of the credit for that. Much, however, has happened *in spite of* the pastor. In a nutshell, archbishop, Joe is an autocrat in an age of cooperation and collegiality. He gives us a vision of a collegial way to be a parish that is based on Vatican II, and then he breaks faith with that Council, and with us, by honoring neither that vision nor years of his own teaching and preaching."

Jim summarized how the longstanding problem had come to a head at the meeting in November.

"I am prepared to take a stand on this matter," he added. "The council did not send me, nor did anyone else. There is no written complaint, no folder full of signatures. But know that I speak for hundreds of people at St. Mary's who have suffered this pastor for too many years."

"I've heard some of these things about Father Joe before—*occasionally.*" The archbishop stressed the last word a second time. "I like to take the long view on things, however, because it's God's hand that guides everything and God is often in no hurry. Changes envisioned by the

Vatican Council also came from God and they remain in God's hands." He refilled Jim's coffee cup and added a little to his own.

"It takes time, Jim. Surely God is at work at St. Mary's. The pastor may not be as effective as either of us might want, but somehow God is using Joe Burns. How can anyone say for sure how God should get things done? I think we have to look at results, and they are there. We have a fine Vatican II parish at St. Mary's."

Jim leaned forward, forearms resting on his knees. He looked to his host, hands spread, palms up. "Even though St. Mary's is a fine parish, archbishop, that is not enough. *How* you make it a fine parish is also important. Because if you do it as a brute or as a dictator, then some very important principles of the Vatican Council are being disregarded. And that is not acceptable. People have understood the message."

"Let me ask you, Jim, what would you do? Be the archbishop for a moment. What would you recommend?"

"The pastor at St. Mary's needs personal, professional help of some kind. I believe he is a very sick man and in his current condition he isn't, he *can't*, be effective. Let me be blunt, archbishop. Joe Burns is divisive, arrogant, and self-righteous. He is a frustrated man, a victim self-proclaimed—a clinic, in fact, in dysfunctional behavior and leadership. I'm sorry, but Catholics today have gotten the message. They will not tolerate or financially support this kind of priest any longer."

"As I said, Jim, I have occasionally heard accusations like this before. Even priests, ones whose judgment I trust completely, have told me that Joe himself causes many of his own problems. But think about it, Jim. Who of us doesn't? I know I certainly do. And you probably do, too— at times anyway." The archbishop smiled at Jim, who got the message.

"Of course, archbishop. I assure you, however, that every word I used to describe this man was chosen carefully. Really, they are not my words alone. I've heard them at St. Mary's for the twelve years I've been a member there. As council chairperson, I feel it's my responsibility to offer some leadership in addressing this situation."

"I don't blame you. In fact, I commend you for it."

"Today, Archbishop Meuncher, if a priest isn't a servant, then he isn't a priest. It's a Church of the baptized before it's a Church of ordained priesthood. The bishops at Vatican II signed on the line for that."

"Jim, I must tell you, it feels like you're beginning to lecture me. Please don't do that. Let me say it again. Being in business yourself, I'm sure you'll understand. I have to look at the results. St. Mary's is a fine Vatican II parish. That's the bottom line."

Jim lifted his hand, asking to speak.

The archbishop raised his own hand, keeping him from doing so. "There's more. Please consider this." The archbishop leaned toward Jim, resting heavily on the left arm of his chair. "We've really got to do more to help and support our priests," he said.

Alarmed at the turn the conversation was taking, looking for a chance to gather his thoughts, Jim grabbed for his cup. It was empty, as was the coffee pot when he lifted it.

"Back in a minute," the archbishop said. He picked up the pot and took one of the three exits from his office, saying he'd draw coffee from a large coffee maker in the kitchen.

Where in God's name do we go from here? Jim brooded. *He listened better than most would have,* he decided, *but what was that last thing he said? Support our priests was his response? To the crisis I outlined! What?*

Archbishop Meuncher re-entered the room, filled Jim's cup, and took a half-cup for himself. He twisted in his chair to face his guest better. "As I was saying, we've got to do more to support our priests, Jim. The men have taken a terrific beating in the last twenty-five years. Most of them like what happened at Vatican II, but they're tired and most of all they're tired of the criticism. It's becoming a thankless job. The work goes on and on; they can never do enough. That takes a toll on a man, Jim."

Confessing that he was talking more than he normally liked to on these occasions, he asked for Jim's permission to continue just a bit longer.

"They're called on to be leaders in so many new ways, to do things for which they've had no training. It's a long list, Jim. Review boards, poverty commissions, parish committees unheard of forty years ago, schools closing, large staffs, salary administration, new forms of liturgy, new music. Many priests never learned how to effectively run a meeting, how to delegate work, how to negotiate a solution. As a result, we've got a hatchet man or two out there. Some people get beat up unnecessarily."

Jim blinked into his cup. Where was this going?

Archbishop Meuncher continued. "It takes time to change, Jim.

Overall, the Catholic Church is healthy. The changes since Vatican II have been good, but for heaven's sake we've got to hold the line on some things. I have supported and promoted all of the documents from the Council. I'm considered to be on the liberal side of things and I certainly think I am. I get scared some times, however. It's going *so* fast. You wouldn't believe some of the things being said and going on today. Don't ask me to explain. Just trust me for now; it's shocking. The faithful would never be able to handle it if they knew what some people are proposing."

"You might be surprised at what we're ready for and what we can handle."

"Sure, Jim. It's easy for you. You're educated. You've struggled with some life issues and personal values, and you have grown spiritually through them and have remained faithful. But the average person in church on Sunday is not that strong or so well educated. We've got to be careful not to lead people too quickly."

"Archbishop Meuncher, I am not suggesting that it has been easy. And while I talk in general about the widespread malaise in our priesthood, the one I really care about today is the current pastor at St. Mary's. That's the only one I can do anything about."

"I don't know how to help you with that, Jim. Obviously I cannot force Joe to be a different kind of person. He is who he is. Joe responds very differently when he is appreciated and honored, instead of being criticized. I've seen it."

"I can tell you this," the archbishop continued. "I will *not* entertain any idea of moving him to another parish. And just as well. There's no way I could promise you a successor who would make everyone at St. Mary's happy. The people at St. Mary's—and you, too, Jim—truly should be thankful. At *least* that. You *have* a priest. Some parishes don't and, sadly, that's going to get worse."

"I admire your compassion toward priests, archbishop. Me, however? I think of the people. Who has compassion for the *people*?"

"What more can I give you, Jim? Tell me."

"What I want is a change at St. Mary's. It's time. At the very least, conduct an investigation, call it an audit, if you will, of parish life at St. Mary's over the last twenty years."

"Out of the question. I never bow to that kind of pressure."

"You could. Priests like Joe Burns have to be recalled and retrained. They no longer fit today's needs or today's Church."

"I assure you, Jim, that I care for all the people at St. Mary's. My love goes out to them. But there's nothing more I can do at the moment."

"I appreciate the time you've given me, sir. However, to dismiss our issues by saying how difficult life has been for priests for twenty-five years...Well, we have to do better than that, Archbishop Meuncher. *You* have to do better. The solutions are not going to be easy or readily at hand. It will take imagination and daring, both of which at this time are more important than the waiting and the patience that you propose."

The archbishop stood. Jim followed suit a moment later. "I'm sorry that our meeting did not work out as you hoped, Jim. Best of luck, in any case." They shook hands. The archbishop helped Jim on with his coat and then saw him to the Chancery's front door.

෩෩෩෩෩෩෩෩෩෩෩෩෩෩෩෩

Instead of going directly to work, Jim walked across the street to the St. Paul Cathedral. There were perhaps a dozen people inside, praying at various places in the cavernous space, which was unlit except for cloudy winter gray filtered by stained glass. At a Marian shrine in the distance, a small group was praying the rosary out loud, but it was almost inaudible from where Jim took a seat.

Looking to the altar, Jim bowed his head, reflecting on the archbishop's years as a priest, nearly half of them as a bishop. *No major position within the National Conference of Catholic Bishops, never an important, highly visible committee chairmanship, no offices; yet considered an effective bishop—always doing what needed to be done, using every means available, from a warm handshake to his considerable skills at listening. Called a glad-hander by some, a great negotiator by others, a successful churchman by almost everyone.*

But he's gutless. Jim folded his arms tightly across his chest. *And too ready to excuse himself from decisive action. A bishop has to be more than a pastor to his priests, a supporter of the producers within a system he wants to maintain. A leader doesn't stand back and let others take the risks. It takes time, he says. It's been nearly twenty-five years, archbishop! People are not going to wait forever. While you wait for change, the institution you are praying for is going to collapse.*

☙☙☙☙☙☙☙☙☙☙☙☙☙☙☙

Back in his office, Jim phoned Sheila.

"How did it go?"

"The man takes you right in."

"Smooth."

"As silk."

"I've heard."

"You think you got anywhere with him?"

"I can't say that. I ended up having almost an hour with him, so it felt like I was able to make the case. The extra time gave both of us the opportunity to listen pretty well, too." He scoffed. "He talked about the hard time priests have had and how long it takes to make changes in the Church."

"And you said?"

"I talked about the need for imagination and for taking risks. I told him that nothing short of a change of pastor at St. Mary's would be acceptable."

"And?"

"That's it. I offered no options and he wouldn't or couldn't come up with any. Said he won't bow to pressure."

"As I've said before, I'm going to deal with this only up to a point."

"I know." He sighed. "The sixteenth of January, then. And no agenda."

"Just the one Joe's bringing."

"That's what scares me."

"Hard to imagine that—you scared. Naw!"

"Believe it."

"We'll handle it when it happens."

☙☙☙☙☙☙☙☙☙☙☙☙☙☙☙

When Joe returned to the rectory from an afternoon with his support group, there was a message for him from Archbishop Meuncher.

"I visited with Jim Jensen today. You are and you will remain, as I told you, the pastor at St. Mary's in Mapleton. No need to call."

CHAPTER 30

Sunday, January 7

4:30 p.m.

Joe arrived at the Roadside Steakhouse half an hour early for his dinner date with Audrey Welch, postponed a week for the holidays. He took their usual table and asked the waiter to hold off on cocktails and menus until his guest arrived.

The window at the table looked west onto the country road that fronted the steakhouse. It framed a view of a barn in need of paint and its companion silo. Scattered clouds in subtle colors floated above and beyond the scene. He entered it, staring, stroking his face for a time, then fingering one hand with the other, softly. This might be why he'd come early, he thought. Before very long, the sun would slide slowly to a point behind the barn, then to the trees nearby and beyond, where he'd lose it, and it him.

At the moment, though, he felt the light that remained shining into his darkness, helping heal him. It had opened his hands on the table, he saw. He left them there, spread slightly, open to both suns, the one at the window, the other inside someplace, seeking him.

He recalled this wonder of creation, this sun, and other times it had offered him a private show, as it were. Stealing across the floor in his study one morning, finding its way finally into the hidden bottom shelf of a bookcase. Coming through a tiny window in the basement to light up a dusty, plastic plant on a small table. On another morning, very early, lighting the underside of geese on wing overhead. And that same evening, the same sun lingering under the eaves of the storage shed in the rectory garden. Peter, his Indian friend, would say something about this, he figured, were he here.

Audrey was a sun of sorts, he thought, shedding light, finding a way into his life. He was *crusading*, she told him, the last time. Without it, she said, he'd be better at what he did. Style shapes the message and is just as important. About that, he wasn't so sure. Not yet, anyway. It had always been good to hear that she found him refreshing, a thing he believed was true. But it was nice to hear it said.

The sight of her car entering the parking lot interrupted his meditation. As she walked to the entrance, she waved to Joe in the window. At the table, they exchanged their usual greeting, hand in hand, a squeeze held the extra moment.

The waiter arrived with menus, took their cocktail order, and left, promising to return quickly.

"So. The first Sunday of the nineteen-nineties," Joe said, smiling. "Ten to the millennium."

"Imagine! I'll be sixty-five."

"I can't begin to. I'll be nearly seventy myself." They both laughed at the idea. He told Audrey he'd been taking in the sunset, sitting, thinking. Audrey admired a final point of light down the road behind the trees. She'd been taken by the sunset, too, she said, as she drove west on the road to Jack's.

"So how are you, Joe, and how was your Christmas? Nice card you sent, thank you. How's it gone with your parish council?"

Their drinks arrived, they ordered their meals, and Joe picked up the ugly story from November, repeating some parts from the beginning, then detailing the tense and bitter, nose-to-nose battles he'd had with Jim Jensen since then, twice insisting that he resign as chairman, and Jim's despicable act of arranging a private meeting of the parish council, in his home, without their pastor.

"Imagine!" Joe exclaimed. "He's had his comeuppance, though. I found out some time ago, the dope scheduled an appointment at the chancery, perhaps thinking he could get the archbishop to replace me as pastor. The fool wasn't aware that the bishop had already assured me that would never happen."

The waiter arrived now with Audrey's filet of salmon and Joe's sirloin. They requested second cocktails. As they began their meals, the pastor resumed the story, offering details about Clarice Morgan and the dilemma she posed for him, combining as she did her outstanding job performance with her brazen bitchiness at staff meetings. He spoke, too, of the high regard he had for Sheila Martinson and how he hoped she would accept his invitation to serve as chair of the council after he got rid of Jim altogether, which would be very soon, he hoped.

"So Jim has not done as you asked. He's still your chairman."

"No, he's not. I will not sit down with the man. I gave him a week to resign after I demanded it a second time and have heard nothing from him, so he's done. I just have to make it stick. I plan to take care of that a week from Tuesday when the council meets."

"Joe, what kind of help do you get from those priests you meet with every month?"

"Yep, my support group. Besides getting together every month, we call on each other whenever it might be helpful. I've talked with Harry Droesch a couple of times about all this."

"How *is* your friend?"

"The one I find most helpful, actually, is Ken Halpin. I'd give my right arm for the peace this man has in his life and for the kind of success he has in his parish."

"You are who you are, Joe. Unhappy comparisons usually aren't very helpful. Tell me, is there a way you can lighten your workload pretty soon? Do you know that when you talk about your work, your eyes often seem about to well up in tears? What is that sorrow about?"

Joe caught the eye of their waiter and reminded him about their request for a second cocktail. He'd forgotten. He hurriedly delivered them, apologizing. Joe held his Manhattan up to Audrey as if to toast her. "And to you, sir," she replied, toasting him and holding it until he smiled in reply.

Turning to lighter fare, Joe told Audrey of his plans to celebrate the diamond jubilee of the parish in June of '91, thereby deflecting and redirecting, or so he hoped anyway, some of the hostility he was feeling in the parish, caused by the parish council, of course, particularly Jim Jensen and Megan Roberts. He'd be appointing a committee to work on it, now that the holidays were over.

"Let the members do it for you, Joe. Your plate is full."

Inexorably, the pastor's mind—and his conversation—turned to the January parish council meeting, a deadline he'd set for himself to resolve what he called "the Jim issue."

"I wouldn't rush it, Joe. Who in the parish can give you the most help this time?"

"I'd say Sheila for sure. Bob Talbot is always helpful, of course, but I want Sheila to replace Jim. She brings a marketing perspective to everything, which makes me a little nervous—you know, business slant and all, as I've told you—but she's a classy lady. She can make a difference for us."

"And how is *she* with that?"

Joe pondered the question. He twisted his glass on the linen tablecloth. Audrey sipped her Whiskey Sour. "Fine, as far as I know," he lied, stuttering on the last word. He backed off. "At least, I'm negotiating that with her. We've talked about it. I can trust her, and I believe she can entrust herself to me for the work we'd do together to make the parish what we want it to be."

Audrey wondered about that. *If Sheila's the person Joe says she is— with her marketing skills and her business sense and all—then how can she be the kind of player Joe wants to work with? Closely. Strong, professional people in churches today want to be consulted, given leadership, and be involved in decisions. Understandable. Is that going to work for Joe? Has it crossed his mind to just give energetic, talented people the room they need— room to give the church the best of what they're good at?*

"Joe, what about letting people take care of more things for you? Just let them go. You could empower parishioners to have full authority in some matters and that would take some of the pressure off you. They have the ability to do that. Priests don't have to be in control of everything in a parish, do they?"

"That'd be nice," he declared. "But you have to be careful when you give people leadership responsibilities and power and authority. That might work in small country parishes, but in large suburban areas there has to be more control. There are standards to meet and the Church knows how to maintain those standards. The Church is one and holy and has a long history. The challenge is to keep it that way."

"People don't wake up in the morning for this stuff, do they, Joe? They don't talk that way, do they?"

Audrey took a last bite of her salmon. Joe pushed aside his plate, a small piece of sirloin still on it. That prompted an appearance by their waiter. "Dessert tonight, folks? I hope you have enjoyed everything so far."

"It's been great," Audrey assured him.

"No dessert," Joe said, after a glance at Audrey, "but we'll have coffee."

"Both black, sir, if I'm not mistaken?" At Joe's nod, their server gathered the dishes and left for the kitchen.

Audrey resumed. "Most people don't care that much about the many things that churchmen consider important. Churchmen have convinced people that salvation comes through their churches. That isn't necessarily wrong, but it can easily become self-serving. Every institution is out to promote itself, understandably. If that doesn't happen, they'd be out of business. And so institutions hold onto everything they can, their control, in particular."

"Two coffees," the waiter announced, setting the cups and saucers in front of them.

"Thank you," Joe said. "We'll need refills, I'm sure. Okay? You'll watch?"

"You bet, sir. I'll keep my eye on it."

Audrey continued, "While the major, mainline Churches have a place in history and God has used them, they make too much of themselves, and those who work for the Churches officially often take it all a bit too seriously. They're not alone. Teachers do it, too. That's human nature. We lose perspective under pressure and then we get ugly. I know you do, too, Joe. That's why it would be great if you could lighten up some. You're so good, so *pleasant* to be with when you're not grinding something out for the Church or when you're not under pressure to be *right* for the Church or to defend it or to get people to do something your way."

"I know you're sincere, Audrey. I appreciate your honesty and that you care enough to bother with all of this. One of the guiding principles of my own life as a priest has been honesty."

The waiter passed and filled their cups again. "We'd appreciate being able to stay awhile to talk," Joe noted. "No problem. Take your time," the waiter replied.

"You're a charming person, Joe, but so often your work has a negative impact on you, on your relationships, and your chances of being successful in what you have given your life to." Audrey sipped her coffee, choosing her words carefully. "I, too, want to see churches be effective, but my sense is that most churchmen—and churchwomen, too—work too many hours and take themselves too seriously. It's important to maintain perspective on it all. If you could do that better, then maybe the Jim Jensens of the world wouldn't unnerve you so."

The pastor reflected for a moment. "*That* I'd have to think about," he said, admitting to himself his irreversible distrust and dislike for Jim Jensen. "I cannot work with this man. In a conflict like this I have to trust the support I have from most—surely the vast majority—of the people in the parish."

"All of this feels like an obsession of sorts, my friend. Your work and your priesthood, they haunt you; they possess you. Jim Jensen, in a way, *owns* you. He has title to you, Joe." She tapped his hand gently and sat back in her chair to observe him. "Human nature does not take well to obsessions. They're always trouble. Obsession takes people past their limits. It disregards boundaries and takes on a life of its own. You get sick from it. Maybe that's what happened to the Churches over the years. Saving people became their obsession, instead of finding out how God is already saving them and then working along with that."

"There are boundaries I cannot cross as a pastor, Audrey. A priest cannot renounce the vocation given him by God and the leadership given to him by his bishop."

"That's the obsession, Joe, right there. I understand, at least partly, what the priesthood means to you and the place you have as a priest in the Catholic Church. But there are certain things you cannot do today, priest or no, and expect to be effective.

Joe sat, reflecting. Was he obsessive? Did Jensen hold title to his life? He drank a half-cup of coffee.

"For twenty years I have tried to work with these people, Audrey. God knows how hard I've tried."

"The key to everything is relationships, Joe. There's nothing standing in your way to building improved relationships. You are a fine, fine person. Relationships are what will make a difference in the Church. It's true in any organization."

"I'll have to give this more thought, Audrey. I'm going to be away for several days, on retreat. It will give me time to think about what you've said."

"That'll be good, Joe."

They sat in silence for several minutes before the waiter brought the check. They split the bill as usual. As they left the restaurant, they peeked into the piano bar. Several diners were dancing to "Lara's Theme" from "Doctor Zhivago."

"Somewhere, my love," Audrey warbled before turning a little more serious. "What about a new dance, Joe? With your parish, perhaps?" In the parking lot, she squeezed him at the elbow and they parted.

CHAPTER 31

Tuesday, January 16

6:45 p.m.

After finishing the hot turkey and gravy sandwich he had prepared for dinner, Joe scooped cat food for Mindy, poured her some water, and turned out the kitchen light. He threw on an overcoat and left by the back door for the parish council meeting. As he walked carefully over the parking lot and schoolyard, lit only by two floodlights high on the school, he prayed for the inner light he'd need over the course of the evening.

At the school, he purposely walked the long hallway in the dark, appreciating the contrast between it and the light he was already beginning to sense inside himself. There'd be no stumbling, not a single misstep. He'd be fine. He snapped on lights for those who would follow.

In the council room he prepared coffee and pulled from the refrigerator four six-packs of soda and two large pound cakes, purchased and placed there earlier that afternoon at his request by Betty Halvorsen. He stepped back, assessing his preparations and the room. Everything appeared to be ready. He began pacing. He'd been doing a lot of it—pacing—since the last council meeting, he realized. So it seemed anyway.

He revisited the decision he'd made. It was the one he *had* to make, he decided again. Every time he'd tested it with the Lord in prayer, the answer had turned out the same. They needed a fresh start. "A priest will not count the cost," he muttered to himself. And he'd never done so. He was at peace.

"Good evening, Father." It was Mrs. Heller, and with her, Mrs. Albrecht. "Hello, Father. More ice by morning," he heard one of them say.

"A typical Minnesota winter, eh, ladies? Good of you to make it despite the weather."

The pastor could count on one hand the council meetings the two women had missed in over fifteen years. When the parish school was closed in 1973, the two had been deeply involved, though on opposing sides. One memorable night they nearly came to blows over it. The controversy cooled after the school closed, but other issues heated up. The two ladies had continued coming to council meetings to stay informed and provide a reliable— they maintained—source of information for others.

"Help yourselves to some cake, ladies." As they did, he paced the room quietly and went over it all in his head again. There would be plenty of support, he assured himself.

He had decided to back down on Jim—sit at the table with him, that is. It wasn't a concession, he reminded himself, but a strategy. A tactic, something he'd come up with while on retreat, nothing more. He'd give in a bit on Jim to keep Sheila. He couldn't risk losing her, couldn't chance it that she would keep her word and leave the parish if he barred Jim from the meeting. He *could* depend on Jim to show up for the meeting, of course. Jim was like that.

He made a turn at the end of the room, musing again on the two ladies there with him now. A smile spread across his face, as he remembered how he thought they'd kill each other that night the council decided to close the school. *And now? The best of friends. Things work out somehow; it's the grace of God, that's what it is.* The ladies told him once they believed that, too.

As members of the council and a dozen other visitors began to arrive, the pastor greeted them warmly, inviting each to take a piece of cake and something to drink. Before long, Bob Talbot stepped up to him and said, in a low tone, "Jim's coming down the hallway."

The pastor turned sharply to watch him as he entered. "Let it go, Joe," Bob urged.

"I have, Bob. I had a good retreat. It's not important any more." He resumed his pacing. The room grew quieter and quieter. Arrivals munched on their cake, refilled their cups, and made small talk about the holidays or wondered out loud about the weather. From the corners of their eyes, they monitored the pastor's effort to disguise his edginess.

Sheila Martinson was the last council member to arrive, right at 7:30. "I see Jim is here," she whispered to the pastor as he came to greet her and shake her hand. "I think that's wise, Joe. Thank you."

"Fine, Sheila, we'll be fine," he replied offhandedly. Then, in a louder voice, "Okay, let's get started here. It's 7:30."

Jim tapped the gavel as soon as Sheila removed her coat and hung it up. Joe took his place at the council table. A few stragglers delayed a moment to take a piece of cake, while others refilled their coffee cups.

"Hold up on that for a minute, will you, folks?" the pastor called out without turning. "We're going to pray now."

People quickly found seats or froze in place. Jim nodded to Rosa to begin. Before she could open her mouth, however, the pastor announced that Tom Andrews would be saying the prayer instead.

"As you know, I like prayers to be spontaneous. I'm sure Rosa would do a wonderful job, as she has in the past. I had Tom in mind for this evening, however."

He watched reaction ripple through the room, Jim snapping his arms into a tight fold over his chest, Megan twisting that ring. From the far end of the table he heard Bob clear his throat. Others looked to Tom, who was as surprised as everyone else but somehow found the words to begin. He prayed for everyone present, asking the grace for each council member to work hard for charity and justice in the world and in the Church, but to leave the results and the timing of those results to God. He looked to the pastor as he finished.

"Good prayer, Tom. Thank you." The pastor heard an "Amen" or two and saw heads nod in agreement.

Hardly allowing everyone present to get settled, Joe looked intently at each member of the council, everyone but Jim, and began. "This has not been an easy meeting to prepare for. It has been quite a burden, as you might imagine."

Jim moved to interrupt. The pastor would have none of it. He extended his right hand, palm up and facing Jim. "Just a minute, Jim. I want to finish."

Jim looked at Sheila. She shrugged skeptically.

"I'm not going to speak for very long on this occasion," the pastor continued. "Because what needs to be said can be said very briefly. I have worked for twenty years to make St. Mary's a successful parish. Sometimes I've gotten the help I needed, sometimes not. But the grace of God has always come through and made available to me good people to help do the work of Christ in this parish. We're a good parish. And, we've done it together. "

Every head at the table was lowered, except for Sheila's. She was staring at the pastor.

"I do not take this council lightly. I believe there is a place for volunteers in the Church. You know as well as I do, however, that matters have gotten out of hand at St. Mary's in the last year or so. I've decided what I have to do about that as pastor. This has not been an easy decision, but I've never refused to take up the cross when it has been necessary."

He sipped from the water he had set on the table and continued.

"The point is, I'm a fighter. There's nothing wrong with that. I refer you to Paul's letter to the Galatians, for example. He and Peter fought like cats and dogs, as the saying goes. They had some furious battles. I like that. Sometimes you have to fight for what you believe in."

Jim stood up. "Sit down, Jim," the pastor commanded. Jim ignored him, walking to the counter to fill his cup. "Anyone?" he asked. There were no takers. He returned to the table.

"Sit down, Jim," the pastor demanded again.

"Go ahead, finish," Jim replied. He sat down. "I won't walk out and I hope you'll show us the same courtesy."

"I'm in charge here, Jim. I'll walk out whenever it's the right thing for a pastor to do, the pastoral thing." He checked faces for agreement. He wasn't satisfied, but continued.

"I want to repeat what I said before: I believe in having lay volunteers for ministry in the Church. I do. There is a limit to everything, however, including how we manage church affairs and, for now, I am disbanding this council."

Jim jerked in his chair, striking an elbow on the table and numbing his arm. Ted Kroenig lifted his shoulders as if to duck inside himself someplace, then slipped away to the counter for coffee. Jittery, irritable silence choked the room, suffocating members and observers alike. Words spun in their heads or gagged them, downshifting everything to slow motion. Bob Talbot, trusted counselor for a lifetime, sunk into his chair, his eyes closed. Dave Hanratty—leader on staff, daring, trained voice for the pastor—saw a blind man walking a short pier.

The priest surveyed the table. *Caught them flat-footed! Not a word, even from the pompous fraud, Jensen —the obstreperous priest without priesthood! Nothing from Miss Roberts either, the bitchy apostate. Both of them, silenced. Good! The way it should be.*

Slowly, the staggering paralysis passed. Jim Jensen straightened in his chair, bristling. "You can't do this."

That turned the room into a hissing cauldron—muttering, whispering, fidgeting, coughing. Pencils tapped here, fingers drummed there; eyes covered, folders closed and, "Aye, Virgen de Guadalupe."

"This is obscene," the chairman declared. "You can't disband this council."

"You're a fool if you think that, Mister Jensen."

"A fool? You'll *see* what fools we are! You'll *see* how fed up we are with this crap. I have spoken with dozens of people—young and old—who have talked with dozens of others since you pulled that stunt with the chapel a year ago. This time we were ready for you. And for whatever your next shenanigan would be. It came in November. And now *this!* We're going to hit you, priest, in your pocketbook. It's been tested. People will support a boycott or something similar. It could even spread to other parishes. It'll be nasty, I assure you. And stop calling me mister, damn it."

"I repeat, Jim. You're a fool."

"No more Sunday envelopes—that's the only thing these guys will understand," Jim asserted, speaking now to his colleagues and the visitors to the meeting. The huge mahogany table moved as he pushed back from it. He rapped the table to punctuate each sentence. "When their world, which we support with our money on Sundays *(rap)*, starts to come apart *(rap)*, it will bring them to their knees *(rap, rap)*. They will listen *(rap)* on their knees *(rap)*. It's the only strategy that will get results."

Bob Talbot grabbed hold of the broad table with both hands to adjust it. "I have to say, Joe, I'm surprised by your decision. This problem won't be solved by what you're proposing."

"I'm not proposing it, Bob. I've decided and, as I said, it's been a hard decision. We simply cannot go on like this. I haven't slept for two months, terrified at what all this means for the Church, for me, and for all of you as well, of course."

Megan Roberts gave a convulsive shudder and leaned into the table, confronting the pastor. "You do not..." she began breathlessly. She paused, struggling desperately for control. She reached across the table, finger pointed stiffly and shaking. "You do not have the authority..."

"I have everything I need on this. And a few things I don't need—like you, Ms. Roberts."

"You need a hundred like me. Now listen."

"I will *not*. There'll be no discussion tonight. I'd like to have a parish council at St. Mary's. I really would. Eventually we will. But we're going to slow this down. This is not your parish. It belongs to the archbishop. And he's entrusted it to my care."

Megan muttered something, muffling it with her hand. Ted thought he heard the words "crazy son of a bitch." He put his hands, palms down, on the table to steady himself.

Joe had heard it, too. "Get out, Megan," he demanded. "You have no place here. None. I have spoken with the archbishop, who is the Vicar of Christ in this diocese. He assures me of his support and that I will be the pastor here for the foreseeable future. That's all there is to it."

He got up from the table. "I'll appoint a small nominating committee in April. That will allow enough time to start over in June, when we normally have elections. I'll be in touch with Sheila about it. She's in line to chair this council. I'm sorry it had to come to this. Good night."

The pastor hurried down the corridor, leaving before anyone who was prepared to argue could do so.

Behind him, the talk turned acrid, loud, and decisive. Even visitors joined the melee. Some of the positions taken and arguments advanced were twenty years old and more.

"He needs some time to think," Ted argued. "He doesn't mean this. Give him some time to reconsider."

"How *much* time?" Jim demanded. "Till he gets a nominating committee together and picks his people, as always? How long, Ted? Till the next blow up? This is the last one. We're going to do something about this. This time we're not backing down."

Noisy cross talk, chairs moving back and forth and people getting up to leave and sitting back down racked the room. Jim banged the gavel for silence. "None of this shouting and arguing is getting us anywhere," he called out. "I propose that the parish council meet at my home again in a week. I'd schedule it immediately, but I have out-of-town business commitments that I simply cannot postpone. And I think we also need to find out where we stand, legally, and consider our options and how far we're willing to go to put an end to things like this."

"To those of you who came to observe the meeting, my apologies. I am sorry both about what happened and that you had to witness it. As many of you know, it's not the first time the parish has had to deal with this kind of behavior. I thought we could make a difference. We've done our best with Joe Burns, and it's come to this."

Most of the evening's visitors already had their coats on. They were halfway out the door, uncomfortable with the tension in the room or eager to confer with one another and convey the news to others in the parish.

"My house, then, a week from tonight," Jim said in a more normal voice. "Same time, seven thirty. Sheila, I'll call tomorrow morning to plan the meeting with you. First, though, let's pray."

Weary from it all, the council members nodded. They left the building and headed for the side door of the church. When they got there, Dave's key wouldn't turn in the cylinder. He tried it again, with similar results. Bob's key, given to him years ago by the pastor for an emergency of some kind, didn't work either.

In the shadows on the back porch of the rectory, Joe watched the council members fumble at the door. *Stumbling and shuffling as usual,* he thought. *Always a step behind.* He'd done the right thing at the meeting, he told himself, and done it well. And he was right to have had Luis change the locks, too. He sank against the wall.

Thoroughly frustrated and disgusted that the pastor had barred them from the church and their customary prayer, the council trudged to the parking lot. There, at a quiet word from Rosa, the members linked gloved hands and bowed their heads. Steam rose from Rosa's lips as she led a short prayer. Moments later, headlights behind the fence flashed narrow slots of brightness around the porch as cars left. The pastor watched to make sure nobody stayed behind.

In his study, the pastor flopped into the recliner and pushed back roughly. The chair squawked and clunked into position. *Always talking, these folks—not everyone, but the talkers get the others going. They need to understand something: You don't learn to do church work overnight; it takes a lifetime.* Mindy leaped onto his lap. *But a good night all in all,* he mused. *A good night for the parish. There were no alternatives.* He drummed his fingers on the arms of the chair.

"They're in the dark, Mindy," he mumbled as he stroked the cat. She purred and settled into his lap. "*Teaching* is the job, cat, next to saying Mass for them and forgiving their sins."

So few of them, when they get bunched, ever want to listen. Too many fixers fixing things these days.

He squeezed the cat, pulled gently at the fur on her neck, and smoothed it again.

CHAPTER 32

Wednesday, January 17

10:30 a.m.

"Sheila! Thank you. I was just going to call," Joe exclaimed when the council vice-chair reached him by phone the next day

"How are you this morning, Joe?"

"Fine, just fine. I'm happy with the way things worked out last night."

Sheila's voice took on an uncharacteristic edge. "Worked out? You unilaterally dissolved the parish council last night. Nothing was worked out!"

"I'm glad it's you calling, Sheila, instead of our former chairman."

"The only reason you're talking to me instead of Jim is that he had to be in Des Moines for afternoon meetings. He'll be out of town till late Friday."

"It's just as well. I cannot work on any project headed by that man or with any group that includes people like Megan Roberts. That's why I had to dissolve the council. Apart from you and Bob, and occasionally Ted, it was a very weak group. Jensen led people poorly—council members and at times other parishioners—and for his own purposes. That won't work, not while I'm the pastor."

"Jim did what he found necessary," Sheila responded, "and I respect him for that. He did it with the best of intentions. Let me make something clear: I will not be party to any 'Get Jim Jensen' movement. Nor will I participate in a 'Get the Pastor' scheme. I want to work this out so that there are winners on both sides."

"I can't imagine you, Sheila, ever being part of a move to get rid of a pastor."

"If that question ever came up, Joe, I would follow my conscience. Most of the time, however, I believe there are ways to improve a difficult situation without steps that drastic. As I always say, winners on both sides."

"All the more reason for a fresh start. People don't want all this trouble. We can start from scratch now. Why not?"

"Because there is a proper way to resolve this—and unilaterally disbanding the parish council is not it. In doing that, you crossed a boundary and assaulted a vision for today's Catholic Church. I will not tolerate that. I'll work with you, but we cannot be successful when we don't follow the rules—rules like the ones you broke last night and back in November and that you have broken around here for years."

"I want you to lead our council next year, Sheila. What can I do to insure that?"

"Listen closely. It is the responsibility and the right of the council itself, by its own by-laws, to name its chair. I will not accept that position from the hands of the pastor. It's another boundary issue. I simply won't do it."

"Then tell me, where are we at on this?"

"Here's where we're at. I will not be party to any maneuvering on your part to name me the chair of the council. Nor am I going to be part of anything that disbands the council or shortens the term of its current chairman."

"You make it hard, Sheila. I want to work with you on this. I'm all for teamwork, but there are some conditions I have to insist on as pastor. If you'll just hang tight, I'll get back to you. I think we can find a way to work this out."

"I want this to work, too, but if you don't propose a workable solution in 48 hours, my letter of resignation will be in the mail. I've already written it. You call me when you've made your decision."

Joe Burns promised to do so.

ᘏᘏᘏᘏᘏᘏᘏᘏᘏᘏᘏᘏᘏᘏᘏᘏᘏ

At noon the same day, the pastor was in his study, planning what he would say from the pulpit on Sunday, when he received a call from Megan Roberts. "Hold for a moment, will you please, Megan?" He set the phone down on his desk and went to the kitchen.

"Yes, I'm here, I'm back," he said, picking up the phone and tucking it between his ear and his shoulder. He opened the refrigerator and pulled out sliced ham and mustard. "What's on your mind?" He pressed on his chest, fighting a surge of heartburn before he reached for rye bread in the drawer under the counter and re-opened the refrigerator for a can of root beer. Snapping it open, he took a long swallow as Megan began to speak.

"It's fair to say we haven't seen eye to eye on a number of things during the years I've been in the parish, Joe. I didn't address many of them because I really had no forum to do so and sometimes no time or sufficient interest. That changed when I was elected to the parish council. That threw us together. I now find myself with both the opportunity and the obligation to contribute to the discussion about this parish."

"Megan, I appreciate your interest and your concern, but right now there is not an awful lot to talk about. There is no parish council at St. Mary's."

He piled ham onto the rye bread and covered it with mustard. He turned to the refrigerator for dill pickles, pulled a plate from the cupboard, and sat at the table.

"I haven't been terribly involved with the Church since I was active in the Newman Center at the U," Megan persisted, trying to maintain a reasonable tone. "But I've enjoyed working with Clarice on the religious formation program. I think she does a great job."

"Yes, she does."

"Anyway, bottom line, this parish council thing is kind of new to me. I don't know the rules. Could you explain this to me then? How is it possible to simply disband a parish council the way you did last night? I don't get it."

The pastor bit into the sandwich, leaving mustard at the corners of his mouth. He reached for a paper towel from the roll on the table and removed it, then took a swig of root beer. "It's simple," he said through a mouth full of sandwich. "Really, it is, Megan. It's what I had to do. The council in every parish is only advisory. It works at the pleasure of the pastor. This council was no longer effective and so we needed to start over." He chewed noisily.

Megan shuddered with disgust, but proceeded. "It always—*often* anyway—feels to me like you are manipulating people, Joe. I can't understand why you think you can do that, at council meetings, or any place else."

"This church does not have a parish council now, Megan. We'll probably have elections again in May. June at the latest. You heard me say that last night. Want to run?" Joe laughed audibly into the next bite of sandwich.

"Joe, I called you with a reasonable concern. I think I'm entitled to a respectful hearing. And a courteous one. May I ask that you wait to eat your lunch until we have finished this conversation?"

"Can't, Megan. Sorry. I've got to be at a nursing home by one o'clock to visit residents there and the sick, and I've got an errand to take care of on the way." Joe dabbed his lips with the paper towel. "But go ahead. I'm listening." He took a quiet sip of root beer.

"I expected something better from you. This Catholic Church of ours, I mean the *whole* Church, not just St. Mary's, is in a heap of trouble. People just don't *believe* the Church any longer. They're not going to continue supporting it. The biggest problem is our priests and the things you men do. You cannot simply keep perpetrating things like last night's fiasco."

The pastor knocked over the soda can, righted it, and reached for paper towels to mop up the spilled root beer. "Listen here, Miss Megan. You have some damn business talking about priests and what we do. You're a sour lady. I don't know where it comes from, and I don't want to. I just see it and hear it..."

"Yes, Joe, I'm angry."

"I said sour, Megan. Bitter. I don't want people around contaminating the parish council with that kind of attitude. Both of you two do so—you and Jensen. That can ruin any barrel of apples, however good, and I believe it has. You've poisoned the council. You and the illustrious chairman. You think you fit on a church council like this, Megan?"

Joe finished wiping up the spill and tossed the wet, caramel-colored towels into the sink. "You've got a small dental office. Big deal. It's easy for you to get along there. This is bigger. It takes more work, and it's a different, more *demanding*, kind of work."

"I *do* fit. You don't, however. You're a dinosaur, a priest from the past," she sputtered. "I don't know exactly how we'll do it, but by God we are not going to sit still for your kind any longer. Don't tell me about my office and my business. You have no idea what it entails. And don't talk to me about contaminating the council. You have infected and debased hundreds and hundreds of people here over the years. We are a contaminated community, laced throughout, in every neighborhood, with people who detest you, Joe."

"This isn't a popularity contest, my dear. I'm okay with myself and with my priesthood. No one is perfect. I've built a good parish here. I get compliments all the time. You're the one out of touch.

"Look, I've got to finish my lunch, Megan." He lifted his sandwich and bit into it, speaking off-handedly as he chewed. "What's your problem anyhow? You'll probably end up on the council when we start it up again. It's not like I'm asking you to resign."

"What did you say? You're not asking me to *resign*?"

"That's what I said; I'm not."

"Why does that even come to mind? You have no right to..."

"I'm *not* asking that. That's what I said. A simple declarative sentence. Why is that so hard for you to understand?" He swallowed more root beer. "And what do you mean—no *right*?"

"You have no right to force a resignation from the parish council."

"Well, that's a different issue. As pastor I certainly have the *right* to do that if I want to. I'm not exercising the right, however."

"You do not *have* the right. You have no right to coerce anyone elected by the people of this parish to resign."

"I can't get into it now. But I assure you, Megan, that I can ask for, and *get*, your resignation if I think it necessary for the good of the parish."

"You could ask forever. If I did not want to resign, I'd never do so."

"If I needed your resignation, I'd have to get it."

"You'd have to *get* it? Why? How? You don't have the power to do that."

"No power, you say? I am the pastor, Megan. There's only one in every parish. I assure you, if I wanted your resignation, I would get it."

"How? By disbanding another council? We'd just meet without you."

"But it's not a parish council then. It's just parishioners. It has no power without the priest. Sheep without a shepherd are just sheep. They're not a flock."

"Joe, somehow you don't buy your own theology," Megan snapped. "I'm no theologian, but I'm not stupid either. I've heard you talk about the Church as the People of God. I've heard you talk about empowering people. I've heard you say that Baptism makes us all holy and that each of us has gifts from God to be used for the good of others. I've heard all that—from *you*, Joe. And I believe it."

The pastor stood up. Grabbing the can of root beer, he placed it on top of the remaining half of the sandwich. Hand flat on its top, he leaned forward on it with his full weight, pressing and twisting the aluminum can into the sandwich until mustard squirted out the sides.

"Don't quote theology at me, Megan." He began stuffing the dill pickle into the mouth of the root beer can. Pickle juice squirted half way up his arm. "Yes, I've taught you well, and many others, too." He pushed on the pickle again, twisting it, forcing it farther into the opening. "I'm teaching you now that there's a limit. There's a right side to be on and a wrong side. Certainly you know what side you're on when you talk like that." He lifted the pickle and, with it, the can. He slammed it down and twisted the dill again.

"I'm not quoting anything *at* you, Joe. I'm repeating what you've told us you believe. It appears that you *don't*, at least not when it puts you in a tight spot."

"I'm always in a tight spot; all priests are today. It's not what we bargained for. You think I wanted this kind of life, this conflict? I just wanted to be a good priest and show people the way to God. They used to call us Alter Christus, Megan. Do you know what that means? It means Another Christ. That's what we are. Other Christs, trying to show people the way."

"You're lost, Joe. Somehow you got lost. I won't buy this kind of priesthood any longer. I saw it when I got divorced. I see it here. I won't take it any longer."

"I don't know what you can do about it. It's divinely instituted, set up that way by Jesus and the apostles. You know what that means, Megan?"

He heard a muffled conversation at the other end of the line, something about a waiting patient, and then Megan's voice again.

"I have to go, Joe, and you have to get to the nursing home. I'll get back to you on this."

"For God's sake, woman, try to relax. There's no need for hysteria.

As I said, you'll probably end up on the new council. I'm not challenging that." He snorted. "Maybe I'll look for you on Sunday after Mass. By then, perhaps, you'll be thinking more clearly about all of this."

He heard her phone slam down. Grinning, he carefully hung up his own receiver. He rinsed his hands of pickle juice and root beer, cleared the table, donned his coat, and headed out the door to the nursing home.

CHAPTER 33

Sunday, January 21, 1990

10:30 a.m.

Joe Burns had continued working on his homily for the weekend Masses and by Friday afternoon he believed he had polished it sufficiently. He went to the church to walk the aisles, to sit and reflect, to picture himself in the pulpit at each Mass. When he left an hour and a half later, the image of himself delivering a perfectly honed message was firmly fixed in his mind.

The outcome wasn't quite what he had anticipated. Aside from the close attention paid by Rosa Perez at the 5:00 Mass on Saturday and Tom Andrews at the 8:00 on Sunday, he saw many yawns, wandering eyes and more apparent boredom than he had expected for a matter so important, and there had been little comment from parishioners as he greeted them afterward at the doors of the church.

Therefore, when he stepped up to the pulpit at the third and final Mass of the weekend, he took time to slowly survey the congregation that nearly filled the church. He was guessing that many members were prepared and on guard, given the response to his message at the earlier Masses, but also because Ted Kroenig had told him before the Mass began about the increased gossip around the parish since Tuesday.

He spotted Jim and Peg Jensen with their children on the left side, halfway back. Bob and Jeanne Talbot were on the right side, near the front. Megan Roberts was there with her two girls, as were Dave Hanratty and his family and Clarice Morgan with her husband. Across the sanctuary sat Ted, serving as Lector for the first Scripture reading. There was no sign, however, of either Sheila Martinson or her husband. He quickly scanned the church again and had to conclude that she wasn't present. He bowed his head briefly, hoping it didn't mean anything.

In their pews, the council members were bracing themselves for what was to come. They knew the stories—had been part of them— about Joe's routine on the Sunday after a major run-in with the parish council. In addition, Rosa Perez had called Jim to tip him off after the Saturday Mass, and he had then informed council members that the pastor's bit from the pulpit would be the customary one.

Joe gazed out over the congregation a final time, using the silence to command their attention before beginning his remarks. He was glad he hadn't rushed into it, sensing that now, somehow, there was more interest in what he was about to say.

"You know, dear people, that I usually preach on the three readings from the Sacred Scriptures for any given Mass. Today, however, with good reason, I am departing from that wholesome practice in the interest of full and open disclosure to the faithful of this parish.

"Though most of you may not be aware of it, there have been notable communication problems between members of our parish council and myself ever since the council meeting held on the second Tuesday of November. Most of the time, of course, these matters are of interest only to those who are members of the council or the staff. I thought, however, that I should inform you about these events so that you will have the facts and not be guided by rumor and gossip.

"Unless you are a complete newcomer to St. Mary's, you know this isn't the first time that a parish council and I have had some differences of opinion—serious ones, at times, yes. That's not news; it happens in all parishes. Differences of opinion serve the best interests of any parish that wants to be a *good* parish and make good decisions. I have never made any apologies or any excuses for the conflict or for standing up for what I believe to be right and true. I have trusted my instincts and they have been reliable. I should also tell you that I spoke with Archbishop Meuncher about the current situation some time ago, a week before Christmas, in fact, and he has encouraged me with his support.

"In these matters, trust in God is *so* important, and, of course, we trust in God by trusting in his Church. That's why I am appealing to you today. I'm not going to go into a lot of detail about this controversy, however. Suffice it to say that there are, at most, only a few unhappy people. There are always unhappy, dissatisfied souls, of course, even if there's nothing going on in a parish that you could actually call a conflict." He inadvertently caught sight of Megan glaring at him fiercely. He hurried on.

"I don't have to remind you that it was upon me that the responsibility fell to first develop an effective parish council at St. Mary's—already in the fall of 1971, shortly after my arrival as pastor. The effort by my predecessor had been a colossal disaster, perhaps for reasons beyond his control. I worked hard to reverse that negative experience and within eighteen months we had a functioning council again, elected by the people.

"So, there is no question that I want to have a parish council at St. Mary's," he explained. "I've been in favor of laypeople from the very beginning. I like to have them involved. They've got something to offer. We've got to have them, especially with the shortage of priests today. Priests can't do it all anymore, so it's clear that I need and that I want help." He shrugged and spread his arms. *Obvious, isn't it?*

"But." He stopped to slowly eye the congregation again from front to back and side to side. "But," he repeated, smiling this time. "It *has* to be done in the right way, my friends. We cannot have strong-willed laypeople running the church. We need true leaders, men—and women, of course, that goes without saying—who can see the big picture. And that, in a nutshell, is why I have struggled with this current council. Things have to be done correctly. I know if I asked you, one by one, you would agree with me. You do not want anarchy. Neither do I. Which is why, last Tuesday, at its regularly scheduled meeting, I found it necessary to disband the current parish council."

He was not prepared for the commotion that raced through the congregation. Husbands and wives exchanged startled looks; children nagged to find out why the grownups were upset. He saw muttering throughout the church and heard groans from the front pews. A kneeler banged to the floor. And then another, as a dozen people got up to leave, one couple dragging their three children.

Cripes! You never know where they're at. Or what they've heard. Or what they'll do. They've been steamed before, but this? It's the rumor mill running rampant since Tuesday. Has to be that. It's got 'em all jacked up— waiting to pounce. Can't have that. I won't let them.

He forged ahead. "I assure you, people—there *will* be another parish council. We just need to get away from the current deadlock so that we can think clearly. I expect to have elections again in May or June, as usual. I encourage you to trust in God. As I said before, we do that by trusting the Church, the voice and the will of God for us all. And may God bless you today." As he left the pulpit, he checked on Megan again. *Still furious. But so be it.* He recalled having suggested to her on the phone that they might see each other on Sunday—when she wouldn't be so hysterical. *Good God, I hope not! Not today!*

He returned to the altar, glad to be there. It hadn't gone well at all. That unnerved him. Was it obvious? he wondered. Did they know they'd given him the jitters, knocked him off his stride? He found himself shaking and hurried to move on.

He nodded to Ted, signaling him to step to the lectern and lead the Prayer of the Faithful. "Grant it, O Lord, we humbly pray," the people replied to each petition.

He intoned the Creed. The people went through it from memory, sat down at his signal, and began to place their offerings in the baskets distributed by the ushers. The pastor proceeded with the Mass.

"Accept this bread.... Receive this wine," he prayed, lifting each. Unaccountably, he was feeling better, back on solid ground. "Holy, holy, holy Lord God of Hosts."

They'll forget and move on, he thought.

"This is my body....This is my blood."

They'll lose interest, as usual. Let the healing begin.

"Through him and with him and in him," he heard himself saying.

"The Body of Christ.... The Mass is ended. Go in peace."

Joe bowed to the altar and left the sanctuary, foregoing his customary trip down the center aisle to greet members as they left by the main doors.

As he disappeared into the sacristy, Megan Roberts made the decision. *This is it. I'm going.* She asked her daughters to wait a few minutes. "I have to see the priest."

She made her way into the crowd that was leaving by the side door. "I'm going to see your *priest*," she whispered to Jim—it was part banter, part sneer—as she pressed through those who had gathered around him in the aisle.

Jim was not himself, she noticed. He'd told her on the phone earlier in the week that he was doing some soul searching at Peg's suggestion. He wasn't sure what he'd do. Even so, Megan had fully expected him to be furious after the pastor's cocksure arrogance at Mass, but when people thanked him for his work he just smiled and when they encouraged him to hold on he nodded briefly.

As she passed them, Megan managed a stiff smile for Peggy, growled softly for Jim's benefit, and stomped toward the sacristy.

Ted was standing by there as the pastor spoke with a young couple who had come to ask about the procedure for becoming members of the parish. Noticing Megan enter, Joe interrupted his conversation with the couple, waving over their heads. "I'll be with you in a minute, Megan," he called to her. "Wait right there."

He took a parish registration form from a nearby drawer and handed it to the visiting couple. "Just complete this for us, please, return it to the parish office, and then someone from our hospitality committee will call on you. Welcome to St. Mary's." They thanked him and made their way to exit the sacristy.

He began to remove the Mass vestments and motioned Megan over. "Yes, Megan. What is it? What can I do for you?"

EPILOGUE

November 16, 2004

10:00 a.m.

Father Ken Halpin, pastor at St. Mary's for fourteen years, processed down the center aisle to the vestibule of the church to meet the casket. As part of his last will and testament, Father Joe Burns had requested to be buried from the parish church where he had served his final assignment as a parish priest. He had also asked to be laid to rest in the parish cemetery and for Ken Halpin to preside at his funeral Mass as the principal celebrant.

As Ken walked the aisle, he scanned faces in the pews, gratified that the church was filled. Lorraine Larson and her husband stood toward the front. During the Mass she was slated to read the first selection from the Scriptures. A few rows back, directly in front of the pulpit, stood Audrey Welch, present to offer a eulogy, as was Bob Talbot—something Joe had also requested before his death. Across the church, near the side entrance, sat Peter Featherstone, in reasonably good health at eighty-three. A walking cane hung from the bench in front of him

He was pleased to see Sister Janine Rowan, who had come from Little Falls, Minnesota, where she was now doing pastoral ministry for the ill and dying members of her motherhouse and, across the aisle from Janine, stood Clarice Morgan and her husband, up from southern Minnesota, where she was the director of religious formation for the Winona diocese. And over there was Megan Roberts, entering down the side aisle from the back, searching the crowd for Clarice. She found her and slid past two other people in the pew to sit with Clarice, who hugged her warmly and held her hand for a short while afterwards. They hadn't seen each other for eight years.

Halfway back on the left he reached out to touch the hand of Rosa Perez. There alone, her husband had succumbed to cancer two years earlier. Several rows later he nodded to Jim and Peggy Jensen, who were still members of the parish. Across the aisle from them stood Luis Alvarez and his wife Ana.

After prayers at the church entrance, the procession back toward the altar began. Pall bearers were Bob Talbot, Ted Kroenig, and Betty Halvorsen's husband, Philip, on one side, and on the other were Dave Hanratty, Sheila Martinson, and James Featherstone, an adult nephew of Peter Featherstone. Parish deacon Tom Andrews led the procession. Lofted grandly above his head was the four-foot Easter candle, its light heralding the light of Christ, seen easily—Tom was certain of it now, on the day of the burial—in the life of Father Joe Burns.

Three dozen priests of the diocese occupied the front two rows of the church, side to side, half of them vested to concelebrate the Mass with Ken Halpin. At the predieux in the sanctuary sat two more concelebrants, Archbishop Timothy McGowan and his predecessor, Archbishop Walter Meuncher, feeble now at eighty-five and almost unable to walk, yet displaying the undiminished charm that was his genius with people.

⌇⌇⌇⌇⌇⌇⌇⌇⌇⌇⌇⌇⌇⌇⌇⌇

Archbishop Meuncher had had no alternative. The day after the assault on Megan Roberts he had removed Joe Burns as pastor at St. Mary's. The priest had made no attempt to deny his actions—and made no excuses for them, either. Nor had he resisted when the archbishop insisted that he immediately commit himself to the psychiatric ward at St. Mary's Hospital in Minneapolis. He was admitted by late afternoon, enabling the archbishop to assure the district attorney when he made a circumspect, unofficial call about the matter that the pastor was receiving help for the nervous breakdown he'd suffered, and that he would be assigned to less stressful duties after he recovered.

Megan Roberts spent three days in the hospital. She had suffered multiple bruises and lacerations to her face and neck and a concussion from the blow to the back of her head. It was weeks before she healed enough to be able to return to her dental practice and the archbishop arranged for her and her daughters to spend the time at an Orlando rehab center where his cousin was the CEO.

To Jim Jensen's surprise, Megan refused to consider pressing assault charges against the pastor. Shaken to the core by the physical violence that she had experienced, she told Jim she couldn't bear the thought of recounting—reliving—the attack for a jury or a judge. She wanted it all to just go away—for *Joe Burns* to go away, go someplace where he couldn't hurt people, psychologically or physically, ever again. Archbishop Meuncher had assured Megan, she said, that he would attend to that personally, just as he was taking care of her medical expenses and the money she'd lose while she wasn't able to work. Jim didn't try to change her mind.

As for St. Mary's, the archbishop quickly appointed a retired hospital chaplain to provide sacramental ministry and other pastoral functions and put Dave Hanratty in charge of staff supervision and all human resources matters as well as maintenance and repair of the parish physical plant. In a letter read at all Masses the following Sunday the archbishop briefly but candidly explained Joe's departure and promised parishioners that a new pastor would be named by summer.

And, indeed, within a few months, Father Kenneth Halpin was named pastor, effective July 1. Within his first thirty days he sat down for an hour-long conversation with every parish employee. He made Dave's new duties permanent, naming him the director of parish operations, and dedicated himself almost exclusively to sacramental and pastoral work, the pursuit closest to his heart and the reason he had sought ordination in the first place.

The new pastor re-established the parish council as it had been constituted at the time Joe dissolved it earlier that year. He commissioned it to serve one full year, until June of 1991, and charged the members to establish by that time a procedure for seating a parish council that did not include elections or voting in any form. An increasing number of parishes with imaginative, enlightened leadership, he explained, were combining voluntary nominations with a discernment process, guided by prayer, that matched names with current parish needs. The new pastor believed the result could be a council that would serve collaboratively with him as servants of the members and help establish a parish vision and a strategic plan that would be reviewed at agreed upon intervals to measure progress made on parish objectives.

Joe remained at St. Mary's Hospital for thirty days until the doctors judged him sufficiently healthy for release. At that time, he accepted an appointment from the archbishop for three months as temporary chaplain to a community of cloistered nuns in a rural community southwest of Minneapolis.

Upon completing that assignment with high praise from the nuns and finding himself feeling better every day, he asked for and received from Archbishop Meuncher an extended leave of absence from active ministry in the priesthood. He requested a period of up to three years to live as a hermit outside the diocese, but close enough to the Twin Cities for easy travel to meet occasionally or as scheduled with his therapist in Minneapolis as well as a nearby weekly support group.

On a tip from Audrey Welch, he was able to secure long-term reasonable rent for a one-bedroom cabin on a small lakeshore lot a few miles north of Hudson. Audrey's proximity and her continued practice of frank conversation with him over dinner were integral parts of his continued recovery.

In addition to three years of complete rest with an occasional follow-up therapy session, the former pastor of St. Mary's took a semester of study at Notre Dame in South Bend, Indiana. It provided him personal and theological *aggiornamento*, a term used by Pope John XXIII in 1959 to describe the need for fresh air and updating in the Catholic Church.

After that, the archbishop assigned Joe as chaplain to the state prison at Stillwater. On the Minnesota side of the St. Croix River, barely ten miles from Hudson, it was convenient to where he was living. It also enabled him to visit with Audrey Welch at intervals they both considered discreet. He served the prison with high praise and appreciation for almost twelve years until he died there in his sleep one night at the age of seventy-three.

ᐣᐧᐣᐧᐣᐧᐣᐧᐣᐧᐣᐧᐣᐧᐣᐧᐣᐧᐣᐧᐣᐧᐣᐧᐣᐧᐣᐧᐣᐧ

Ken Halpin ascended the stairs to the sanctuary and moved around the altar to face the congregation.

"During this liturgy of Christian burial for Father Joe, let us all reflect on the great mystery and the generous gift of life and of death. Consider how you knew Joe Burns, ever a challenging person and priest, and what the nearly twenty years he spent here at St. Mary's meant for you. Consider what he accomplished during his time here—and in the years after he left. There is a Joe Burns story to be told for every day he lived; each of you has one you could tell. Let us remember and be thankful for this man's life. And let us pray in gratitude to God. Joe Burns has found his peace."

After Lorraine presented the first reading from the Scriptures, Ken proclaimed the second and then he preached a brief homily, expanding on the words with which he had begun the Mass.

"Joe Burns was a student of the future—someone who embraced original thinkers, whether philosopher, theologian, scientist or poet. Vatican II, in the first instance, opened doors for him to potentially immense freedom in every area of life and priesthood. It was his enlightenment—sparking here, exploding there in bolts of power and brilliance.

"The spirit that drove the revolution of the 1960s reshaped the mind and the soul of this priest. It propelled him into the called-for and necessary reform of the Catholic Church. He lived and died for that reform, for change that would include shared leadership in the Church, a vision for stewardship ahead of its time, stirring, lively parish liturgy, a fairly—that is, justly—paid staff with benefits. He encouraged solid, thoughtful questions about a restored permanent diaconate and enthusiastic support for a priesthood where celibacy could be a choice, not a mandate, thereby increasing its witness. He considered a financial commitment to social justice a principal priority for any parish. And all of this, mind you, some years ahead of any other parish I know of.

"It did not come without struggle, as many, perhaps most of you know. Joe was a perfectionist of serious dimensions—and that did not always serve him well. In some ways and on many occasions, I think it's fair to say, human nature pulled him down. We all, of course, have a dark side. Like Joe, we continually fight the tragic side of human nature and human existence. We live wistfully, longing for a better condition, because here and there, now and then, we've gotten glimpses of a better day.

"Personally, I often get that glimpse from good music. I think, for example, of the memorable concertos and symphonies of the great, in my opinion, totally unique master, Wolfgang Amadeus Mozart. When we permit ourselves to get overwhelmed by the human condition, when we take ourselves all too seriously, as though there is no tomorrow, then it's easy to miss the magic and the haunting beauty created by an incomparable genius like Mozart.

"I think of *waiting* for Mozart and his perfect music as a metaphor for the resolution of conflict and the healing of the human condition. It is *important* for us to be good at waiting. With time and with a universe in motion there comes a *shaping*—expanding and restricting, reforming and revising, forcing here powerfully, there gently—that presents us with endless possibilities for adaptation and growth. The shaping comes with words spoken and actions performed with the right tone of voice and in the right key, done *on* time and *in* time, with half steps and grace notes played perfectly or at least *better* as time passes.

"May Joe Burns rest now, fully in God, fully at peace."

ᑫᑫᑫᑫᑫᑫᑫᑫᑫᑫᑫᑫᑫᑫ

At the end of the Mass, Ken Halpin invited Bob Talbot and Audrey Welch to the pulpit for their eulogies. Bob was first. He spoke without notes.

"A writer quoted years ago in the *New York Times* said that where the human race is concerned, the odds are nine to five *against*. Period. That's all he said. Meaning that when you're talking about human beings and the human condition, your chances for *anything* are not all that good.

"As I look back on the life of Father Joe and the time he spent with us here at St. Mary's, I recall a full-credit course on the human condition. We were *human beings*, a mixed bag of goodness and dedication as well as a whole lot of frailty. We were honest, faithful and practical. We got angry, and we were stubborn and close-minded—*all* of us, including the man we celebrate and lay to rest today.

"I knew Father Joe very well. I was a co-worker in the parish. I was also a counselor and a confidant, a truthful sounding board for him or someone to wrangle with when that was what he needed. Because he found reasons and a way to trust me, I found ways to be there for him, for the parish, for *myself*. When Joe Burns asked for my help, he took hold of my very soul. Who would not reach from the boat for a guy who was drowning?

"Joe trusted me and that was a gift. There were other gifts, too. The seeds planted by Vatican II transformed the man's spirit, and that was something to behold! There were ups and downs, of course, and at times I witnessed the man in tears, weeping for his inability to implement the vision. The sight of that was a gift to me, uncalled for and unexpected. It was a gift, too, in that it showed me that I needed to sharpen my own focus on the vision. What things were optional, which crucial, for a reformed Roman Catholic Church? Just imagine for a moment the significance of that phrase: A reformed Catholic Church. My! No wonder it was stressful!

"He was a man of great vision, of pure passion, endless energy. There were times, however—and let's be honest—when Joe was himself a laboratory in how *not* to get something done. This was tragic, as all of us *are* sometimes. He made some mistakes, as we all do when the odds are nine to five against us.

"Yes, we struggle mightily with the prohibitive odds on the human condition. I often wonder how human beings can be conscious and self-aware—the marks that distinguish us among all the living creatures we know of on earth—and still somehow get it wrong about God? That is, make the mistake of thinking *we* are the gods?

"How can we do better? How could we all, including Joe, have done it better back then when he was with us? I have reflected on that for some fourteen or fifteen years now. There must be a way to shorten those odds. To move them back, one day at a time, one meeting at a time, in one conversation and then the next. What can I do today or tomorrow, I ask myself, to make the odds eight to five or perhaps seven to five? Is there a way to *even* the odds? How would I do that? What would it take?

"Here's what I've learned—and thank you, Joe, for the lesson, one that came in by the back door, so to speak. I've learned that the only day worth living is the day I do something to bring people together. Every day, that's the issue. We need to be saved from our narrow selves. It was true for Joe Burns. It's true for me and, I dare say, for every one of us present here this morning.

245

"We are given our gifts from God and we return them by doing the tasks waiting for us as we live our lives on this one planet, within this one great, great galaxy. There are different gifts for different times. *Whatever* a person's gifts are, compassion and communion are the desired outcomes, in every case.

"May God give this priest rest. He worked hard for us and with a lot of success—better than nine to five overall, I'd say. He was not perfect, but there is no such thing as perfection in the human condition. May Father Joe rest in peace now."

֍֍֍֍֍֍֍֍֍֍֍֍֍֍

Peggy Jensen reached to squeeze Jim's hand. He squeezed back. She wished there was a way, a chance, to tell Jim's story, start to finish—not to rival the pastor's story on the day of his burial nor Bob Talbot's moving eulogy either, but just for the record, just for Jim, her dear husband. She knew what she'd say, having rehearsed it silently at home before coming to the church for the funeral.

My husband Jim was, and to some extent still is, a man driven by a some-times unbelievable passion to get things right. It goes back to his training—Catholic parochial school through the seminary and then ordination to the priesthood. I can tell you today, however, that he has learned over the years that there are different, less driven, but still excellent ways to live. And he's liking that more and more.

The night the pastor disbanded and dismissed the parish council we talked about this until daybreak. Jim wept like a child when he came home and he wept on and off all through the night. The situation at St. Mary's was out of control, and so was Jim, lying in my arms there in our bed. He was overcome, not with rage, but with grief—destabilizing, total grief.

I took the opportunity to raise matters we had discussed on other occa-sions. I asked whether he could live with the idea that there might be more to life than Vatican II and the reform of the Catholic Church. Could he see that often God doesn't give much of a rip about all of our reform, all our rightness? How's about relaxing more? I asked him. What about being less tee-totally committed to fixing the Church?

The events of that night forced him to do some serious soul-searching and he began to make some changes in his life. Jim knew the rules and prin-

ciples for a negotiated settlement all along—be hard on the problem, go easy on the people involved; work at reconciling interests because each party has them; defeat the problem, not your counterpart in an argument; know that there are opponents for whom every disagreement is visceral.

It was that last part that Jim—and a lot of people back then, including the pastor—couldn't manage. When you're in the heat of things, it's hard to remember that war almost never brings peace. You forget that you can't be a reformer if you think in terms of them and us. That way, everyone loses; nobody finds the Grail. You get fixed on final, forever-like answers. You write the last chapters when the story is still unfolding.

When you do that, or try to, you end up being less effective than you might have been—short on patience and disregarding of other people; seeding resistance by the very way you walk, the look on your face, the way you carry yourself and deliver your message. A different attitude about whose world it is can give you a sense of humor, a lightness that gets results, a charm that makes people want to follow you, no matter how high the bar.

I'll remember that night forever. Jim's hour of redemption had come. He began to slow down a bit, to do less sometimes. He started going to the park for a walk when it called him, to the backyard where he would sit to study sun and shadow. Many days he wouldn't plan any work for the evening. He began to follow the natural rhythms of the day, in fact, getting to bed earlier and getting up earlier—with the sun in summer and with the first pink light of day in winter.

As for the Church, well, Jim has come to terms, better terms anyway, with that, too, and with the great disappointment of his life, his great windmill, the mystical dragon he's been stalking for some forty years now—the reform of the Catholic Church. He sees the Church now more as a story, a people with a history, a movement never intended to be what it became. The Church is the road we walk, he says, and we can be thankful for it. Fix the road where you are able, but know that it extends a long way behind you and ahead at least to the next turn. Stay on it, but know it's just a road. It leads someplace, but at times it's shrouded in fog and is unrecognizable, even up close.

Jim meant it that night when he declared to me that he would learn to ease up on things. It was the first step. We don't talk about it much any more, but I know that Jim regrets now that he was not able at the time to care in the least about the pastor's problems or whatever his sickness may have been. The time for change had come, Jim believed, pain or no. There was no turning back. The struggle was not intended to roast the priest or the Church, although that happened sometimes. That wouldn't be right and Jim has confessed to me that on the occasions when it did happen, it did not help.

⤚⤚⤚⤚⤚⤚⤚⤚⤚⤚⤚⤚⤚⤚⤚

Bob Talbot remained at the lectern for a full minute, head bowed. He turned to the prelates in the sanctuary, then to the casket in the center aisle, bowed slightly and returned to his place beside his wife. She grabbed his hand and squeezed it.

In the pew ahead of them, Audrey Welch turned, reached back to shake Bob's hand and thanked him before making her way to the pulpit. She opened the folder carrying her eulogy.

"I am a stranger to all of you, I know, but it is a pleasure for me to be here for the funeral Mass of Father Joseph Burns. I am the superintendent of schools in Hudson, Wisconsin. I have known and been a friend of Father Burns since we attended a management seminar in Minneapolis twenty-five years ago.

"It was a seminar on the art of supervision and the skills required to do it well. Over the next six to eight weeks, we had a number of follow-up conversations by phone about what we'd learned there and how to apply it to our work. Shortly after that, at my suggestion, we had dinner together for the same purposes. Eventually we began to meet once a month at a restaurant outside of Hudson to discuss the challenges and rewards of teaching and ministry. Just so you know, we were friends, nothing more—colleagues on different paths, with different careers, doing different work, but with common interests. We continued dining together monthly up until his death.

"The eulogy I offer you today is something Joe Burns wrote and asked me to read at his funeral. It contains conclusions he arrived at over quite some period of time, not easily, not quickly, and definitely not lightly. It is his last word to the parish he loved dearly. He gave it to me just a month ago, about a week after it reached its final form, he said, and asked that I read it at his funeral celebration. That was *his* word. *He* called it a celebration. I guess he hoped it would be one. Perhaps what he wrote will help to make it so."

She pulled out several sheets of paper and began:

There is no easy way to live through and manage relentless, inexorable change, especially change of great importance. I, certainly, never found the right way to do it well. Mostly, I didn't have the skills to lead other people and I didn't learn fast enough or understand deeply enough how big this Vatican II thing really was. In the end, I have to say, I was a poor vessel for the treasure which that Church Council gave us.

Of course, I also brought to the situation my personal stuff—my temperament, my compulsive work habits, and the idiotic idea that people are stupid. As a result, I could not develop the relationships I needed in order to cope with change. I realize now that relationships were the key to everything. I didn't see it then, though, and if ever I had an inkling, I didn't trust it.

I was also a cleric and celibate—a male celibate cleric! My! That *could* be three strikes against a guy! Surely each easily carries some bias. As I learned it first, my job was to save the people. Then, with Vatican II, it was to reform the Church to save the people. The mistake all along, of course, was to believe that priests save people; they don't.

The stress was unbearable at times. For relief, I used to get into my car and just drive and drive, for a whole day, into open air and freedom. I'd head up Minnesota 95 and over the river into Wisconsin and then take Highway 35 north through beautiful, wonderful country to Superior. Coming back over the bridge into Duluth, I'd cruise back down the Minnesota side. I was driving too fast to be safe, even on the interstate, but running free, chasing a dream for all of us as I pressed on the gas pedal—a dream breathed on us by a pope who knew what he wanted and what the Church needed. Fresh air, he called it. Reform. Change. The things

I made the business of my life.

Vatican II was so liberating for me personally! I could not for the life of me understand why every single priest and every last bishop could not get on board right away with the Council, with the freedom and new opportunities it gave us. Why couldn't they just walk away from all the nonsense we learned as young men and get on with it and move forward freely with the reforms? So much delay, testing and waiting! It was going to take forever with all the backsliding, negotiating, and playing games. It destroyed the potential created by that glorious, freeing Council. It was personal for me, this reform. It called my heart as nothing else ever did. I was disappointed— crushed, in fact, and scandalized—by the slowness to get on with changes that the Church so desperately needed.

And so I got tied down holding the line, slowing things down myself, trying to be faithful to the Church, to the leaders, playing ball, being patient with clerics, many of whom, in fact, were reactionaries and liars. I got caught up with being 'an organization man.' How I hated that term born in the Fifties! And then to discover and be forced to admit that I myself was just a good organization man on behalf of the Church I loved and served as a priest! When I finally realized that, I couldn't get over it—churchmen, myself included, holding back the Church of the people! That was a conflict I never resolved while I was with you. It sometimes made me an awful person to work with and to be with, I know. It all came apart for me because of how slowly it was going. I became part of the problem for many of you because I began to hold back in order to be faithful to the Church.

I know that now. I see it. And so, I encourage you. Keep moving ahead at St. Mary's. There are more changes coming. Make them. Keep doing the work. It doesn't end. I wasn't able to get my part of it done with you. I should have read and studied the report I requested from the parish council. That was a horrendous mistake and I accept the blame for it. I am sorry and I ask your forgiveness. I will help now, as best I can, from wherever I am when you hear this read.

God bless you all and, as ever, Father Joe.

༺༺༺༺༺༺༺༺༺༺༺༺༺༺༺

The Rite of Christian Burial concluded with the final commendation of Joseph Burns to God and divine goodness and mercy. Burial was in the parish cemetery, two blocks from the church. Megan and Clarice walked together in the procession, conversing quietly but constantly, filling in gaps from phone conversations they had had during the years since Clarice moved to take the position in Winona.

"It's *so* good to see you, Megan. You—both of us—struggled fiercely with this man and you look like you've moved on and healed completely. His attack on you was criminal and he should have paid for it. It's only a strong and determined person like you who could have survived that and be healthy again."

"I'd fight him again, Clarice—but differently, I guess; more civilly, maybe. The new pastor made a big difference around here. He was very instrumental in my recovery."

"You've done beautifully."

"It took lots of therapy to get over the shock and the violence but, yes, overall I'm doing well—still a member here, too, but not active in parish affairs, except for Sunday Mass."

On the way back from the cemetery, the topic changed to Megan's two girls and how well they had done in college, but they talked mostly about Clarice's work in Winona.

Ken Halpin invited all of the parishioners and visitors back to the parish for lunch in the school building, prepared by the women of St. Mary's Funeral Guild, a ministry, a work of mercy, initiated by Joe Burns thirty years earlier, in the fall of 1974.